Beyond
The Veil

Book #1 in
The Veil Series

Pippa DaCosta

ISBN:1494242354
ISBN-13: 978-1494242350

Paperback Edition.
US Edition.
Ve

Chapter One

I should have known he'd be trouble as soon as he walked into my workshop, but I couldn't have known he'd be the death of me. He wore a three-quarter length red leather coat, had platinum blond hair long enough to sweep back out of his eyes, and sported scuffed Timberland boots, but if the goose bumps shivering across my skin were anything to go by, he was clearly not as human as his appearance had me believe.

At first, I tried to ignore him, refusing to give him the satisfaction of seeing me hesitate. A quick glance at my dusty clock told me it was late, past midnight, and I'd be damned if I was going to drop everything just because he'd invited himself in. I continued to work on the sword resting on the anvil before me. I hammered out imperfections in the blade's surface with renewed vigor, metal singing at each blow. Behind me, the coal forge roared. Rolling waves of heat branded my back. I told myself it was sweltering temperatures sprinkling perspiration across my face and back, making my scruffy tank top cling to me, but in truth, it was fear.

Picking up the unfinished sword with gloved hands, I turned and plunged the blade into the glowing coals before facing my uninvited guest. He'd given himself the tour of my cramped workshop, seeming to admire the various swords on display, some unfinished, some as close to art as I was ever going to get. Shame I couldn't wield them as well as I could craft them.

"Well?" I managed to instil some genuine irritation in my words in the hope it would disguise the anxiety building inside me. I tried to flick my hair out of my face but a few strands stubbornly clung to my sweaty cheek.

"Impressive." He nodded once and turned arctic-blue eyes on me before flashing what he probably thought was a knee-weakening smile.

If my *guest* expected me to gush and swoon, he was in for a shock. "Who are you, and what the hell do you want?" It was late. I was tired. He wasn't human. I figured I was within my rights to be blunt.

His expression tightened. "You're Muse, right?" He tossed a gesture at the stuffy workshop. "I was expecting something...else."

I hadn't heard that nickname in years. Muse was a tag left over from dark days I didn't wish to revisit.

Approaching me, he reached inside his coat. I caught a flicker of light slide over a handgun tucked into his waistband and tensed. An unusual motif, like entwined scorpions, adorned the grip. But he didn't reach for the gun. He withdrew a sword and rested it on my anvil. "I want you to read this."

I tugged off my glove and skipped my fingers over the smooth surface of the blade. The metal burned cold against my insolent touch, as though the sword resented my presence. It was a wonderful piece of workmanship. The ripple - or *hamon* - below the surface of the carbon-steel blade hinted at Japanese origins, and the tempered edge was sharp enough to slice through flesh with little effort. An intricate hand-forged guard and leather-wrapped hilt betrayed the sword as functional but with a flair for the dramatic, and yet it was clearly a weapon meant for combat, not ceremony.

A thin snap of power danced up my fingers, and with a small hiss, I snatched my hand back. This sword would not easily give up its secrets. "What's in it for me?"

"What do you want?"

Now there was a loaded question. I didn't know what or who he was, and had no idea how much he could afford or what the stakes involved. "It depends on what I'm going to find. If we're talking murder, then I want danger money. If it's just a lovers' tiff you're interested in, a few hundred should do it. I'm assuming you want recent information. If you need me to go back more than five years, it'll be another two hundred."

"Or I could walk out of here now and tell the world where you are. I know there are a few unsavoury characters from your checkered past who'd be very grateful for the heads-up on your whereabouts." His smooth voice and slight smile belied the threat in his words.

I smiled tightly, my first smile since his arrival. "Now, there, you see? We were having a civilized conversation, and you just had to go and spoil it by threatening me."

"Why don't you just read the blade, and I can leave you to get on with your–" he cast a glance about him, "–work?"

And now he'd insulted me. "I'm not telling you anything until you give me more to go on." Who did he think he was talking to? Some back alley half-human woman who would fall over her own feet to do his bidding? He might know my name, but he obviously didn't know me.

He blinked, before turning back on the charm, as if I could be bought by a handsome face. "You're right. I'm sorry. A few hundred, was it?" He dug deep into his coat pocket and pulled out a wad of cash. Without counting it, he tossed it onto the anvil. "That should cover it."

I tugged my glove back on, pinching the heatproof fabric between each finger. "I think you should leave."

He narrowed his eyes. "Just read the sword, Muse."

I didn't have time to humor assholes, especially those of the demon persuasion. "Get out."

He pulled his distinctive gun on me, finger resting firmly on the trigger, aim rigid. "You will do this for me." It wasn't an order. It was fact–at least as far as he was concerned.

"Go back to hell," I sneered, before reaching around and snatching the blade from the forge, flinging both the half-finished sword and some hot coals at him. He recoiled, cursing as the embers bounced off his coat. I dashed for the doors. My hand was on the handle, when he slammed into me, knocking the breath from my lungs.

He thrust the gun under my chin, freezing me rigid. "Why do you have to be so difficult?"

I really didn't want this to escalate. Bad shit happens when *she* comes out to play. The darkness slumbering at my core began to unfurl, opening like the petals of a flower, but its intent was far from delicate. The trickling touch of power spilled into my muscles. Heat flooded through my body. The warmth of my element embraced me, threading itself through every part of me, the lure of chaos undeniable.

He abruptly released me and took a few steps back, gun up. His narrow glare measured me.

I pressed my back against the workshop door. Power dripped from my fingertips. I couldn't see it—the human part of me was blind to the energy—but he could. His arctic eyes blazed with a promise of conflict.

He appeared to consider his next move and then, quite unexpectedly, laughed and lowered the gun, tucking it back into the holster inside his coat. "You're right. This isn't worth it." With his hands up, as if in surrender, he turned and retrieved the sword in question before weaving his way back around workbenches toward me.

"I'll leave you in peace."

"What?" His sudden change in mood completely disarmed me.

"Step aside. I'm leaving."

Surprised by his abrupt surrender, I did as he asked and watched him slide the door open and step out into the night. A sharp winter breeze invaded the heat of my workshop, rousing me from my muddled stupor. Confused and somewhat disappointed, I followed him out into the alley. The raw energy he'd aroused began to fizzle out. Its departure left me with a sickly chill and bitter sense of loss.

He climbed into the driver's side of an old Dodge Charger with rust-bruised red paint. I had no idea who he was, where he'd come from, how he'd found me, or what lay hidden in that damn sword. And he was leaving. That couldn't be right. Didn't I deserve some sort of explanation?

"Hey!" I ventured further into the street.

Headlights bathed me in twin beams, forcing me to shield my eyes. He gunned the engine, jammed the box into reverse, and swung the car backward into a J-turn before speeding off, fat tires squealing on wet asphalt.

I stood in the street, hand on hip, head tilted to one side and breathed the crisp night air, clearing my lungs of forge-dust. Then the shockwave hit me. The explosion lashed across my back. I must have briefly lost consciousness, but the furious pain in my back quickly summoned me from the depths. A whine drilled into my skull. Alarms sounded from the industrial units around me.

I turned my head toward the heat, grit digging into my cheek as I peered into the smoke bellowing from the hollow gap between two buildings.

My workshop had gone and with it, my attempt at a normal life.

Chapter Two

I sat in the reception area of Phoenix Developments, biting at the quick of a nail until it bled. The tiny jab of pain paled in comparison to the abrasive grate from the dozens of cuts that riddled my back. Bruised, battered, but alive, I'd spent the night trying to salvage what scraps of work I could find in the remains of my workshop. A fruitless task.

As I sat in the waiting area, the world around me continued as normal. The working day had begun. I felt numb. The chrome-plated arms of the leather chairs glinted under halogen lights. The receptionist occasionally glanced my way over rimless glasses, her lips so thin they were barely there at all.

She didn't trust me. I couldn't blame her. Despite having showered, I could still smell the smoke in my hair. I also wore knee-high boots over skinny jeans, something that clearly didn't compliment the pinstripe suits and slicked-back hair of the 'city boys' milling back and forth through the glass doors.

It was nine a.m. Not an hour before, I'd been slumped in the back of an ambulance while the police rattled off their box-ticking questions. Were there any witnesses? Did I have any idea what had caused the explosion? Were there any hazardous materials on site? I told them what they wanted to hear, neglecting to mention my less-than-human visitor. Once you mention demons, the authorities get twitchy. I'd wanted to blame my uninvited guest, but until I knew what—or who—I was dealing with, I couldn't risk the repercussions.

As things stood, I didn't know what had caused the explosion, but I doubted Mr. Asshole's timing had been a coincidence. It had been years since I'd heard the name Muse—even longer since I'd spoken with someone less than human. He'd shown up, thrown money around, made demands, then left rather sharply. I found myself face down in the road seconds later.

The receptionist's phone buzzed. She snatched at the receiver and listened for a few seconds before thanking her caller. She looked at me. "Charlie Henderson, was it?" Her voice was as tight as her beanpole frame.

I stood, brushed down my top, and approached her glass-topped desk. "Yes."

"I'm sorry, but Mister Vitalis is in a meeting all morning."

I attempted to smile sweetly, but it's not easy when you've just survived an explosion that's ruined five years of hard work. I'd lost more in that blast than I cared to think about. "He'll want to see me."

"He's in a meeting."

"Yes. I know. You just told me that." I tapped my fingernails on the glass desk. "Okay, look. Tell him it's Muse."

She narrowed her pin-sharp glare. "Muse?"

This woman took her job far too seriously. "Yes. It's a personal thing. Just tell him... please."

She gave me one long look. I smiled as best as I could, and she finally picked up the phone. It wouldn't have surprised me if she'd jabbed a security button and summoned the heavies to escort me from the premises.

"Yes. I'm sorry about this, Mister Vitalis. Now she says she's called Muse. Yes...yes... Well..." She looked closely at me, the glare of her beady eyes drilling right through me. "Yes that looks like her. Very well. I'll send her up." She hung up. "Mister Vitalis will see you in his office in ten minutes."

Victory. I beamed. "Thank you." And hurried to the elevator.

***

A wall of windows framed a spectacular view of the city. Sunlight glinted off the adjacent high-rises. His office hadn't changed in the several years since my last visit. Polished glass, brushed aluminum and supple leather all vied for attention, as if each style attempted to outdo the others. At one end of the room a large desk housed a single Mac computer, at the other, black leather couches huddled around a glass coffee table. Not a single photograph adorned the walls—no strategically placed pot-plant, no personal touches whatsoever. The office was austere. Not unlike its owner.

The glass doors hissed open, and Akil Vitalis strode in. My skin prickled, human senses alerting me to danger. How right they were.

His dark eyes briefly checked me before he made sure the door was properly closed behind him. Then he faced me, hands clasped behind his back, face impassive.

My heart hammered a little faster, nerves fluttering in my chest, shortening my breaths. Time seemed to drag, and I began to worry. We hadn't parted on the best of terms, and I hadn't spoken a single word to him in five years.

Akil's smile, when it finally came, allowed me to breathe again.

"You look good, Muse." He crossed to a cabinet. From inside, he collected a crystal decanter and two glasses. Without asking if I wanted a drink, he placed them on the coffee table and poured two fingers of whisky in each.

I swallowed my nerves and approached the back of the nearest couch, digging my fingers into the cushion to hide my trembling hands. "You too." And he did. He wore a gunmetal gray suit, jacket unbuttoned with no tie. A few of his shirt buttons were undone, revealing the natural bronze of his skin. He appeared to be in his late twenties or early thirties. Nobody would guess an immortal being resided in that suave exterior.

"How's the blacksmithing business going?" His fingers lightly picked up his glass.

"You knew?" I wasn't surprised, not really. Nobody escapes Akil.

He took a generous drink and smiled but didn't reply. He didn't need to. "So tell me; to what do I owe this pleasure?" He shrugged off his jacket.

As he offered me the glass of whisky, I considered where to start. I owed Akil everything. He'd been my teacher, my guardian, but more than that, he'd saved me. Without his intervention, I'd be dead in a ditch somewhere. Another half-blood consigned to an early grave. And yet I couldn't trust him, not completely. He, like most of the full-blooded demons I'd known, had his own motives.

"I had a visitor last night, and I wondered if you might know him."

"Oh?" Akil arched an eyebrow and leaned back against the couch. "I take it your visitor wasn't human?"

"I don't know what he was," I admitted, taking a sip of the whisky. The alcohol rolled across my tongue, smooth, mature, and no doubt as costly as the loan I was still paying off on my workshop. I took another sip, needing the reassuring warmth.

Akil saw my hand shake but was polite enough to pretend he hadn't.

"He—er... He wanted me to read a blade. I would have, had he not been so rude about it. Either he was rusty at playing human, or he's just naturally an arrogant—" I stopped before my anger got the better of me. "Anyway, we had a little tête-á-tête and then he left. Ten seconds later, my workshop exploded, almost taking me with it." The warmth of the whisky soothed my rattling nerves as the shock of my close call really hit home.

The kindness in Akil's eyes hardened. "What did he look like?"

"Tall. Smug. A thing for red leather. But it was the sword that was interesting." I finished my whisky and let Akil refill my glass. "It was hand crafted." I recalled the tease of power I'd felt from the blade. I rubbed my fingertips together, the ghost of its touch like pins and needles beneath my skin. "Similar to a Japanese katana but it had an elaborate guard. It's unique."

"Did you read it?" He returned to my side.

"No." I flicked Akil a smile as I took my refreshed drink. "You know, the more I think about it, the more I wonder why he came to me. He asked me what payment I wanted for reading the sword. I told him, but he threatened me instead of just giving me the money. Why would he do that?"

"He wasn't there for the sword."

I was beginning to realize the same. "He was testing me. I thought it was odd at the time. He deliberately pissed me off to get a reaction." I frowned. "Why?"

"It's obvious." Akil's smile was one I recognized well. He was waiting for me to catch up. "It wasn't about the sword. You weren't meant to leave that workshop. He wanted you dead."

But that didn't make sense. "He had plenty of easier chances." A gunshot to the head would have done it.

Akil inhaled, leaning back and rolling his shoulders. "When have you known our kind to do anything the easy way? If he's any kind of demon at all, he's not going to execute you without having his fun. It makes perfect sense to me. He went there to kill you, but he wanted to get his kicks. Maybe he'd heard of you. Did he call you by name?"

"Muse? Yeah."

"Then he knows who you are. Someone hired him."

Akil's words rang true. How else would Mr. A have known my demon name? Only those from my past knew I'd been given the name Muse by my former owner as a cruel joke.

"Shit," I hissed.

"Indeed." Akil licked his lips. "You should stay with me."

Hell, no. I immediately looked away, smiling awkwardly. I felt his gaze on me, roaming where it shouldn't. This was not why I was here. I couldn't do this, not again. I owed Akil everything, but I was just a half-blood demon. His world had nearly killed me before. I couldn't go back to that.

"Muse." He sounded apologetic until I saw his smile.

I pushed away from the couch—away from him. "You know what, don't call me that." I tried to make it sound like an order, but the nervous tremble in my voice undermined my intentions, reducing the words to a request. "I left for a reason, and I'm not coming back."

"You think your assassin won't try again?"

"I'll take my chances."

He winced a little, his smile twisting into something darker. "How long do you think you'll survive out there, Charlie? You've got power but not nearly enough to stop them all."

"I did it before. Five years, Akil. I had five years without you—without them." It had felt good. The freedom. The life. The normality of it all. I paid bills. I drank coffee. I even had a cat. Life. It was real. A tangible dream, one I'd worked hard to hold on to. He wasn't going to take it from me, and neither was Mr. A. I was sick of running because they deemed me some half-baked mistake, tired of fighting those who thought me an abomination.

"He's out there, you know," Akil said.

When I looked at Akil, watched him walk slowly toward me, I knew he wasn't talking about the assassin. My heart sank, and my dream of normality slipped away. I lifted the glass to my lips and finished off the potent whisky, wincing as it burned a path down my throat.

Akil stood a little too close. The proximity of him stole my breath away. A trickling current of power stirred within me, my demon half recognizing him as her savior. He tipped my chin up, perhaps sensing my reluctant defeat and brushed the back of his fingers down my face. "Your brother sent that assassin. You know he did. Stop fooling yourself. It was never going to last. Your workshop is gone. Don't let him take your life as well."

Mention of my brother wasn't going to scare me into staying, although it probably should have. Akil was right, but he was also plucking at my weaknesses, reminding me why I needed him. Not so long ago, I'd have let Akil lure me back in. It seemed like an easy decision to make. He'd protect me, give me everything he thought I needed, but it wasn't as simple as that. For much of my life, I'd been someone's property, pushed from pillar to post, toyed with and exploited. Akil could disguise it behind an offer of kindness, but he was no different.

I turned my head away. "No. I'm sorry." I wasn't. "I'm going home, Akil. Don't try to stop me."

Chapter Three

I twisted the key in the lock and shoved the door open, sweeping back the mound of mail that had gathered on the floor behind it. Depositing my keys and mail on the kitchen countertop, I swept a hand back through my hair, holding it there as I scanned my tiny apartment. Everything looked as it should: a few faux suede cushions strategically scattered on the couch, a collection of generic canvas prints on the wall, but it felt different. Or perhaps it was me. I felt different.

I flicked on the LCD TV, letting the comforting murmur of background voices fill my apartment, and largely ignored its chattering until a news reporter caught my eye as she challenged a stiffly poised official, *"...how do you explain these freakish events, such as the flooding near Beacon Hill in July? We're hearing reports of demons; is this true? Are there demons in Boston?"* I reached for the remote and turned off the TV. I'd had about all I could stomach of demons for one day.

It was only in the last few years that the word 'demon' had become headline news. No longer content to hide in the shadows, they hid in plain sight, walking among us. I'm proof of that. The public were largely misinformed, perhaps deliberately so. For most, demons were a curiosity. A mild annoyance. Unless cornered, they looked human, and talk of their 'powers' had been toned down, made to look like bizarre coincidences or blamed on climate change. Snow in summer is a dead give-away.

While their numbers were scarce, the government had a hope of controlling the rumors, but they had no idea that, for every demon caught, another ten had successfully infiltrated daily life.

Demons were just the beginning. Existence of the veil—the invisible barrier between our world and the demon realm—was not public knowledge. The government was keeping a lid on that particular bag of snakes. Demons are one thing; another world neighboring ours? A netherworld, where the sky broils, and the air flows with the elements of chaos? People weren't ready for that.

I shrugged off a creeping weariness, rolling my shoulders and dragging my hand down my neck, trying to ease the stiffness in my muscles. I ached in places I didn't know could ache. Shock and physical damage had taken their toll, as had the meeting with Akil. At least he'd let me leave and had even offered to throw some feelers out to see if my assassin could be identified. Going to Akil had been a risk. I'd turned my back on him, and wasn't someone who took that sort of denial lightly. I'd pay in some way for asking for his help. He'd make sure of that.

I flicked my gaze to the bunch of flowers in the lounge window. The heads drooped. A few brittle leaves rested on the sill beside the vase, a sure sign I'd spent too much time at the workshop lately. I retrieved the flowers and dumped them in the trash, rinsing out the vase and upending it on the drainer.

I leaned back against the sink. Everything was so quiet. The double-glazed windows stifled the constant drone of the city, but today I almost felt as though I needed the noise. The city lived. It breathed: the blaring car horns, the rapid shrill of the pedestrian crossings. Walk, don't walk. I didn't want to walk. My apartment, as small and insignificant as it was, felt like a real home. I'd never had that before, and I wasn't about to walk away from it.

I opened the window, breathing in the South Boston air. The sounds of children playing drifted from nearby Buckley Playground. I caught snippets of a conversation from a couple passing beneath my window. A car rumbled by, and I soaked up the familiar sounds of life. The cacophony of human activity grounded me firmly in normality.

The meeting with Akil, although brief, had rekindled an ache I thought I'd long ago cured. He exuded power, wore it like cologne, and the primal creature curled at my core refused to ignore the attraction. My demon, she's all about need, and she made it clear she needed Akil. It didn't help that Akil was one of the Seven Princes of Hell; demon catnip to the likes of me.

Flicking on the coffee machine, I grumbled a few choice words. They could all go to hell, or the netherworld, to give it its proper name. I wasn't giving up my life, not for anyone. It might seem quaint to the many varieties of demons who stalked me, but it was mine.

Opening the fridge, I took out the milk and closed the door. A creased photo caught my eye, the corner trapped against the fridge with a cat-shaped magnet. Sam and me. I smiled. He had his arm around me, his broad grin genuine. The picture had been taken a few months ago, in the summer. We'd hiked up a woodland trail and found a small waterfall off the beaten track. Water rushed just out of the shot. Sam's jeans were wet with the spray. His salt-and-pepper hair had a damp and ruffled chaos about it. How I loved to run my fingers through his hair.

The flowers I'd just thrown away had been from him. An apology for something he didn't need to apologize for. I'd lied to him. A lot. Especially about why it was never going to work between us.

While pouring the milk into my coffee, I caught a glimpse of a blinking light from my antiquated answering machine. *Six messages, more than I usually get in a month,* I thought, taking a sip of coffee. The machine wasn't the most reliable at the best of times and had a tendency to delete or overwrite messages.

I jabbed PLAY on the machine.

"New message received Sunday, eleven-fifteen-pm," an automated female voice said. "Hi, Charlie." Sam's deliciously smooth voice instantly soothed my strung-out nerves. "You really need to get a phone at the workshop, or get a cell phone. Everyone has a cell these days. Even my Aunt—and she's nearly eighty." He talks too much, always has. "Anyway. Look, I can't make Tuesday. A potential contract has come up...you know how it is. I can't say no. I'm really sorry." He paused, his silence weighted with unspoken words. "I want to see you. Miss you." He hung up.

I groaned. Break ups are never easy, especially when neither party really wants to separate. I shouldn't have agreed to meet him even though our planned 'date' was a friendly one, no strings attached.

Tuesday? Today was Tuesday. I clasped my hands around the hot mug of coffee. My slouch deepened. Now that he'd cancelled, I realized how much I needed to talk to him. Sam made me forget myself, who and what I was. He had such a light-hearted outlook. So quick to smile. He loved his work as an architect, and his enthusiasm for life infectious. It was one of the reasons I'd let our relationship go on for as long as it had.

"New message received Monday, nine-oh-nine-am." Silence followed.

Strange.

"New message received Monday, nine-oh-eleven-am." Silence, then static and click. "New message received Monday, nine-oh-fifteen-am." More static.

I frowned into my coffee and glared at the answering machine. Its digital display blinked PLAY back at me. The messages continued to play their static nonsense until I reached the sixth, received an hour before I'd arrived home, a message from the police asking me to visit them at the station. Non urgent.

I stopped the machine, my finger hovering over DELETE ALL, when something possessed me to listen again. It was the third message I was interested in. I set my coffee down on the countertop and listened. It wasn't silence. There was something in the background. Muffled noises, static, then a click as the caller hung up.

I hit REPLAY. There was someone there. I could hear scuffles, like the sounds you hear when a caller hasn't hung up properly, and he's dumped the phone in his pocket. With a shrug, I picked up my phone and coffee and walked into the bedroom, tapping out Sam's number.

"Hey, this is Sam Harwood, Architect. Leave a message, and I'll call you back between the hours of nine and seven." His voicemail beeped and waited for me to speak.

"It's Charlie. I got your message." I sat on the edge of the bed, cradling the phone between my chin and shoulder and placing the coffee on the bedside table. "Sorry I didn't call sooner..." The seconds ticked, and the silence urged me to speak. "Something has happened at the workshop and... It's all gone." A knot twisted in my throat. A swell of emotion choked me. "I've not been exactly honest with you. Can you call me?" The phone beeped, cutting me off.

I couldn't tell him everything, but he deserved to know the break-up hadn't been his fault. Humans cannot date demons, even half-demons like me. The history I carried—my family, my past—was too dangerous. If he knew what I was, had any inkling of what lay at my core, it would destroy him. Like most people, he knew about demons. He tolerated their presence, but to be sleeping with one? He'd never look at me the same again. It would ruin what was left of our friendship, and I'd be alone again.

I lay back on the bed, resting the phone beside me on the pillow and closed my eyes. Sam had been a mistake, one of many I'd racked up over the years, but at least I had the memory of our relationship: the dinner dates, the movie nights, the simplicity of it all. That had to be worth something.

I fell asleep with the comforting thoughts of Sam in my head and the warmth of my normal life around me.

***

Jonesy nudged my cheek, purred, then sniffed my lips in that irritating way cats do. I swatted him away, only for him to dive back in and nuzzle my chin. His purrs vibrated through his furry little feline body.

I dragged my eyes open. The gloom around me came as a surprise. My digital clock read 9:20pm. I'd slept all afternoon and into the evening. Jonesy continued to pester me as I rose from the bed like the walking dead. He darted around my feet, weaving around my shins, mewing softly.

"Yeah, yeah, yeah, cat. I get it."

The phone on my pillow rang, its screen glowing green in the dark, one name flashing on the display.

Akil.

I picked it up. My thumb hovered over the answer button. Just seeing Akil's name sprinkled traitorous shivers through me. It hadn't been a day since I'd left his offices, and already my body felt the effects of demon-withdrawal. The damned darkness inside wouldn't let me deny what I'd experienced seeing him again. They do that to you, demons. They know your intentions, your needs, your desires, and they play them like musicians play their instruments. The demon inside me—she knew I wanted Akil on a level I didn't dare admit. But thankfully, I'm not all demon; I still had a measure of self-control.

I answered the call.

"Muse." His voice teased through my sleep-addled mind, rekindling sparks of desire. "Are you alright?"

Was that something like concern in his voice? Surely the all-powerful demon property developer wasn't worried about little ol' me.

"Yes, I'm fine," I croaked, the remnants of a deep sleep clawing at my voice. "Why? Shouldn't I be?"

Jonesy weaved about my feet as I headed for the bedroom door. Some part of him arcing back to his big-cat origins, he tried to playfully lunge at my boots.

"Your assassin... Did he carry a gun with a scorpion motif on the grip?"

"Yes." My heart thudded a little faster.

"Where are you?"

"At home."

"I'll tell you in person. Will you invite me in?" The way he asked, slipping it so easily into the conversation, you'd have thought it was a flippant request. It wasn't. Akil is full demon. A Prince of Hell, no less. Without an invite, he couldn't physically enter my apartment, but only idiots and mad men invited demons into their homes, and I was neither.

I couldn't invite him in and was about to say as much when I stood on Jonesy's tail. He yowled and shot through my bedroom door in a blur of black fur. I stumbled after him, falling against the doorframe, and froze.

"Muse?" I heard Akil's voice from the phone at my side, but dared not lift it to my ear.

Sprawled on my couch, an arm draped along the back, boots propped up on my coffee table, sat Mr. A. The pale glow pooling through the window bathed him in a cool crisp light, casting shadows across his face that darkened his arctic blue eyes. That same light played across his hair like water shivering over ice.

"Muse?" Akil growled. His distant voice at the end of the phone snapped me out of my reverie.

I lifted the phone to my ear, my unblinking stare never leaving my uninvited guest. "Yes," I hissed.

"What's going on?" Akil demanded.

"Nothing. I'm fine," I replied, each word hollow.

Akil fell quiet. "Goodnight, Muse."

"Goodnight." The forced nature of our farewell was a clear indication that not all was well.

I hung up the call. It wouldn't take Akil long to arrive. I just needed to buy time.

Mr. A hadn't moved. No human could sit as still as that. He might as well have been carved from stone. But there was definite amusement glinting in his otherwise frosty glare. His lips ticked into a crooked smile.

Jonesy, my traitorous cat, leapt onto the couch beside him and then proceeded to nudge Mr. A's hand, purring like a V8.

"Your cat has taste." The velvet tone of his voice crept through my defenses, stirring my reservoir of energy. He had power in his voice, but the sense of power didn't stop there. Like an iceberg, the man I saw was just a fraction of his true self. I felt his restrained energy prickling my skin, but what the hell was he?

"It's widely known that cats are half demon. So what are you?" I asked, pleasantly surprised by my casual tone. The fact that he was in my apartment, sitting very comfortably on my couch, meant he wasn't a full-demon. No invite—no entry. He was something else or a half-blood, like me.

I snaked my arms across my chest and leaned nonchalantly against the doorframe as though I hadn't practically fallen over my own feet a few moments before.

Mr. A. dropped his hand and gave Jonesy an obliging tickle behind the ear. My cat fell over himself, soaking up the attention, utterly oblivious to the rising tension in the room. Mr. A fought a smile before he planted his boots on the floor and leaned forward. "Can I trust you, Muse?"

I almost laughed. "Trust me?" I shoved away from the door, feeling his eyes lingering on me with every step. "No. You can't trust me."

His confident smile faltered as though my answer might actually matter. He broke our mutual stare and stood. Numerous buckles rattled against the supple leather of his coat. I caught a glimmer of light as it slid across the gun in its holster, but no sword.

"Where's the sword?" I stood between him and the front door.

"Somewhere safe."

"Why did you destroy my workshop?" My attempt at remaining calm began to fail. My voice quivered. "I don't know you. I've done nothing to you. Why would you do that to me?"

He cast his gaze over my shoulder at the front door behind me then dragged it back to meet my accusations. "I know you. You're the half-sister of the full-blood demon, Valenti. The illegitimate child of Asmodeus—one of the Seven Princes of Hell. You were sold at birth as a plaything for lesser demons."

My power began to stir despite my best efforts to keep it from awakening. A tightening heat seeped outward, the touch of it rolling across my skin. I knew what I was, but hearing the disgust behind his words roused deep-seated emotions I'd tried to keep locked away.

"A half-blood abomination," he snarled. "An embarrassment to demons everywhere. By all rights, you should be dead."

The heat broke over my skin. My demon stretched her tendrils outward, entwining herself with my human form. "And you don't know the half of it," I growled. He had come to kill me, but he wasn't going to find it easy.

I welcomed the blaze of power, letting it burst white-hot across my fragile human flesh. Demon and human blurred together as one. My human body was a shimmering apparition, intangible amid the raging heat. Writhing power lanced up my spine, the pain blinding and yet invigorating. It sought release. My physical flesh restrained it, containing it behind reality. Now that I'd revealed my demon, there would be hell to pay.

I summoned the city's elemental heat. Human activity provides an endless supply of energy, an energy I can summon the same way the ocean calls the tides. The streetlights outside flickered before blazing bright then bursting one by one before wilting on their poles like the long-dead flowers I'd thrown away. Heat swelled inside of me, the power brimming over. It wasn't all I had, but it would be enough to make Mr. A to think twice.

He had backed up a few steps, shielding his face from the heat with crook of his arm, but he made no attempt to retaliate. He hadn't even reached for his gun.

Molten power dripped from my body, fizzling to nothing once it separated from the inferno lashing inside of me. Half-blood, half-demon, I stood between two worlds, summoning the darkest of energies from the fabric of this reality, but it was restricted, captured, and tethered in my human form. Bound as I was, I could still incinerate him if he made one wrong move.

"I'm not your enemy, Muse." He flinched and staggered back a few steps as the sheer weight of the heat bore down on him, but still he didn't summon the power I knew he must have.

"No? Then prove it." My voice no longer resembled my own. It hissed and spat, lashed and snarled. He wouldn't see me as human, not any more. What he saw, the thing that occupied my body, was a hellish visage of anger and hate, of the years I'd spent cowering at the feet of others. He saw a beast ablaze in flame, a female silhouette tethered by the blanched-white chains of power.

With each step, my intent grew. The demon inside me reared up, demanding satisfaction. She wanted the chaos that came with summoning the elements. Her elation spurred me on, her lust for destruction tugging my conscious thoughts toward maddening freedom.

Mr. A. pressed his back against the window and lowered his arm. Refusing to look away, his jaw worked, teeth grinding. His fists, clasped rigid at his sides, gave away the effort control took him. He was deliberately holding back, refusing to rise to my threat. His restraint was commendable, but it wouldn't stop me from hurting him.

"Be careful what side you choose, Muse." He turned and ducked out of my window in a flurry of red coat.

In a blink, I was at the window, hands splayed either side as I peered four floors down to the street below, but Mr. A was nowhere in sight. Sirens wailed, a fire truck blasting its horn somewhere close.

With the threat gone, the mass of elemental energy inside me had no outlet. With the promise of retribution stolen, and the lure of devastation no longer achievable, it turned every drop of its displeasure on the woman anchoring it to this world: me.

I knew what was coming, but short of leveling a city block, I had no choice but to let it ride over me. I could have released the chaos, could have walked right out of my apartment building and swept a wave of destruction in my wake, but if I did that, I'd be no better than the demons I despised. As my demon turned the weight of pure elemental energy on me, I buckled under its pressure, falling to my knees and burying my head in my hands. Like the devastating force of a hurricane, it tore into me, metaphysical talons slashing through my cowering soul, tearing out any strength I might have had to resist it.

I hugged myself tighter, trying to escape the relentless assault. Lashings of fire snapped over me, through me. I heard my own cries in the maelstrom, but they were distant and detached, belonging to another woman. A pitiful human woman, weak of mind and soul.

"Invite me in, Muse." Akil. His voice broke through the storm of chaos in my head. The slightest touch of him was enough to soothe the madness.

I didn't need to speak the words. All it took was a moment of intention, a brief flicker of defeat, and he was there, beside me, gathering me into his arms and holding me close against him. I fought him at first, trying to desperately hold on to whatever remained of normality, but it was pointless. I had neither the strength nor the inclination to deny him, and he knew it.

He cradled me against him as I sobbed, ignoring the pulsating waves of heat spilling from me. A wretched trembling wracked me. My muscles cramped. With each lash of pain, I bucked, teeth snapping shut. Akil's strong arms held me firm as he whispered words in a language I didn't understand and didn't care to.

I don't know how long he held me, but eventually reason and reality returned. I listened to Akil's heavy heartbeat as the sounds of the city drifted through the open window. A cool breeze slid over my flushed skin. No physical indication of what I'd just been through remained. My demon rarely wounds me physically; she knows better than to damage her human counterpart.

"He was here," I said.

He shushed me, making words redundant.

"He was here. He got in. He's not a full-demon. He's something else..." Barely coherent words tumbled from my lips.

"I know."

I closed my eyes, resting my cheek against the warmth of his chest. It felt good to be held by him, to know that nobody could touch me. I was safe in his arms, and I wondered why on earth I'd ever wanted to be free of him. Who was I fooling? I couldn't live like a normal woman. I had a force of nature inside me, a demon consumed by need with a deliberate lust for chaos. She was me. I couldn't hide from her and didn't want to. I wanted her. I wanted to awaken her, to embrace her. My attempt at normality had been the madness, but now I was home, in Akil's arms once more.

"You did well." His fingers stroked lazy circles on my shoulder.

"I shouldn't be here." I could easily have unleashed that explosive force of power. All it would have taken was my surrender, and innocent people would have died. With that much energy, my demon would have raged against anyone and anything in her way.

"I know."

"Take me home," I whispered.

Chapter Four

When I'd first turned my back on the netherworld, nightmares had plagued me. Once I had a taste of what it meant to be human, the full horror of what I'd been forced to endure overflowed inside me, and my subconscious succumbed to the memories. The terrors became so bad that I began to fight sleep, to force myself to stay awake and avoid reliving the things I'd spent a life time running from. I tried to drink myself into hiding, but that only made it worse. I dabbled in drugs. Anything and everything to run from the demons, both metaphysical and tangible, that hunted me. Eventually, the nightmares tired of me, then stopped altogether. The demons never found me. I was safe in hiding. I'd found a way out. I would survive.

But when I let Akil back into my life, the nightmares returned.

***

I woke tangled in pure white sheets. My heart fluttered, my breaths coming in short gasps. I couldn't fill my lungs. Panic stole my ability to think. Sunlight flooded in through the floor-to-ceiling windows. Virgin white drapes rippled in the breeze. But as serene as it all appeared, I saw demons in my peripheral vision. They leered at me, talons reaching outward, obsidian claws digging into my flesh.

I scrambled from the bed, the dream still very real in my mind, and stumbled over the sheets, dragging them with me. I fell and landed firmly on all fours. It was only then, hunched over and trembling, that I realized I was safe. There was nothing in the bedroom, and there never had been. They were in my head. Memories.

I saw the room for what it was: just an innocuous room. Clean. Modern. Nothing to indicate a malevolent presence. Clutching the sheets to me, I managed to stand on unsteady legs and stagger to the window. Boston harbor sparkled in the early morning sunlight. Luxury yachts bobbed in the marina fifteen or so stories below. I recognized the opulent high-rise buildings as Atlantic Wharf, Boston's financial district and home to The Atlantic Hotel, Akil's hotel.

I stepped away from the glass, and the fluttering in my chest intensified. He'd brought me home, right back into the very heart of his world. Of course he had. I'd asked him to.

A bubble of laughter escaped me. Panic laced my veins with adrenalin. I spied clean clothes folded on the end of the bed and quickly dressed. The navy blue dress would have been modest had it not been for its short, figuring-hugging cut. I didn't care what it looked like. I could change when I got home—my home.

I ran my fingers through my hair, trying to work out some of the knots, then plucked my boots from beside the door and stepped barefoot out into a marble-tiled hallway. Moving lightly on my feet, I breezed down the hall, slowing as it opened into a vast lounge. The lounge area was easily four times the size of my entire apartment. A sunken area housed a scattering of cream leather couches. Art adorned the walls, splashes of color among an otherwise stark interior.

I listened, but besides the soft hum of the air conditioning, the apartment was quiet. I was alone. I jogged across the lounge, feeling as exposed as a criminal outside the prison gates, then entered the entrance foyer.

With a sigh of relief, I tugged open the door
leading to the elevators and met the bright smile of a
woman clutching a file to her chest.

"Hi. Good. You're awake." She breezed by me,
her rushed words chasing one another from her lips. "Akil
sent this over for you. He wanted me to drop by, make sure
you're okay."

My hand lingered on the door handle. Freedom
was so close.

"I'm Nica. Akil's assistant."

I glanced back, finding her bubbly enthusiasm
distracting. She held out her hand. She was human. At least
I didn't get any indication of power coming from her, but I
doubted Akil would employ a human assistant.

"It's okay." She tucked her short honey-blond
hair behind her ear before offering me her hand once more.
"I won't bite." She certainly looked friendly enough, her
enthusiasm just about ready to burst, but I'd been fooled
before. You don't have to be demon to be lying.

I shook her hand. Her grip was firm. "Where's
Akil?"

"Working. He asked that you have a look at this
file. I'll answer any questions you might have."

Nica appeared to be one of those people who
could brighten any situation with her presence alone. The
file, her friendly approach, and the fact she was a human
personal assistant to a Prince of Hell had me intrigued
enough to abandon my escape attempt.

I dropped my boots by the door and followed
Nica back into the apartment. She wore cream trousers
with sandals, as though it was the height of summer and
not the tail-end of October. Her white blouse billowed
loosely around her slim physique.

She stepped down into the sunken seating area
and waited for me to join her before handing me the file.
"His name is Stefan."

I flicked open the file and immediately came face
to face with my would-be assassin. The black and white

picture showed him walking away from the camera, his face in profile. If his distinctive leather coat didn't give him away, the car he had been captured approaching certainly did: the same battered old Charger he'd parked outside my workshop.

"Stefan..." I whispered, perching myself on the edge of a couch and splaying the various photographs, documents, and notes across the coffee table in front of me. Half a dozen images caught him in motion, but few were close enough to allow me to examine the details of his face. Either he was apt at avoiding having his photo taken, or the photographer didn't want to get too close.

A black and white image of a familiar motif caught my eye: entwined scorpions, the same emblem as on Stefan's gun. "What is this mark?"

"His identifier." Nica lowered herself on the couch beside me, brushing the creases from her trousers. "His brand," she said, gathering from my confused expression that I had no clue what she was referring to. "Given to him at birth."

I frowned at her curious choice of words. A brand implied ownership. "What do you mean?"

"He's a hybrid, like you. From what we can gather, he was given that mark when he was handed over to his guardian, probably shortly after birth." Half-bloods were routinely killed at birth. Those who weren't were sold among the demons as curiosities. Few survive. I'd never met another.

"I don't have any marks like that," I said.

Nica smiled sympathetically. "He was taken in, Muse. Trained. Tutored and reared for one purpose. Somebody cared enough to brand him."

"Why?" Half-bloods are thought of as worthless monstrosities. Why would someone bother with him?

"He's a tool, a mercenary. If you look through the file, you'll see we can place him as a suspect in countless high-profile demon attacks and one successful assassination. It appears he was trained well."

I picked up the black-and-white photo that had first confirmed Stefan as my Mr. A. Even frozen mid-stride, he carried a confidence that no half-blood had the right to. I'd seen evidence of that smug attitude at both my workshop and my apartment, where he'd made himself at home while I'd slept, blissfully unaware of his presence.

"If he was hired to kill me..." I paused, uncertainty stalling me. "Why didn't he kill me at the workshop or at my apartment?"

Nica shrugged. "Perhaps he's playing with you."

Akil had said the same, but I wasn't so sure. If Stefan was a mercenary, then surely he would only receive payment on my death? So what had he been waiting for? Sure, at my apartment, I'd given him a taste of what I was capable of, but prior to that, I'd been asleep. Considering how relaxed he was, sprawled on my couch, he could have been there for minutes, hours even. He had plenty of opportunity to kill me and collect on the contract, but he hadn't. He'd waited.

No, he wasn't sent to kill me. I was sure of it. He wanted something, and the sword was the key to finding out what.

"So he's half-demon." I nodded firmly. It felt right. I'd known he had power, had felt it the moment he'd walked into my workshop, but his half-human nature had confused me. "What demon sired him?"

Nica scratched at her cheek, briefly dropping her gaze to the scattered images. "His father was human. His mother is Yukki-Onna, also known as the Snow Spirit."

"Snow? As in an ice element?" No wonder he and I didn't get along. While I was born of fire, my power fuelled by flame, his stemmed from the exact opposite. He and I were poles apart, elementally destined to repel one another.

"From the feelers Akil put out," Nica said, "she continues to have a relationship with her son. It's all rumor, of course. Officially, she denies he even exists."

I had to smile. If my father, Asmodeus, acknowledged my existence I'd soon be wiped from the face of the earth like a bug from a windshield. But then my father was one of the Seven Princes of Hell, so he had a certain reputation to adhere to. Lucky for me, he chose to deny my existence, and nobody dared question him. It was a shame my brother couldn't follow in our father's footsteps and ignore me.

"Akil believes my brother sent Stefan to kill me..." I hadn't seen my brother for a long time, but the specter of his intent to kill me followed me everywhere. A full-blood demon, born of a pure bloodline, he considered my existence an abhorrent freak of nature. My life offended him.

"In all honesty, it could be any number of demons. No offense, Muse, but you're not exactly popular among your kind." She offered me a half smile.

Because I dared to be different; the obtuse little half-blood who had somehow managed to slaughter her owner. Yeah, that was me, and I'd do it again in a heartbeat.

Nica was right. My brother Val could have sent Stefan after me, but so could any number of pissed off demons who would have taken offense at my ingratitude at being owned. How dare I snub them? Had I just insulted them, things might not have been so bad, but to kill my previous owner, yeah... There was no coming back from that one. I had a target on my back, and there was no escaping it.

It did make me wonder why Akil had protected me and continued to do so.

"You'll be safe here," Nica offered, reading my pensive expression as one of concern.

"Yeah, about that... I can't stay here. I can't just leave everything I had." I tossed Stefan's picture back onto the pile of documents. "I have a boyfriend. Well, did have. We sort of...we broke up. Anyway, I can't just leave."

She stood with a sigh. "That's between you and Akil."

"And a cat. Jonesy. I have to make arrangements for him. Bills need paying. The police want to talk to me about the workshop. I can't just walk out one night and never go back."

Nica looked down at me, and I swear I saw pity on her face. "All I know is, once you're in, there is no out." Her bright smile was back, and the pity I thought I'd seen might as well have been imagined. "It was nice to meet you. I was expecting a bitter and twisted woman on the verge of insanity. You seem pleasantly coherent to me."

I laughed, not entirely sure whether she was joking or not. "Thanks, I think."

"Take care, and if you have any more questions, just give me a call. My number's on the front of the file."

"I have a question."

"Oh."

"What are you? You're not demon. You referred to demons as my kind, so what are you? I'm just curious, is all."

She chuckled. "Well, I'm just a personal assistant." By way she spoke, the slight tip of her head, a glint of mischief in her eyes, she made it perfectly clear she was not just a personal assistant.

After she'd left, I browsed through the file on Stefan, absorbing and digesting every piece of information I could find. At least when we next met, and I was under no illusion—there would be a next time—I'd know who I was dealing with.

Chapter Five

Jonesy's throaty purr resonated around my small kitchen. I envied my cat's simple existence as I tickled him behind his ears. He chomped merrily through his bowl of kibble, oblivious to my turmoil. I'd made arrangements for my landlord to temporarily take him on, but I really didn't want to leave him. I'd taken on the responsibility of having a pet, and it felt like failure to hand him over to someone else; a little like I'd be shoved from one owner to another. It didn't sit well with me. While discussing temporary ownership of my cat, I let my landlord know the electrics in my apartment appeared to be on the blink (not mentioning it might have something to do with the energy spike from a half-blood demon) and paid him two months' rent in advance while giving him notice of my intention to vacate.

I lied and told him I'd secured a metalworking contract half way across the country. He said he was sorry to see me go, and I believed him. In the three years I'd been there, I hadn't once been late with the rent. I didn't hold rowdy late night parties and barely had any visitors at all. The model tenant.

That would all change if I'd stayed.

The few items I considered important fit into a shoebox. Photographs, mostly. A note from Sam that he'd left at the workshop one evening, asking if I took commissions. He'd been recommended by a friend and had seen my work online. I didn't sell swords from a website. I was pretty sure that would raise some eyebrows, but I did craft metal pieces for private clients. Gates, candlesticks, art. It paid the bills, and I was damn good at it.

I'd realized I could read metal during my time as another demon's plaything. A curious skill, to say the least. I couldn't explain it, not really. Some might call it psychic, but how could metal retain a memory? It doesn't, but that doesn't stop me from seeing the people who might briefly have come into contact with a metal item. Perhaps the metal creates a bridge between the past and present, and being an elemental demon, I could cross that bridge. Whatever it was, the demons who controlled my chains very quickly learned about my skill. At first, I'd thought it might mean they would afford me some respect, but all it did was give them another means by which to hurt me.

Reading the metal requires a sacrifice of blood, specifically my own blood. To get any kind of image at all, I must bleed, and it just so happens that all demons ever want to read are weapons. Swords, daggers, axes. Demons aren't known for their subtly. Make me bleed, make me read. It had been Damien's mantra. Come see the curious half-blood who can read your past; bring your own sword.

I shivered just thinking about him, preferring instead to file those memories away in the 'Do-Not-Enter' part of my mind. Damien, my ex-owner, was dead, my past and the woman I had been, long dead with him. If it hadn't been for Akil, I might have still been there, sobbing on the end of those chains, my demon soul spent and my body abused.

"You shouldn't be here."

I yelped in surprise at Akil's voice. He stood in my apartment doorway, leaning against the doorframe and had never looked as wickedly divine as he did in that moment. He wore a perfectly tailored tuxedo, jacket unbuttoned over a fluid white shirt. His crooked smile topped off the sophisticated demeanor, so he simply exuded confidence. He held a bottle of red wine in one hand. A cocktail dress still inside its clear wrapping was draped over his other arm.

He sauntered over to me and deliberately stood a little too close, leaning past me to place the bottle of wine on the countertop. As he straightened, he made no attempt to move out of my personal space.

He smelled like cinnamon and cloves, like a fireplace on a cold winter's day, and it was all I could do to gape up at him. His hazel eyes appeared almost black as he looked down into my wide-eyed stare. As he breathed, I felt the energy radiating from him and had to fight not to reach out and place my hands on his chest. I could soak up that power, draw it into me, but once I did that, I wouldn't be able to escape the lure of his control.

I took a few light steps backward, extricating myself from his clear intent to distract me. "I er—I can't stay with you, Akil. I just can't." Along that path, bad things slumbered. If I gave in to him, let him control everything again, it would be like walking toward a black hole, knowing it would swallow me whole but unable to break free. I couldn't give up my control. It was everything to me.

"You can't stay here."

"I know that." I gestured at the shoebox as though that explained everything. I sounded irritated, but in fact was more annoyed at my traitorous body and the stirring of desire that did odd things to me. For a start, I couldn't breathe properly.

I marched across the room and flung open the same window Stefan had escaped from the day before. Outside, the sun had dipped behind the high-rises, the warmth of the day seeping from the air as the dark of night loomed.

Akil stood beside me, leaning against the wall by the window and snaking his arms crossed. "Your little show of power melted the streetlights." He was enjoying this, could probably read right through my stubborn attempt at denying I felt anything. "It made the news. A power-surge. I've never seen a power-surge melt the post. Have you?"

I shifted awkwardly. I could see one of the streetlights in question outside the window, just off to my right, its damaged head drooping low. No, that wasn't normal. The elements of chaos are slippery, difficult to rein in, always demanding freedom.

"Every demon worth his name knows something happened here, Muse, and you're right in the middle of it." He closed the distance between us with a single stride and swept a fallen lock of hair from across my eye. "You can't come back here. I can't lose you again."

I fell into his eyes again, my body possessed by the hunger he roused in me. A shiver of power danced across my skin, and the fine hairs on my arms stood on end. He might look human, but that was where the similarity ended. The demon inside his male exterior burned with primal needs. It devoured, it stole, it consumed. He was all greed and desire, always hungry. And I knew his real name. Mammon, Prince of Greed.

It was the human in me that resisted him, always had been. Perhaps that's why he'd saved me. To my knowledge, I was the only demon, half or otherwise, brave or stupid enough to walk away from him. Most cowered at his feet.

I found myself moving away again. As if in a slow waltz, we drifted about my apartment only to be irrevocably drawn back together again.

"You're going out?" I squeaked, clearing my throat and cursing my female urges. Goddamn him. How was I meant to think clearly with this much power in the room? I planted both hands on the cool kitchen countertop, admiring the little red dress folded there, with its short ruffled lace hem. If he thought I was wearing that, he could go straight back to hell. Unless I could wear it with boots, of course.

"I was hoping you'd join me. A little human party I've thrown together."

I turned my head, smiling. "I don't think that's wise. Do you? I've got a killer after me, not to mention all manner of demons who would like to take me down a peg or two, and you want me to party the night away?"

He raised an eyebrow and shrugged a shoulder, before retrieving the bottle of wine and beginning to search my cupboards, I assumed, for wine glasses.

"Nobody would dare threaten you in my presence." He found the glasses and planted them in front of me. He tore the foil off the wine, paused as if briefly considering searching for a corkscrew before he decided not to bother and instead placed the palm of his hand over the cork, summoning it from the bottle with a satisfying pop.

I watched the red wine pool in the glasses as he poured. With a twist of the wrist, he straightened the bottle, and placing it on the side, he slipped the stem of a glass between his fingers and presented the drink to me.

"What do you want from me, Akil?" I smiled my thanks and took the glass. I'd asked him the same question many times over the years and had never received a satisfying answer. In my last few years by his side, I'd stopped asking altogether, but by then I'd stopped thinking for myself too.

"All I want is for you to be safe."

"But why?" I tasted the wine, finding it satisfyingly warm.

He picked up his glass and tapped a finger on the dress. "Will you come?" His smile twitched as he saw me hesitate. "How long has it been since you really enjoyed yourself, Muse?" He leaned forward. "I mean all of you." The delicious purr of his dulcet tones stole my breath.

What harm could it do? A human party, he had said. Nothing to worry about.

Leaving my wine on the countertop, I scooped up the dress, and casting him a playful smirk, I disappeared into my bedroom to change.

A party might do me some good, I thought. A chance to unwind, to forget my would-be assassin and the abrupt end to my normal life. Perhaps I could treat it like a farewell of sorts. One last hurrah before I stepped back into the world of demons and their devious machinations.

After dressing in the little red number, I checked my reflection, reaching behind me in an attempt to zip up the dress. I couldn't do much about my pale complexion or the hounded look in my eyes, but with a little splash of lipstick, I might resemble a woman in control.

Akil's reflection behind mine snatched a gasp from me. Before I could protest, I felt the press of him against my back. The aura of power that he wore wrapped its warmth around me as he trailed his fingers down the curve of my neck. I tiled my head to the side, my gaze locked on his, daring him to proceed.

He slid a hand around my waist. His palm pressed against my hip as he pulled me back against him. My own power unfurled, tentative ethereal tendrils reaching outward, entwining around him, through him.

He growled low in his throat and broke our stare by bowing his head. I couldn't help leaning back against him while his lips trailed painfully delicate kisses down my neck. He slid the dress from my shoulder and nipped at my flushed skin, sending tremors rippling through me. The demon in me purred, slipping into my skin and spilling the heat of otherworldly energy across my flesh.

I heard him suck in air through his teeth, breathing in energy and felt his body quiver. I watched his reflection as he dragged his stare back up to meet mine. To know that he wanted me, a being born of magic and chaos, an ageless and powerful Prince of Hell, was all the excuse I needed.

He saw my acceptance, or felt it and turned me suddenly in his arms, pinning me back against the mirror. I laughed or growled or purred again. Either way, I was lost. He clasped my head in his hands. The sudden urgency made it difficult for me to breathe. I expected him to kiss me, for his mouth to hungrily devour mine. I knew where it would roam from there, the trail of wanton destruction it would leave across my body. I groaned for it, but he kissed me so gently, lips so frustratingly soft.

I snarled. His teasing just about drove me insane, and I lunged at him, tasting him, teasing him. Arms around his neck, I pulled him down to me, and this time he didn't hesitate. When he drove me back against the mirror, the glass cracked. Hitching a leg around his thigh, I locked him against me, fisting my hands in his hair as his biting kisses skipped over the rise of my breast.

The phone in the kitchen rang.

He snarled something that didn't sound human before finding my mouth again. My body baked in the heat rippling between us. Power spiraled around us like an entirely new force of nature. I knew what it meant to be lost in Akil, to forget the fragility of my human flesh and succumb to the overwhelming power he commanded.

The phone continued to ring, its shrill alarm sounding all the more persistent for being ignored.

Akil planted a hand against the wall beside me and met my stare. His dark eyes simmered with energy. An inferno raged within. He dragged every breath through clenched teeth, as though struggling to contain the energy broiling the air. I have to admit, it felt good to have him like that, knowing I could pull him back in. He might not be human, but the vessel he had chosen was, and I could give him one hell of a ride.

The phone cut off, and my recorded voice jabbered on about not being home, please leave a message.

I leaned into him and licked at his lips, teasing my tongue ever so gently between them.

"This is a message for Charlotte Henderson. Charlotte, I'm Detective Mark Bergin. We need you to come down to the station. We have a witness who's given us a description of a man we believe to have been at your premises shortly before the explosion and... well... we would prefer it if we spoke to you in person. You need to call me back. This man is potentially very dangerous."

I heard the detective's voice chattering away in the other room as he left his message. I'd have ignored it, but the mention of a man I could only assume was Stefan instantly doused my desire. Akil must have sensed my distraction. With a resigned sigh, he leaned against me, his cheek resting against mine. The power we had summoned between us began to fizzle away, crackling and spitting its displeasure as it retreated. I felt its departure keenly and ached to have it back, but the moment was gone.

When he pulled back, the swirl of power I'd seen in his eyes had vanished, and his smile was a little despondent.

"Tonight," he promised. "After the party. We're going to finish this."

He said it like a threat, and my insides fluttered, a sliver of desire peeling the last little groan from me before Akil released me.

Chapter Six

Streetlights flickered on as Akil's limo inched forward through the rush hour traffic. The car was so well insulated that, while I could see the city bustling by us outside, I couldn't hear a thing. Throngs of people flowed back and forth over the sidewalks in their rush to get home. They had no idea one of the most powerful demons ever to have existed sat a few yards from them behind the limo's black privacy glass.

Akil relaxed in the seat opposite me, leaning an arm on the wrap-around shelf. His gaze slid across the anonymous people outside. Lost in thought, we had barely spoken a word since leaving my apartment. I felt the tug of desire every time I let my gaze linger just a little too long. Occasionally, he'd flick his dark eyes to me, and I'd see that hunger slumbering there. He didn't need to speak to make me to squirm in the leather seats. It took every ounce of my human stubbornness to stop myself from pouncing on him. My imagination worked overtime to supply me with the sort of images that brought a rush of color to my cheeks.

"Would you like me to accompany you?" He leaned forward to reach for the door.

The unimaginative blocky structure housing the police department loomed outside as the driver pulled the car to a halt against the curb. I peered through the soundproof glass at the entrance, reaching for the door handle. My fingers brushed his. A spark of energy bolted between us, providing enough of a shock for me to snatch my hand back.

He held my gaze. Words were superfluous against the wolfish grin on his lips. He opened the door, stepped out, and held it open for me.

It felt good to step from the car back into the bustle of city life. I breathed deeply, tasting the metallic residue of the city air on my lips. The clamor from the traffic grounded me firmly back in reality.

Akil looked at me as though waiting for an answer. It took me a while to remember what he'd asked.

I glanced up the steps at the police department doors. "No, I'll be fine. Will you wait?"

"Of course." He closed the car door and shrugged off his coat, before sliding the expensive garment around my shoulders. He hesitated, bunching the jacket together below my chin and looking down at me. His smile faltered, and the briefest glimmer of concern tightened his expression before he retreated to lean against the car. Despite the chill in the air, he wore only a shirt. The cold wouldn't bother him. Such human afflictions rarely did, and yet something clearly concerned him.

I climbed the steps and entered the building, feeling somewhat over-dressed in my red cocktail dress and knee-high boots. In the cramped waiting area, plastic chairs lined one wall. A water-cooler butted up against the reception desk. I registered my arrival with the uniformed officer at the desk and asked for Detective Bergin.

I didn't have long to wait. Detective Bergin introduced himself with a handshake firm enough to bruise. A big man at six foot plus, he towered over me. A barrel chest and booming voice declared him alpha, whether he knew it or not. He was the kind of guy people instinctively move out of the way for.

"Have a seat." In an interview room, he gestured at the metal chairs before pulling one out from beneath the table and lowering his muscular bulk into it. The chair creaked.

The room was little more than a concrete box. A fluorescent light spilled a sickly glow on its four mauve walls. I couldn't be sure whether it was the room or the man, but a slither of unease had worked its way beneath my skin.

"Thank you for coming." His voice boomed far too loud for the small space we shared. He gestured again for me to sit, thrusting out a large calloused hand as though it was not a request but an order.

I planted a hand on my hip and stayed on my feet. "That's okay. You said someone saw something at my workshop?" I didn't want to stay any longer than necessary. I had a hot date, literally, and my distaste for the detective was growing by the second. His very presence left an odd taste in my mouth, like the gritty aftertaste of spoiled fruit.

"Yes." He snatched at a thin file from the table and flicked open the cover. "Do you know this man?" He pinched an 8-by-10 color photo between his thick fingers and holding it up for me.

It was Stefan. "No."

The same distinctive red coat, but the image had been enlarged. The quality suffered because of it. In the photo, Stefan held something at his side, a sword perhaps, a very different one from the katana he'd brought to my workshop. With no identifying date or time stamps and a blurry background, I couldn't be sure when or where the image had been taken.

"We have a witness placing this man outside your workshop minutes before the explosion. Apparently, he got into a red car. Do you know anything about that?"

"No."

Bergin's cracked lips peeled back over coffee-stained teeth in a mockery of a smile. "You don't remember watching him leave prior to your workshop going up in smoke?"

I glanced at the door and back at Bergin. "Are you asking or telling me?"

He blinked slowly, leaning back in his chair and chomping his lips together as he deliberately raked a filthy gaze over me. "This man, he's wanted for murder, numerous assaults, wilful destruction of public property, and more parking offences than you can shake a stick at, and yet he continues to elude us—not to mention destroying your place of work. So I was wondering if you might remember seeing him and whether you'd be kind enough to tell us where we can find him."

"I don't know that man. I've never seen him before in my life." Why was he so insistent? Wasn't I meant to be the victim here? I certainly did not like how he looked at me or how he implied I was lying. Despite the fact that he was right.

Bergin refused to look away as I deliberately pinned my stare on his. He might think he could bully me. In fact from the sordid gaze, I could tell he wasn't thinking much beyond what lay beneath my dress. He had no idea what he was dealing with.

"Are you done?" My fingers twitched at my sides. I could spill a little power into my touch if I needed to. He'd wake with one hell of a headache.

He snorted a laugh. "You half-bloods are all the same."

I looked away, plastering a grin on my lips. Apparently there was more going on here than a simple Q and A. Now that he'd revealed he knew me, we could cut to the chase.

He stood, the chair legs scraping across the floor, and steepled his fingers on the table before him. He bowed his head but kept his eyes on me, like a wolf hunched, ready to attack. "You think Akil can protect you?"

I summoned a little heat, pooling it in the palms of my hands. If he noticed any change in me, he didn't show it.

"He's not here now." Bergin's voice began to slur and grind his words, no doubt something to do with the elongated teeth cluttering his mouth.

Demon. I had no idea what sort, but knew I was about to find out.

The exit door stood at about the same distance away from me as Bergin. If I made a dash for it, the table between us would slow him down.

He straightened, muscles cracking as he shook off his human guise. The bulk of him shimmered indistinctly. My limited human eyesight blurred the full depth of his transformation, but I saw his form expand as though he'd gained a few more pounds in a few seconds. His flesh peppered with scales. His mouth and nose stretched outward, elongating into a snout. His curved fangs drooled saliva. A forked tongue flicked.

He hunched over, arms pinned to his sides as his body stretched. Scales latticed the length of him until nothing of the detective remained. The huge serpent reared up, mounting the table in one fluid ripple of its smooth body.

"I shall be rewarded..." Its hideous voice clawing through my thoughts.

I thrust a bolt of energy down my right arm and cast my hand out, lashing a whip-like tendril of heat across its scaled form, then sprinted for the door. I managed perhaps two strides, before it slithered in front of me, blocking my path. Serpentine eyes blazed green. A black tongue flicked, tasting the air, forcing me back.

"You should be dead," It quite literally hissed, spittle streaming from its fangs, but I heard the words clearly inside my mind. "...your throat cut the day you were born. That is our way. You are a monstrosity!"

"Look who's talking," I snarled.

I dipped my chin, looking up at the demon through hooded eyes. Thrusting both arms down at my sides, I summoned power, drawing it into me while the darkest part of me spilled into fragile flesh.

The serpent-demon rose higher, jaws opening into a glistening grin. It lunged forward as I threw everything I had at it. A furious blast of energy funneled through me, slamming into the beast with enough force for it to ripple backward, shaking its whiskered head with a wrenching scream. I backed up again, the power planting itself inside every limb, pooling in muscle, bolstering my fragile flesh. It rushed through me, a burning elixir spilling through my veins, bringing me to life. And this time it had a target.

I lashed out, casting a lance of power toward the layered scales of the thing's chest. The blanching white heat passed through it, tearing a hole. The demon lifted its head and let out a keening cry that drilled into my skull.

I staggered. Its cry shattered my momentary enjoyment like shards of glass thrust into my skull. I had no choice but to cover my ears. It was no use. The cry resounded within me.

Hunched low, I willed it to stop. My power rattled about me, seeking a target but finding only chaos. I couldn't focus, couldn't hear, could barely breathe, and then it was gone. Like the snap of a light switch chasing away the plummeting darkness, it was over, and when I opened my eyes, I saw why.

Akil, or rather his true form, Mammon, stood before the serpent-demon. He had thrust an ethereal broadsword made entirely of an undulating electric blue light through the serpent-demon's scaled body. The bloodied, intangible tip of the sword protruded from its skull. I stumbled, falling to my knees, as always, finding Akil's true nature difficult for my human eyes to focus on. The suffocating weight of his considerable power filled the room. The overwhelming pressure of it crushed the air from my lungs. I forced myself to look at him, refusing to let weakness steal my consciousness.

Akil's broad multi-jointed wings of tanned leather bowed against the ceiling, a dusting of embers raining from their arched edges. As those wings flexed, the muscles in his broad back rippled. Every ounce of flesh looked as though it had been sculpted from obsidian, every muscle lean and powerful.

"Vos inhonesto mihi." Akil's growl thundered around my aching skull. *You dishonor me.*

I watched his right shoulder bunch, one wing jerking a little as he altered his grip on the sword and twisted the blade deep in its snug-fitting wound. The serpent demon grunted, skewered as it was. It was only when Akil tore the sword free, ripping open the chest of the beast, that it collapsed forward, tail twitching. A dark pool of blood bloomed around its hideous body. Its green eyes hung open, unseeing. Dead.

Akil turned, and I caught a glimpse of his true face before I bowed my head. Cut from the very fabric of the elements, his face barely resembled the man I'd left beside the car. He appeared more beast than man with spiraled horns twisting from his forehead, his wide gaping mouth brimming with jagged teeth. Dark wrappings of power thrashed around him, seeking their next victim. An aura of energy simmered against his flesh. The thin veil of reality fizzled into dust at his feet.

I'm not ashamed to admit that I cowered on my hands and knees before him. The other part of me had slunk away into the farthest corners of my mind, curling herself into a tiny insignificant flutter in my chest, hardly there at all.

He crouched before me, thick muscular arms resting on stocky knees slick with a sheen of energy. When he held out a hand, elongated fingers tipped with curved claws, I had no choice but to take it. My delicate fingers curled in his, my human flesh so pink and fragile. His writhing tendrils of power curled themselves up my forearm, snaking around my elbow before leaping to my shoulder. I had enough time to realize the darkness had entwined itself around my legs like creeping vines, before the weight of it dragged me down. I fell, and the darkness rushed up to greet me.

Chapter Seven

The party had spilled out into the hotel foyer. The inebriated guests wore masquerade masks ranging from vampires to ghosts and demons. Akil's idea of irony, I guess. It would have been hilarious, had I not just seen one of the originals of those so-called myths slice a serpent demon in half.

Akil sat in the center of the head table like a scene from a modern day last supper, leaning crookedly in his chair as he laughed at something the woman beside him said. They all wore masks, so only mouths and eyes could be seen. The more subtle expressions remained hidden. He had given up trying to catch my eye and now appeared to revel in the role of charming host. His mask sported a pair of devil horns. Those around him had no idea that the beast sat among them. He played the part of a human a little too perfectly, but nobody would suspect him. He was too charming, too successful, too influential to be anything other than the city's most successful developer.

I poured myself some more wine and slumped in my chair. It wasn't as if I didn't know what he was. I felt the power in him every time I shared the same airspace as him, but it's one thing to know and another to see. I'd deliberately forgotten who and what he was for the sake of my sanity. My half-human mind couldn't keep up with what I'd seen, despite the fact that much of the same elemental energy ran through my veins. The human brain struggles to comprehend the truth about demons. The netherworld exists beyond our spectrum of understanding. Our senses are struck dumb by its extremes. Thankfully, the netherworld is locked beyond the veil, out of human reach, but while humans can't survive there for long, demons can and do live among us here. Higher demons can cross the veil at will, but most prefer their homeland to ours. Aren't we lucky?

Akil had walked me out of that police department without another soul seeing us. The people had parted in front of us, veering around us without realizing anything was amiss. He had simply peeled the visible reality around us so that we emerged outside the building without so much as catching a sideways glance from the dozens of people on the sidewalk.

Hands planted against the roof of his car as though to steady himself, Akil had stripped the demon from his visible form, shedding layers like a snake sheds its skin, revealing the male vessel inside. Watching him emerge like that—his human form reborn like a moth from its chrysalis—turned my stomach. By the time he'd sat me in the back of the car, I felt numb. When we reached his hotel, I still trembled like a leaf clinging to an otherwise naked branch. Without so much as a word of explanation, an apology, or an 'are you okay,' he handed me a cat mask and escorted me inside.

That had been over two hours ago.

If he knew of the turmoil spinning in my head, he hadn't once mentioned it. For him, it was as though nothing untoward had taken place. Another day at the office.

Nica slipped into a chair beside me, sporting a very fine leopard-print ankle-length dress and a witch's mask, complete with a cute crooked hat. "Hey there." She beamed. "Akil said you were coming." Perhaps my smile came off more as a grimace than I'd meant it to because she flinched, her bubbly mood evaporating. "Did you read all the information in the file?"

It took me a moment to even remember what file she was referring to. I hadn't thought of Stefan since Bergin had mentioned him prior to turning into a snake-demon and trying to kill me. Now I wondered what the police would be asking. They wouldn't find a body—of that I was pretty sure—but Bergin wasn't coming back from a sword through the gullet, and I was technically the last to see him. How would Akil cover it up? Would he even bother?

"You look a little pale, are you okay?" Nica asked.

The concern in her voice roused me from my recall of events. "Yes, I'm okay. Just tired." I mustered a warmer smile and downed my drink.

She shrugged and refilled my glass. "Something has happened between you and Akil. Am I right?"

I swallowed, reaching for the wine. "What makes you say that?"

She looked past me, down the table to where Akil and a small crowd were gathered. "He looks content, but you see how his fingers are tapping on the base of his glass?" She nodded encouragement, so I had to look.

"He hasn't touched his drink. That's the same glass of wine he's been nursing all evening. And that crowd—some of them are the most influential people in this city, and yet he hasn't once engaged in business talk. He's avoiding it, skirting around the topic, which is not like him at all. We both know how greedy he is, but tonight, there's nothing here for him."

I looked at Nica with newfound respect. "You know him well."

"I have to." She lowered her voice and reached out a hand to clasp mine. "If we play with fire, sooner or later, we all get burned." She slipped off her mask, revealing a wrought expression. Lines of worry etched into her fine features. "Nobody plays with Akil unless they're prepared." She lifted her glass, inviting me to do the same.

"To the survivors," she suggested. We clinked our glasses together.

"You're right." I finally admitted. I sensed the warmth of Akil's gaze on me but refused to rise to the bait. "Something happened."

"Well, don't let him fool you. Whatever it was, it bothered him." Nica grinned and dipped her head low. "Whatever you did, good on you. It can't hurt to remind them who holds the true power, right?"

"Who?" I laughed.

"You, us, women. He loves you, Muse, and that's more powerful than anything else in this mockery of reality."

That was absurd. Akil didn't—couldn't love me. Demons were capable of many things, but love wasn't one of them. "How much wine have you had?"

She arched an eyebrow and admired the swirl of red wine in her glass. "Not nearly enough. Finish off this bottle with me, will you?"

Chapter Eight

As the night wore on, a live band began to play. The crowd got merrier by the minute. Much of the exuberance had rubbed off on me, or perhaps it was the wine. I'd begun to relax a little and mingle with the guests. Most were human, but some were not. I caught a few leers from behind the anonymous masks and silently cursed Akil. He'd made a point of telling me that no demons were on the list, and yet I'd counted at least five blending with Boston's elite. They, of course, looked just like anyone else, but there were clues. Demons move with a fluid grace, as though every step, every gesture, is measured. Nothing is wasted. When still, they might as well have been smartly-dressed mannequins and were equally as disconcerting because of their inhuman stillness. Humans are constantly in motion. Demons are not. They stalk. It's part of makes them so efficient.

I gave the demons I'd spotted a wide berth. Akil seemed confident nobody would dare hurt me in his presence, but that wouldn't prevent one of them driving a dagger into my back before he could stop them. I admired the generous buffet food, wondering if I should eat something from the perfect plates of sandwiches arranged in geometric shapes. Some had yet to be touched, and I had to fight the urge to upset the precise design just for fun.

A hand slipped around my waist from behind, and immediately a sliver of fear trickled down my spine.

Akil must have felt me tremble because he bowed his head, whispering against my cheek. "Do I frighten you?"

I didn't dignify his query with an answer and turned to face him, driving back the fear with sheer determination. He still wore the ridiculous devil mask. I flicked it off to reveal his playful expression beneath, then tossed the mask away with a mischievous grin.

"Dance with me." It wasn't a request. His fingers had laced in mine, and he pulled me toward the dance floor before I could concoct an excuse. Thankfully, the music was slow. I had no idea how to dance. They didn't teach party etiquette where I was raised.

He pulled me against him, hand slipping down to the small of my back to hold me close. I giggled. Alcohol had gone a long way toward soothing my fears. Stumbling a little, I looked at my feet, wondering what on earth I was supposed to do with them. Akil tipped my chin up.

"Just lean into me and relax."

I obeyed, preferring to let him guide me than risk complete embarrassment. I found the slow beat of the music calming. Or was it standing so close to him that banished my worries? Either way, I let him hold me close as we swayed gently.

"Are you alright?" His deep voice rumbled through me as the music played around us. There were others dancing, but I barely noticed them. I listened to his heartbeat, losing myself in its rhythm.

"I'm okay," I whispered, and I really was. Akil had that effect on me. "I had that serpent demon where I wanted him, y'know. I was just about to finish him off when you showed up."

I felt Akil chuckle. The delicious ripple of laughter ignited desire at the very heart of me. "I very much doubt that," he said. "The detective was a Dahaka servant." The exotic pronunciation rolled off Akil's tongue, revealing an ancient accent he usually kept hidden. "A particularly aggressive example. He would have relished devouring you, likely feet first."

I stopped swaying in time with Akil and looked up. He smiled, but I got the impression he wasn't joking. With a trembling sigh, I rested my head against his shoulder. "I wanted to leave all of this behind."

His fingers gently stroked my back. "You can't."

"I know, but I could have pretended."

"Your five year folly almost got you killed." His arm snaked around me.

I closed my eyes, my grip on him tightening. I'd wanted to be free so badly that I might have gladly died for it. The demons and their ways weren't me. I belonged in the nine-to-five working day with the Starbucks coffees and kicking back on the couch, Doritos in one hand, TV remote in the other. I enjoyed the mundane. At least that's what I told myself. It wasn't exactly true. I could never run from the half of me that danced in the dark.

"Let's go." He looked into my tired eyes. "Wait here. I'll make my excuses, and we'll go back to my apartment."

With a nod of agreement, I reluctantly let go of him and cast him a little curl of a smile before he turned and let the crowd swallow him up. He'd promised a night to remember, and the thought of being alone with him with no interruptions—exploring, tasting, teasing—warmed me in the most intimate of places.

A shoulder nudged mine, forcing me to stumble back, just as an arm hooked around me, reeling me into a crushing embrace. I opened my mouth, about to launch a verbal assault on my unwanted dance partner, when I felt the brutal nudge of a gun poke up under my ribs.

"Scream and I'll pull the trigger." Stefan drilled his gaze into mine.

We were moving, swaying to the music like those around us, his grip so tight against me that I had no chance but to step with him. "You won't leave here alive," I hissed.

"No?" His azure eyes scanned the crowd around us. "I don't think you know me very well."

I squirmed in his grip. The pressure of the gun began to bruise me. "I'd have thought you'd have had enough of your games by now."

He met my gaze as though something I said surprised him. "You're in danger."

"No shit."

"You have to come with me. Now."

"I'm not going anywhere with you." I squirmed again. His grip tightened further, wrenching a gasp from my lips.

He suddenly bowed his head, his hair tickling against my cheek and whispered, "You must have realized by now that I don't want to hurt you."

Anger flash-burned through me. "Then you're failing miserably because you have hurt me. You took away the only thing I've ever really owned. You stole my life." As he faced me, I saw his eyes narrow, as though I'd hurt him with my words, but for the life of me I couldn't imagine why. "Who are you?"

"Please, come with me now. There are others here. You aren't safe."

I followed his gaze among the sea of party guests and saw the demons approaching, parting the dancing couples like lions stalking through long grass. Stefan jerked an eyebrow and then the pressure of the gun was gone. His cool grip tightened around my wrist, and before I could protest, I was jogging after him. He led me through a fire door. The music from the party thumped the air and echoed down the stairwell. Fluorescent lights hummed above us.

"Wait." I snatched my wrist free, forcing him to turn. His long leather coat rippled around him. "Just tell me what's happening." I rubbed my aching wrist.

"They're coming."

The fire door burst open behind me. I had a moment to recognize one of my suspected demons from the party before he launched himself at me. He sprang off his legs in such a way that he literally pounced, hands and feet slamming into me, throwing me back against the wall. My head smacked against the block work, dizzying me and stalling my reaction. He threw his head back and yawned, revealing a mouthful of razor sharp, needle-thin teeth. Repugnant ocher venom dripped from their points, dribbling over the distorted flesh of his chin.

I flooded my body with power, but it wouldn't come quickly enough.

A gun blast cracked the air, and the side of the demon's skull exploded in a burst of blood and bone. I blinked, ears ringing, and struggled to comprehend what was happening as the body collapsed in a lifeless mound at my feet.

Stefan stood a few steps down, gun poised in one hand. He snatched at my hand and tugged me stumbling down the stairs behind him. We didn't stop until we burst through the doors into the basement parking garage. Orderly rows of cars lined the bays, their glossy paintwork shining beneath the orange strip-lights. I saw his battered, old car ahead.

I pulled back, but his grip tightened. "Wait." He didn't stop. "Wait, dammnit!" I dug my heels in and snatched him back. "I can look after myself."

He rounded on me, his smile devoid of all humor. "Are you serious?"

"Who the hell are you, and why do you think you can drag me around like this?"

He snorted a derisive laugh. "I just saved your life—again—and you doubt me?" His voice echoed around the parking lot, bouncing off the walls and returning with just as much derision in its tone.

"What do you mean, again?"

He looked as though he might have answered when a blood-curdling howl sounded throughout the parking garage. I turned, sensing the source was somewhere behind me. I knew that sound. The beast it came from was no friendly dog. Fear flushed through my veins, adrenalin spiking, racing my heart and ratcheting up my breathing.

Another howl went up, followed quickly by another. The wretched baying echoed.

"Muse! C'mon!"

I searched the shadows among the parked cars but couldn't see anything, but then I wasn't going to. I was too human to see them. Then I heard the panting, the tick of claws on concrete, and the thump of heavy pads.

I swung a glance back at Stefan. "They're for you!" I hoped they were because Hellhounds cannot be outrun.

He dipped his chin and shook his head once, then lifted the gun and fired over my shoulder. The gunshot cracked the air, the deafening boom followed by a dire whine. I trembled even as I summoned my element because I knew it wouldn't be enough. I couldn't see the hounds—they were constructs of pure demonic power—but I could hear them. My imagination unhelpfully filled in the blanks.

Stefan grabbed my arm and tugged me backward. I finally found my nerves again and ran beside him, heeled boots skidding on the concrete as I ducked around Stefan's car and tugged open the passenger door. "Can you see them?" I panted, throwing myself into the seat.

"Oh yes." He turned the key in the ignition, and the engine roared to life. Thrusting the stick into reverse, he flung the car from its parking bay and stamped on the brakes.

Twisting in the passenger seat, I peered out through the back window but couldn't see anything. The car suddenly bucked, the roof above caving inward. Four gashes ripped through the roof as though it were paper.

"Hold on!" Stefan planted the accelerator to the floor, lurching the car backward again.

I snatched at my seat, clinging on as the invisible hound on the roof tumbled forward, cracking the windscreen and denting the hood on its way down. Stefan locked an arm around the back of my seat. His unwavering glare focused through the rear window, and his other hand twitched the steering wheel. I had a moment to wonder where we were going when the rear of the car plowed into a sizeable chunk of nothingness. The hound yowled.

"Is it dead?"

"Nope. Just pissed." Stefan slammed the car into gear and yanked the steering wheel, accelerating hard toward the exit ramp. The rear end fishtailed, tires squealing, before the car finally found traction and lunged forward. Its raw horse-power threw me back into my seat.

We burst onto the street, narrowly missing passing traffic. Stefan fought with the steering wheel. The car slid sideways, but he didn't ease off the accelerator. Engine revving, the car gobbled up the road. Buildings blurred past us. Weaving between the sparse nighttime traffic, Stefan swapped the car from lane to lane. Horns sounded around us.

"Put your seatbelt on." He stared ahead, his attention divided between the road and mirrors, before changing gears to squeeze yet more acceleration from the engine.

I fumbled with the seatbelt, watching the needle on the speedometer creep higher. Glancing out of the rear window, I couldn't see anything but the angry flash of headlights from other drivers as they resented our disregard for traffic laws.

"I can't see them."

"Take this." He tossed the gun into my lap before dropping a gear. The car roared, and we burst through an intersection, the red lights little more than a blur in my peripheral vision.

I picked up the weighty gun. "But I can't see them."

He stole a brief glance my way. "Call your power. You'll see them."

Stefan jerked the car to the right. I clung on, leaning away from the turn as the car drifted toward oncoming traffic. If the hounds didn't kill us, his driving would. I caught him smiling and frowned at him. He was enjoying this.

Straightening the car out, he said, "You might want to start pointing and shooting about now."

I twisted in my seat, gun heavy in my hand, and peered out of the rear window. Spilling a little of my element into my body, I let it pool outward, dropping a warm veil over my vision. At first, very little changed. As the car twitched and jerked, I struggled to focus. Then I saw the glass windows blow from the ground floor of a nearby building. Ahead of the devastation, a parked car bounced sideways, an entire side caved in. I tried to focus on where I thought the beast to be, using the wake of destruction as a pointer, and saw its hazy outline shimmer into existence.

It was huge, the size of a small car and hairless except for several razor-edged spikes running down its back. Its hideous bulk bounded toward us, bouncing off the city obstructions like a dog through an agility course. I tried to steady the gun on the seatback but the constant twisting and lurching made aiming impossible. "I can't get a shot."

"You want me to pull over?"

"No!" I saw a gleam of mischief in his eyes and swore at him. Sarcastic and arrogant, what a charmer.

"It's gaining!" The hound had our scent, its crimson eyes wide with fury as it chased us down.

I pulled the trigger. Nothing happened.

"Flick the safety off," Stefan helpfully suggested, suppressing a laugh.

I fumbled with the safety, yanked the slide on the barrel back, and fired. The recoil nearly tore my arm off. The bullet punched through the shatterproof rear window, but the shot went high, completely missing the hound. To make matters worse, its pack-mate raced up the street, leaping over slow-moving traffic without breaking its stride.

Stefan's car slowed. "Don't slow down," I said, "They're almost on us."

He checked the mirrors and cast a glance ahead at a tourist bus lumbering its way down the street.

I looked back and yelped. The hound's snout was level with the rear of the car, black tongue lolling, saliva foaming around its mouth. It snapped at the rear fender, bumping its head against the metal. The car broke away, threatening to spin. Stefan steered into the slide, regaining control as we drew level with the bus. The hound slammed a muscular shoulder into the rear door, growling through bared teeth. Head level with Stefan's door, it thrust its skull into the window. Glass exploded over Stefan. Great gleaming jaws snapped together inches from Stefan's shoulder.

"Shoot!" he yelled.

I fired out through the rear passenger window, hitting the hound clean in the rump just as Stefan tugged against the steering wheel and slammed the car into the beast, pinning it against the side of the bus. Shattered glass and screaming metal assaulted my senses, but we swerved free of the coach as it veered off the road, smoke bellowing from its brakes.

Behind us, the stunned hound slumped on the road, its hollow whimpers lost among the squeal of brakes and the traffic fast backing up behind us. The second beast didn't hesitate as it galloped past its fallen pack-mate.

"Go, go!" I screamed.

Stefan fumbled with the gear shift, and the car shuddered forward. He muttered something, then found the right gear and rammed the accelerator to the floor. The Dodge growled as Stefan demanded every ounce of horsepower from its engine. As we thundered forward, the hound snapped its jaws at my side of the car. It missed then struck again. This time, its teeth crunched into metal, tearing out the entire rear light cluster and tossing it aside.

As our speed increased, the hound fell back. We were pulling away. I watched the beast closely. The street blurred, and the engine roared in my ears. The Hellhound had me in its sights. Its penetrating stare held me transfixed. Stefan was right. It was after me, and if it got to me, those vicious teeth would tear strips of flesh from my bones. I shuddered and called more of my element.

"You can't stop it." Stefan must have sensed the change in me. He probably felt the ambient temperature rise.

"I've got to try."

"We—"

A horn blared. We both looked out the driver's side just as the truck t-boned into the side of the Dodge. The massive grille and blinding headlights were the last things I saw before my entire world spun. Metal and glass shrieked, groaned and shattered. Abrupt needles of pain dashed against me from all sides. I don't recall exactly how Stefan's car ended up on its roof. It's likely I blacked out and only reawakened when Stefan tugged on my seatbelt.

I heard him calling to me, his voice flowing in and out with the ringing in my ears. Peeling my eyes open, I realized I couldn't see, at least not at first. My muddled mind tried to comprehend which way was up. I blinked rapidly, clearing my right eye. The car no longer resembled a car at all, just a twisted hunk of metal entombing me. I pushed down on the roof, scraping my bare arms against serrated metal.

"The belt!" Stefan reached in through the compressed passenger window and tugged on my seatbelt again. "Quickly."

I smelled fuel and heard the tick of the cooling engine. Panic spilled ice water into my veins. "Oh god." I fumbled at the latch, jabbing at the red button to release me, but my own weight pulling down on the belt trapped the buckle in its latch.

A monstrous howl rippled through the night.

Stefan snapped his head up then pulled back out of sight. I whimpered in frustration, tugging on the damned seatbelt. Weren't these things meant to save lives? My breath rasped in short sharp gasps. My heart galloped behind my ribs. The tingle sensation of my element trickled forth. The source of it at my core broiled in response to my panic. Considering how I hung upside over a pool of gasoline, the last thing I wanted was fire or heat of any kind, but my instincts weren't listening. Damnit, I wasn't dying there, trapped in a steel coffin. I hadn't survived years of torture and countless assassination attempts to die like that. I was stronger than that, better than that.

Rage chased away the debilitating effects of fear. I screamed at the damned seatbelt, punching the buckle until it finally released me, depositing me unceremoniously upside-down amid the mangled wreckage. Twisting around inch by inch, I managed to get myself into a position where I could grab the passenger door and drag myself through the tiny gap that had once been the window. My head barely squeezed through. My cheek grated against the shattered glass. I reached out with a hand, clawing at the pavement to try and find purchase so I could pull myself free.

I saw Stefan.

He kneeled on one knee in the road. Sparkling vines of ice rooted him to the ground. His entire body, clothes and all, glinted sharply with fragments of ice. But it was the wings that held me spellbound. They rose from his back, insubstantial, not quite solid enough to touch, but very real. Each feather appeared to be made of ice. The light from the streetlights fractured through each fine barb, casting multicolored shafts of light on the black asphalt surrounding him.

I watched, awestruck as he hunkered down, wings flexing behind him while he summoned a sword of ice into his right hand. Jagged fragments of crystalline ice layered one on top of the other, creating a long, thin weapon. I'd been mistaken. It wasn't a sword but a spear.

A snarling growl tore my attention from Stefan. The remaining hound stood within leaping distance of Stefan. Its monstrous head hung low, lips rippling over glistening teeth. Drool pooled on the road just ahead of its substantial paws. The spines along its back rippled, making a hideous hissing as they scraped together. It stood still, leg muscles bunched, ready to spring forward at any moment.

Then it saw me and cocked its head to one side. Its leathery lips formed a grin.

"Hey. Not her! Me!" Stefan stood, ice cracking off him. Fragments of it tinkled against the road surface.

I heard sirens nearby, but the authorities were the least of our concerns. Clawing again at the road, I attempted to drag myself free, but every movement drew the hound's attention right back to me.

Stefan growled and flung an ice shard at the beast. It shattered against its thick hairless flesh, doing little damage. I realized we were probably about to die. You can't kill them, and you can't stop them. What chance did we have?

He flung a second shard of ice. A third. The hound snarled its fury then sprang off its feet, leaping at Stefan. He hunkered low, wrapping his right arm around the spear and thrusting it up right through the belly of the hound, using its own momentum to fling it over him. The beast yowled, slamming into the road with a heavy thump. Its front leg pawed at the air. Its keening whimpers hollow and chilling.

Stefan came for me, tossing aside the ice spear as he reached down, and clasped a bitterly cold hand around mine. He tugged me free of the wreckage just as the police cars squealed into the street behind us. As his icy visage melted away, wings dissolving into snow and dissipating, he scanned our surroundings. The buildings lining the street huddled closely together.

"There, the alley. Go."

I ran, adrenalin fuelling my fight or flight response, and kept up with Stefan as we ducked into the alley. A chain-link fence blocked our path. He didn't hesitate but clambered up a dumpster and leaped over the top. I scrambled after him, landing awkwardly on the other side. Then we were off, sprinting across the small open space of a children's playground. A howl resonated around the empty space. I managed to find an extra burst of speed, and bowing my head low, I sprinted with every drop of physical strength I had left.

Reaching the other side of the park, Stefan dropped down a set of steps alongside a building and kicked in the door to someone's basement apartment. Once inside, he slammed the door closed and plucked an aerosol can from his coat pocket. Giving it a token shake, he flicked on the lights and sprayed red paint over the door and wall, creating a large circle with swirling symbols inside. Done with one wall, he proceeded to spray the same mark on the opposite wall.

I heard another howl. The sound sent a shiver crawling across my flesh. "It's close."

He didn't reply, just continued to spray the paint on the wall. Then he shoved the couch into the center of the open-plan lounge/kitchen and stepped onto the cushions, resting one boot on the back of the couch while reaching up to spray paint the ceiling.

I hugged my arms against me and watched the door. If the hound came through, we were dead. I still panted hard, lungs burning in my chest. A full-body ache asserted itself. I hadn't even noticed I was injured. The adrenalin had worked so efficiently to keep me moving, but now I'd stopped my limbs didn't quite feel like my own and a throbbing pain tried to punch out of my skull.

Stefan also breathed hard, sucking in air through his teeth. He shook the can and reached up to finish the mark, then hissed and winced, clearly in pain. Blood bloomed across his shirt.

Jumping off the couch, he crossed to the kitchen area and proceeded to spray the kitchen units with the same mark.

"Will these marks stop it?" I brushed my hands up my arms, trying to rub off the goose bumps.

"Yes," he replied gruffly. "This symbol, it restricts elemental magic. More precisely, demon magic. By placing it around us like this, I've created a cocoon, cutting us off from the elements. Once the Hellhounds lose our scent, they'll return to their master."

I nodded. That sounded good enough for me.

"It also means you can't go nuclear on me. So don't bust a blood vessel trying."

So, I was trapped in there, with him, unable to call my power, until the Hellhounds got bored. Great.

Only when Stefan had finished marking all four walls, ceiling and floor, of the small basement apartment did he finally stop. He tossed the spray can on the small kitchen countertop and slumped against the cupboards. "We're safe. For now."

I couldn't help glancing back at the door, expecting the horrid things to come crashing in at any moment, but as the seconds ticked on and nothing happened, I breathed a little easier.

Chapter Nine

The beige patterns and cream overtones of the small basement apartment were comfortable enough, and thankfully the owner wasn't home. Perhaps it was a weekend bolt hole. Either way, I was glad I didn't have to explain any of this to people not accustomed to demons barging into their lives. I roamed the lounge area, admiring the photos of a man with two young girls who I assumed to be his kids, and felt a pang of guilt for vandalizing his apartment.

Stefan had shaken off his coat and slung it over the couch. The red bloom of blood on his shirt hinted at a wound beneath. "Are you alright?" His expression was almost one of concern.

I didn't reply immediately. I was trying to work out what was happening. My thoughts ran amok. He had saved me, again. There was no doubt in my mind; Stefan wasn't sent to kill me, but I was a long way from trusting him. "I think so."

He crossed the room and reached out, as though about to touch my face. I flinched away, moving around the couch, shivering in my torn and bloody dress.

"You're hurt... You have a cut over your right eye. I was just... Never mind." He returned to the little kitchen and stood with his back to me. I caught the memory of his wings and averted my eyes. He hadn't looked like any demon I'd ever seen before. He'd looked... glorious.

He shrugged his shirt off his shoulders, letting it slip down his back then peeled the fabric away from the jagged gash in his side. A fragment of metal protruded from his skin with blood oozing around its sharp edges. Gritting his teeth, he gripped the shard and yanked it free with a hiss.

"Thank you," I said, trying not to wince in sympathy. "You didn't have to do any of that for me."

He grunted an acknowledgement and tossed the bloodied fragment of metal in the kitchen sink where it rattled. Finding some paper towels, he tore a few sheets free of the roll then dampened them before pressing the wad of paper against the weeping wound.

He turned, leaning back against the countertop. I admired his physique before I could stop myself. I might have glanced away if a tattoo hadn't caught my eye. On the muscular plain of his navel where his jeans hung low, two entwined scorpions had been tattooed into his smooth skin. I couldn't help staring. So many questions went through my mind, but I wasn't sure I had the energy to ask, knowing the answers wouldn't be easy. Exhausted, bruised, and battered, I didn't want any part of this madness. I wanted to go home, but didn't even have one anymore.

"Will you let me take a look at that cut?" he asked after allowing me a few moments to collect my thoughts.

I shook my head. "Stay away from me."

"Fine." He tore off more paper towels and proceeded to clean himself up while I watched. I wanted to hate him. Ever since he'd entered my workshop, everything had gone wrong. That wasn't a coincidence, and yet I was beginning to believe he didn't want to hurt me. I couldn't have survived what we'd just been through without him.

"You were right," I perched on the edge of the couch, hands clasped together on my thighs, knuckles white. "They were sent for me."

He gave me a cool glance before returning his attention to the wound. "You have many enemies, Muse."

"But you aren't one of them?"

"No."

"Akil said you were."

Stefan snorted. "Akil. Right." He rummaged through some drawers and found a small tube of Loctite. "I could use your help... if you can stand to be within two feet of me."

I stood and approached him. Considering everything he had done, I could hardly say no. "What do you want me to do?"

He handed me the glue. "Would you mind?"

I looked at the small tube then at the two inch wound in his side. "Really?" His arched eyebrow told me to get on with it. I pinched the lid free and tentatively touched the nozzle to the puckered flesh around the wound.

He immediately hissed in a breath. I winced. "Sorry."

"No, I'm good. Just..." He planted both hands on the edge of the countertop, bowing his head, and smiled. "You're hot."

I blinked. "Huh?"

"I mean—your touch—it's hot, physically." He laughed lightly, a trickling chuckle that summoned a reluctant smile from me. "Never mind."

I pinched the wound together, watching lean muscles ripple with tension. Fighting a smile, I squeezed the glue into the wound and held the skin closed for a few seconds. "Best not glue myself to you, huh? I'm not sure how I'd explain that to Akil."

"Do you love him?"

I frowned. The abrupt question caught me off guard. "That's personal."

Stefan looked right at me, his smile gone. "I need to know the answer." His cold stare could have pierced stone.

"Why?"

He hesitated, his sharp blue eyes searching my puzzled expression. "Because if you do, then it makes my task all the more difficult, and I need your help."

"What does any of that have to do with whether I love Akil or not?"

He moistened his lips and straightened so that my hand fell away from his side. I looked up into his eyes, sensing the cool energy thrumming inside him. A trickle of power rippled inside me. The warmth embraced my weary limbs, but that was as far as it could get. The marks on the walls surrounding us prevented the power from manifesting outside of me. I felt my demon butt up against my skin, unable to break free.

"Who do you think sent those hounds?" Stefan's voice deepened.

"It could only be my brother, Val. I don't know much about Hellhounds, but they're difficult to summon. Only pure demons can do it, even then they're virtually impossible to control. Val has wanted me dead for years. Summoning Hellhounds would just be the last in a long list of things he's done to me."

Stefan briefly touched my forehead with his fingertips, probably an instinctive touch, but the dance of power that ignited between us immediately jerked me back. The spark had been so intense that it tugged a great wave of energy from inside, briefly staggering me. I reached for the countertop, steadying myself as Stefan stood firm, his cool gaze heavy with intent. What that intention was, I couldn't be sure.

"Akil sent those hounds, Muse." Stefan's voice had lost all of its jovial lightness. The arrogance was back, his tone cold.

It was my turn to laugh. "You don't know what you're talking about. Akil and I... it's complicated."

"I don't doubt that." He raised an eyebrow, implying a great deal with that one gesture.

I tossed the glue on the side and snaked my arms crossed, attempting to control the flicker of anger flaring inside me. "How dare you judge me? You don't even know me." He shrugged a dismissive shoulder, further infuriating me. "You have no idea what I've been through. You were looked after. Someone cared enough about you to keep you safe, to train you. I had none of that. I was sold, virtually given away to the demons as a plaything. I was raised beyond the veil. Do you even know what that means?"

His hard expression softened a little. He rested a hip against the cupboards, his head bowed a little. "Who told you I was kept safe?"

"It doesn't matter. What matters is, I don't know you, but I do know Akil, and he's done nothing but look after me."

"He's a demon, Muse."

"What are we?"

"We're human." He ground his teeth, flicking his hair out of his eyes to glare at me. "And believe or not, we hold more power over them than they've led you to believe. Why do you think he keeps you so close?"

Because he loves me? I didn't speak the words, but they'd been there, right on the tip of my tongue. Stefan didn't need to hear it. He saw it in my expression, in the hopelessness on my face. He shook his head. "I had hoped you'd be stronger than this."

"Oh, screw you. You're impossible. You know that? Like a goddamn force of nature. You waltz into my workshop and ruin my life, and now you pity me? I'm sick of it. Sick of you." I headed for the door.

"You can't leave. Not yet."

With a sigh, I stopped a few feet from the front door, feeling the chill of his gaze on my back. "If you're not an assassin, and you're not here to hurt me, then what are you?"

"Whatever Akil told you is a lie. I'm an Enforcer. This tattoo you so readily admired proves it. I wasn't 'kept safe,' Muse. I was plucked from my home, stolen from everything I'd ever loved, and forced into this way of life, but you know what, I love it. I hunt demons and thrive off it. I kill the bastards who step out of line, the ones who breach the human world and wreak havoc, and I need your help to kill your brother."

"I don't believe you." I ignored the 'kill your brother' bombshell for now because it was insane to even consider it.

"It doesn't matter what you believe. It's the truth. Akil means to kill you. Your brother isn't behind any of this, and I can prove it."

Stefan watched me closely, waiting for my reaction. I couldn't believe him. Akil wouldn't hurt me. He'd saved me from my owner, given me the tools I needed to slaughter the bastard. Akil had been there ever since, my guardian in a world that despised me. No, Stefan was lying. This was Val's doing. My brother was capable and had a motive. There was no mystery here.

I sat on the couch with a disgruntled humph and dropped my head back, closing my eyes against the physical and mental aches and pains. "Thank you for everything, but when I leave here, I don't want to see you again."

"Muse, if you go back to Akil, he'll kill you."

Pinching the bridge of my nose, I squeezed my eyes closed. My headache pulsated. "He's not going to do that." Akil wouldn't hurt me. I'd seen the passion in his eyes, felt the warmth of his arms around me. There was no malice.

"You traded one owner for another, and you're too blinded by Akil to see it."

"Shut up."

"Just because he doesn't beat you, doesn't mean he's not controlling you."

I snapped open my eyes. "Stop it."

Stefan glared back at me. "Why can't you see it?"

"Because..." I winced at my own foolishness.

"Because you love him?"

Maybe I did, but it wasn't as simple as that. Without Akil, I was nothing. I wouldn't survive a night without him. The detective at the police department had proven that. "He keeps me safe."

Stefan smiled bitterly. "You kept yourself safe for five years."

"It didn't last. You turned up and ruined it all."

"I was the reason you were standing on the street when the explosion destroyed your workshop, remember?" His smug grin was back. "Akil set you up. You pissed him off, Muse. You turned your back on him and walked away. Did you think he was going to let you get away with it?"

"Stop it. Just—stop. I don't want to hear any more of your lies."

Finally, Stefan gave up trying to force me to believe his propaganda. He came and sat on the couch next to me, resting his boots on the coffee table and propped an elbow on the arm of couch beside him. He leaned away from me, shuffling down into the cushions and closing his eyes.

"You're going to sleep?"

"It's that or listen to the Akil fangirl speech."

"Asshole."

He snickered at my insult but kept his eyes closed; the conversation was over.

I watched his chest rise and fall, confident that he couldn't see me doing so. Stefan's lean body was built to kill, and evidently he had no qualms about doing so. He'd executed the demon in the stairwell without hesitation and on the run from the Hellhounds. He hadn't once stopped to consider his actions. He took it all in his stride, like it was part of his day job. I sat there, in a room where the walls were covered in symbols I'd never even seen before and didn't have a clue what they meant. But they'd worked. He was well trained, that much was obvious. Even the stunt with the superglue, which I was pretty sure he could have done himself, hinted at his no-nonsense get-the-job-done attitude. So he'd been trained, but I'd never heard of 'Enforcers'; shouldn't I know about them? Were there more of them? Who trained them? It sounded like fantasy to me. Half-bloods didn't have the power to go up against demons. It was impossible.

When he'd called his power, let it ride over him, I'd seen the demon that resided at his soul, and it had been astonishingly beautiful. There wasn't a rule that said demons couldn't be stunning. They came in all shapes and sizes, but I had never seen anything like him. The wings alone; jeez, you could understand where the angel-myth came from. I had wings, well, used to. Now only one remained, but they had never been as beautiful as his. My owner had sheared my missing wing off with a scimitar. When I went 'nuclear' as Stefan had called it, when the demon rides me so completely that you can't tell us apart, my remaining wing appears, but it's a sorry specimen, ripped and useless.

Stefan's breathing had slowed. Asleep, with the Hellhounds at the proverbial door. Typical. I twisted side on to face him and blatantly let my gaze wander across his fine physique. Honed to the pinnacle of physical fitness with an athletic grace, he wasn't all muscle, but might as well have been. I skipped my gaze down to the tattoo and had to stop myself from reaching out to touch it. That mark had to be significant. His branding, tattooed into his skin and on his gun.

I gave in to curiosity and reached out. My fingers hovered over the tattoo as it rose and fell with his breathing. Sliding my gaze higher, I deliberately let it linger on his body. A curious urge to touch was proving frustratingly difficult to ignore. Just a little touch. Would his skin be cold or warm? I'd never met an ice demon.

I rested the tips of my fingers lightly on his chest and found his skin to be warm. Resting my hand over the ripple of his abdominal muscles, I let the warmth of him soak into my touch. His breathing continued to slowly ebb and flow. He wouldn't know how I'd admired him in more

ways than one. He was a half-blood, just like me: human
but for the demons slumbering at our cores. Ever since I
could remember, I'd been deemed unworthy, a lesser
being, a mistake, but Stefan oozed confidence. He carried
himself as though he didn't give a damn about what he
was; almost as though he knew he was better in some way.

He had hinted that he knew about my past, that
my owner had beaten me, but he didn't know the half of it.
It had been worse than that, night after night. Beaten,
raped, cut, abused. I'd only survived because Damien
wouldn't allow me to die.

As the memories flowed unbidden, I pulled my
hand back from Stefan's alluring body and stood up,
moving away to roam the apartment, my thoughts
darkening. Finding a single bedroom, I opened the
wardrobe door, looking for some clothes to change into but
found only suits and shirts. Come to think of it, the
apartment was lacking a woman's touch. Perhaps the
owner was a single guy, separated, who saw his kids on the
weekends. I began to feel inexplicably sad for a man I
didn't even know before realizing the sadness I felt wasn't
for him; it was for me.

For as long as I could remember, I'd been in
chains. Occasionally, Damien had released me, finding it
amusing to let me go and then parade me in front of his
peers. I spent so long with him that it became all I knew. It
was life. It was normal. So I took the abuse, only
summoning the demon inside me when Damien wanted it,
so he could torture her too. She is me and I her, irrevocably
connected and yet different entities occupying the same
human body. And oh, how he despised my human body. I
bore many scars, only a fraction of which were physical.

I'd met Akil through Damien. So proud of how
he'd beaten his pitiful half-blood into submission and kept
her like a pet, Damien had presented me to Akil one night,
showing off his accomplishments to one of the Seven
Princes of Hell. I'd looked at Akil, at the smartly dressed
business man and saw only another anonymous face

leering at my disgusting existence. But he hadn't leered. He didn't do anything at first. Then he asked Damien to 'lend me' to him. Damien couldn't refuse one of the Seven Princes, so he handed me over to Akil.

I'd expected a whole new world of pain to begin, but Akil hadn't touched me. All he did was look at me cowering on the floor. He didn't speak, didn't do anything, but he watched. In some ways, that had been more terrifying. I didn't know his name, didn't know who he was or what he was capable of, but I felt the elemental power radiating from him. I expected him to leap from the chair and kill me with one swift, decisive moment, but he didn't move a muscle.

The second night, he crouched in front of me, holding out a hand. But I'd just peered up at him through the rats-tails of my hair, trembling and mute.

I began to look forward to our meetings. I was terrified of him, of the power coursing through him, but he hadn't hurt me, and my time with Akil separated me from Damien. Eventually, Akil coaxed me into speaking. Damien didn't like to hear me talk, but Akil did. He wanted to know my name.

He calls me Muse. I was Damien's muse, as though I inspired hatred and disgust in him. My existence gave him leave to hurt me in ways I didn't even know he could. I was art to him, a bloody, damaged, and violated piece of fragile art. In some sick and twisted way, he thought he was liberating me, that I should be grateful for lashings that split my flesh.

The memories turned my stomach, and my reflection in mirror above the sink paled. I clasped my hands either side of the washbasin and peered at the woman looking back. The gash across my right eye had scabbed over, but the bloody mess down the side of my face was worse than I'd expected. I had glass in my hair and dozens of grazes across my arms. My dress was torn and bloody. Patches of oil or gasoline splattered across the once vibrant red fabric. No wonder Stefan had wanted to clean me up.

I scrubbed my hands with soap and tried to wash the blood off my face. I'd spent a great deal of time washing the filth from my own skin, imagined and real. My hands shook, perhaps from the late onset of shock, or from the assault of memories. Either way, I needed to get a grip of myself. This wasn't over. I was safe for now, hidden behind Stefan's clever graffiti, but as soon as I stepped outside that door, I was a target, and it was open season on me. By now, word would have reached the demons. Not only was I still alive, but I wasn't with Akil. They wouldn't care that he'd forbidden killing me. Look at the detective at the police department. He hadn't cared. He'd just wanted me dead. They were all the same.

At least Stefan was different. He'd survived. He may or may not have been protected, but he could clearly look after himself. Nobody had bothered teaching me a damn thing. I only had a name because my owner found it amusing.

"Damnit!" The blood wasn't coming off. I fell against the sink, gripping the white porcelain so hard that my fingers blanched. My stomach churned as my body rebelled against my attempts to remain calm. What Stefan didn't seem to realize was that without Akil, I was dead anyway, so what did it matter? What did any of this matter?

I stumbled from the bathroom and dropped my weary body on the edge of the bed. The apartment was alien, the man who'd brought me here had his own dubious motives, and I had nothing.

"You okay?" Stefan's voice held a softer tone than I'd heard from him.

I didn't turn, couldn't find it in me to look at him. He probably stood in the bedroom doorway and could stay there for all I cared. Head bowed, body trembling, I knew how I looked. He'd think me weak, just as he had earlier. Maybe he was right.

"You're not like me." I flicked my head around to glare at him. "You don't know me. You don't know anything. I'm not helping you kill my brother, an impossible task by the way as he's immortal. I don't care what your issue is with him. I don't even care that you think you have proof Val isn't behind this. I don't want to know."

He looked as though he might say something; clearly, he had some sort of witty retort on the tip of his tongue, but he swallowed it back. Without another word, he left the bedroom. I was glad he'd gone. His presence only served to remind me how pathetic I was in comparison.

I growled and flung myself back on the bed, falling into a fitful sleep within minutes.

***

The quiet was complete beyond the veil, the netherworld air thick, like soup. I had to drag it through clenched teeth to breathe. Ripples of pain rode through my body. My fragile human skin glistened with perspiration beneath the touch of moonlight, but I had come to embrace the agony. It meant I was alive. I could see my owner's silhouette only when I lifted my gaze through matted hair. He might have appeared human but for the huge bat-like wings that relaxed behind him.

A flash of pain darted down my back. The wounds he'd inflicted gaping like hungry mouths. The chain coiled around my owner's right hand dripped with my blood. I couldn't see him smile. His face was lost in shadow, but I knew it was there. Clouds broiled in the dark sky, briefly smothering the blue moon, snuffing out its waning light. My mortal eyes failed to pierce the complete darkness, but it didn't matter. I knew what was coming.

When the washed-out light from the moon flowed once more into the clearing, he towered over me. I reared up, baring blunt teeth in a snarl. He could beat me all he wanted. I was not giving up without a fight. He pulled the chain tight in front of him, links rattling. I had enough time to fill my lungs with the cloying air before he wrapped the chain around my neck and pulled it tight. My demon clawed within me, thrashing against my restraint in a bid to be free, but I held her back. I would not let him win. Her talons sunk into my resolve even as my chest burned for air. My head throbbed.

He leaned in, tugging me off my knees, clutching me close to his leering face. When he laughed, the sound boomed about the clearing. Nobody—nothing would hear us. Even if something did, it wouldn't care.

"The Prince believes he can claim you." The snarling voice drilled into my skull. "You are mine."

***

I woke with the memories still bubbling in my head, threatening to spill over into reality as they had at Akil's hotel. Sitting bolt upright, I reined in my fears and swept them back into their mental box where they belonged, sweeping my hands down my face to chase the remaining fragments of the nightmare away.

Thoughts grounded in the now, I realized I was alone. Nothing unusual there, but I knew Stefan had left the apartment. The room was warmer, for a start. Sunlight streamed in through the high basement window, instantly brightening my mood. I had no idea what day it was, or where I was, or what I was going to, but it was okay because I was alive.

The lounge looked the way I remembered it: trashed. Perhaps I could mail the apartment owner some cash. He was going to need it.

On the countertop, Stefan had left a note, scrawled on an unopened letter.

Gone for the evidence. Stay here. Do NOT go back to Akil.

No, 'Love from Stefan,' Ha. If he was gone, that meant the hounds had gone too. I tossed the note aside and strode out into the daylight. No money. No phone. My only choice was a long walk. Dressed as I was, blood-splattered and disheveled, I soon caught a few wayward glances. Some people even crossed the street to avoid me.

Retracing my steps from the previous evening, I came across Stefan's wrecked car. Crime scene tape flapped in the breeze, cordoning off the crumpled barrier and dented lamp post. Gouges in the pavement further up the street and a trail of shattered glass made it clear where the car had rolled. The truck remained, front end caved in, awaiting recovery. I ducked on by with guilt sitting heavily on my shoulders. At least it didn't look as though anyone had been seriously hurt.

After I'd walked for twenty minutes, a black limo pulled up beside me. I stopped, planted a hand on my hip and admired my bedraggled and distorted reflection in the privacy glass. The door opened, and Nica smiled up at me. "Wow, rough night?"

"I've had worse."

"Get in."

It became clear she had no idea what had happened to me. Akil had asked her to take a car and driver to the street she'd picked me up on. Apparently, he was working. My invite would have given him knowledge of my whereabouts. She fished for answers, but I was in no mood to talk. I feigned tiredness and pretended to sleep the rest of the way.

Chapter Ten

Left alone until that evening, I was grateful for the time to clean myself up and to think. Nica had left some clothes for me, asking if I wanted to have my things brought over from my old apartment. I smiled and didn't answer. 'Some clothes' turned out to be a black lace dress. I groaned and rolled my eyes at Akil's choice of clothing. Give me jeans, and I'm happy. Dresses just felt plain wrong, but tonight I had a plan.

I held the dress up against me in front of a full-length mirror. Considering what I had in mind for the evening ahead, it was the perfect combination of intricate lace with conservative coverage. I dressed and left the bedroom, scrunching my damp hair in my hands as the tinkling of piano keys drifted down the hall. Fantasia in D-Minor, Mozart. A peculiar mix of haunting melody and light upbeats. One of Akil's favorites.

I followed the sound of the music, padding barefoot down the hall, passing the lounge until I reached what appeared to be a study. A speaker-dock on a shelf played the music. Equalizer bars jumped on the docked phone. A fire flickered in a modern alcove fireplace, and glass across the front sealed in the dancing flames. Books sat neat and orderly on their shelves, some very old with weathered spines and tanned leather covers.

Then I saw him, suited up and seated leisurely in a high-backed chair, glass of red in one hand, open book in the other. His laden gaze rested firmly on me. I swallowed, vision briefly blurring. The weight of his stare quickened my pulse, stealing away the confidence I'd embraced all day. I bit into my lip, feeling as though I were shrinking in size with every second that ticked by.

The music stopped. The fire crackled behind its glass cage.

Only when he looked away did I breathe again. He closed the book, stood, and placed it neatly on a desk. An eclectic collection of swords displayed on the wall behind the desk drew my attention: six stunning swords from various locations around the world, although one appeared to be missing. Its brackets were bare.

Akil set down his glass of wine, fingertips teasing across the rim, making the crystal sing. He came toward me with clear intent in those dark eyes. Fear threaded through my limbs so that I stumbled back. I may even have yelped a little right before he clasped my face in both hands and kissed me. The urgency of that kiss surprised and excited me. I responded in kind, devouring him as the fear quickly turned to fire in my veins. His element called to mine, sinking heated tendrils through my flesh and drawing the slumbering power out of me. I pulled him tight, needing him close, grinding my hips against him while his hands slid down my back, cupping my behind. He lifted me, and I instantly hooked my legs around him, throwing my head back as his mouth teased kisses down my neck.

He carried me to the desk, sweeping its contents aside before planting me on the edge. His sultry touch rode up my thighs, hitching back my dress. The demon in me purred her glee, curling power around my flesh and reaching out to him. As I let down my guard, my element flared within me, spilling over my human body, revealing the truth about me: a human-demon hybrid. The unfurling of my one insubstantial wing completed the transformation. I flexed my power outward, stretching my ethereal wing higher. It felt like stepping out into a glorious summer's day. The weight of control lifted from my shoulders. With Akil, I could be me—all of me. I didn't need to pretend.

Akil growled low in his throat, fingers teasing out the ribbon of my dress. He sunk his other hand in my hair, holding it there as his mouth found mine once more.

"I thought I'd lost you," he breathed. "I searched..." He pulled back enough to peer into my eyes. "Don't ever do that again." His growl teased my desire even higher.

I grinned and nipped at his lip, fingers fumbling with his shirt buttons. I gave up and tore it open, pressing my warm hands against the sculpted contours of his chest. I felt my own magic flexing around me, my one deformed wing trembling as he slipped my dress from my shoulders. Arching back, I let his mouth roam, his occasional nip sending ripples of pleasure through me.

His hand on my leg pressed higher, easing my thighs apart. I wanted him, but it was more than desire, I ached for him. Human and demon, all of me. I was his. His touch smoldered against my skin. His hands awakened wave after wave of power, calling it from every cell in my body. I blazed with energy, and he wanted it. I could see the hunger in his eyes. His power raged an inferno inside him. Blinded by the all-encompassing heat of desire, I couldn't have resisted him if I'd wanted to.

He tore my underwear free, jerking me off the desk against him. The short-lived dress slipped down over my hips and pooled at my feet. He backed up a few steps. His heated gaze devoured me, drinking in my hybrid appearance. Where others had considered me grotesque, he had always enjoyed the intimacy every time I laid all of me bare.

I stepped up to him, clutched his torn shirt in both hands, and pulled him into a fevered kiss. His hands found my hips, but I knocked them away. He growled a warning just as I turned him and shoved him back against the desk. He panted through clenched teeth, lips pulled back in a wolfish grin. I stepped up to him, sliding my hand down his chest and dipping it below his waistband. It was his turn to arch back. A humble groan escaped him.

I had power over him. Nica had been right, but it wasn't something I could use lightly.

Withdrawing my hand, I held his stare as he lifted his head, then shoved him down onto the desk. He didn't resist but opened his arms, completely giving in to me. I tugged his trousers lower before climbing over him, trailing moist kisses up his navel, tongue teasing across his rippled chest before swirling around a nipple.

"Muse..." he growled my name, bucking a little.

I reared up, stretching my wing high behind me, and straddled him. He groaned something, the words lost as his original accent slurred them, before locking his molten gaze on me. I began to rock my hips. I had him. All of him. Utterly and completely at my mercy and I liked it. My element spilled from me, rolling in and out like waves on a beach, as his reservoir of power flooded over me, into me. I lost myself in it. My memories, my fears, my suspicions, they were all chased away by the insatiable need to have him inside me. The rush of delight rode higher. The lights above flickered. The fire in the hearth roared. I summoned the residual energy into me, calling to the latent element found everywhere and letting it bloom inside of me until I couldn't take any more The pressure released, snatching a cry from deep within. Akil bucked, fingers digging into my thighs as he threw his head back.

He didn't see me falter, but he heard me whisper, "Would you ever hurt me?"

He cried out, the human part of him spilling his seed into me. But I saw what I needed, the glimmer of uncertainty in his eyes, the briefest flicker of doubt. He'd answered my question before he could stop himself, too lost in desire to lie.

I fell forward and kissed him hard, deliberately nipping at his lip and drawing blood. He pulled me down and turned me onto my back, so he had the advantage. As his kisses burned down my breast and his fingers kneaded,

I blinked back tears, quickly sweeping them aside before he could see. I feared the truth and what it meant, feared that Stefan had been right.

Akil was lying to me.

I had to find Stefan, but first, there was one last thing I needed to do: talk to my brother.

***

Moonlight spilled through the drapes, its milky caress draining all color from the room. The quiet seemed complete, as though the world outside had been smothered while I dosed. Carefully easing the sheet off me, I sat up in bed, slowly turning my head to look down at Akil. Moonlight lay across his face and chest. The sheet bunched around his middle, one arm cast behind his head. He was like temptation personified, which of course was deliberate on his part. Nothing about his male physique was an accident. His vessel hadn't been born in the natural way of things. It had been constructed in the image of this era's notion of perfection. It was an act—a mask—deliberately designed to seduce, and it worked on me. Sure, I knew what he really was, but I certainly wouldn't have jumped his demon-bones if had he revealed his true self. My head was too full of human desires for that.

I ached in all the right places, my lips flirting with a smile. I could so easily have lain back down, eased my arm across that delicious body, and stayed that way until the demands of the real world pulled us apart, but that was the coward's way out, and a coward was one thing I had never been. I gently rose from the bed and tiptoed out of his room before jogging quietly back to the guest room where I quickly dressed in jeans and a sleeveless top. I had a jacket somewhere and would need it. It was approaching 3am and would be near to freezing temperatures outside. I found my suede jacket and tugged it on, peeling my hair from inside the collar. A figure in the doorway blocked my exit.

"It's late," Akil said. "Or early, depending on your perspective." He paused, giving me a moment to fill the silence with an explanation.

In the low light, it was difficult to see his expression, not least because I couldn't ignore the fact he was naked. My wide-eyed gaze roamed all over him. "I er... I was..." My voice quivered, a croak fracturing my attempt at confidence. "My cat." Yes, blame the cat. "I need to feed Jonesy. I've not been home and he's—"

"Resourceful, I'm sure."

I definitely detected irony dripping from those three words, or was it barely concealed anger? He sauntered toward me, the light from the window silhouetting his body. I didn't move, didn't dare to. That stare of his crawled over me while his expression remained impassive. He moved around me, circling me, easing closer with every step until he stood before me and tilted my chin up.

"Why did you ask me whether I would ever hurt you?"

And there I was thinking I'd gotten away with that little gem. I couldn't lie to him, not when he glared right into my eyes. He'd know a lie immediately. I chose instead to stand firm and glare right back at him. "I don't trust you."

"When have I ever given you reason not to trust me?"

His teeth appeared perfectly white. His eyes were a little brighter than the ambient light could account for. Even his expression had lost its human fluidity. His whole body tensed. He had never given me a reason not to trust him. That was what made all of this so difficult to digest, but he couldn't deny his very nature; could he?

He released my chin and stepped back. "What did he say to you?" I blinked, trying to pluck one of Stefan's pieces of advice from my memory, but I'd already hesitated too long. "Don't lie to me, Muse. I will not tolerate lies."

That was rich, coming from a demon masquerading as a man.

Akil clench his right hand. "You were with Stefan. Were you not?"

"Yes," I replied, struggling to retain my stubborn bravado. "He saved me from the Hellhounds."

Akil arched a single eyebrow. "Ingenious, isn't he?" he said dryly.

Ingenious indeed. "Why didn't you help me?"

Akil regarded me, eyes narrowing a little as he considered his reply. "Your brother Valenti sent those hounds. You know I cannot interfere with his intentions."

The convenient 'gentleman's agreement between demons' excuse. The Princes had agreed never to dabble in each other's lives. Apparently immortality bred contempt. They lived too long to get along, so instead they agreed to disagree and moved on, preferring to dabble in the lives of humanity. The same agreement bound the Princes' offspring, Val, being the son of Asmodeus, was obliged to follow the same ground rules. Akil could no more meddle in Val's machinations than Val could in Akil's. Didn't seem to stop Val from trying to kill me though, a crime for which one detective had recently been skewered.

I dropped my gaze, unable to carry the weight of Akil's stare on me any longer. "Those hounds could have killed me. Stefan was there. He saved me."

"What lies did he tell you?" He seemed more concerned about what Stefan might have said than about the fact that I could have been killed.

"Akil." I smiled thinly. "What is this? Why are you behaving like this?"

"I'm not the one sneaking out the door." Akil moved closer again, taking both my hands in his warm grip and lifting them between us. "He told you I sent those hounds. Didn't he?"

A shiver rippled through me. I closed my eyes. Somewhere amid all the uncertainty, the doubts poking holes in my perception of Akil, the seed of mistrust had been planted. Its creeping vines strangled my conviction.

"What else did he tell you?" His voice had softened, but as soon as I opened my eyes, I saw the barely suppressed anger tightening his smile. I would need to tread carefully, like walking on hot coals.

"Let me go." I yanked my head free and staggered back. "He said you sent the hounds—okay—then told me not to come back here." I threw up my hands. "What do you want from me? It's not like I wanted to be there with him. I had no choice. You're lucky I'm here at all, Akil. Those hounds..." My stomach flipped just thinking about how close they'd been. Stefan had faced one of those creatures head-on. Who does that?

Akil had fallen quiet. I could have left it at that, but I knew of one more chink in his armor, one last little shard of truth that would unnerve him. "Stefan said I'd swapped one owner for another. To be honest, right now it's beginning to feel that way."

Anger immediately flared in Akil's eyes. "Do not ever compare me to your previous owner—that despicable excuse for a demon—Muse."

I took a deep breath. "Stefan said you were too demon to love me." I watched Akil flinch back as though I'd hurt him. "That you were just playing with me, a cat with a mouse. He implied that when you got bored of me..." I shrugged a shoulder. "You'd kill me."

For a few seconds, neither of us spoke. I watched him closely for any clues as to what might be going through his head, but he'd locked away his emotions. Then he quite unexpectedly laughed.

"He's got balls. I'll give him that."

I frowned. Laughing hadn't been the response I'd expected. Fury, I'd expected. Akil's crooked grin confused me. Why wasn't he angry? He stopped before me, bowing his head so that his lips brushed mine. "He is nothing, Muse. How can he possibly understand what we have?" The words whispered against my lips, tugging at the embers of desire settling inside of me.

I chased the tease of a kiss as Akil pulled back a little, leading me in to him.

"He cannot know you, Muse. Not as I do. I would not have bothered with you in the beginning if I didn't see something in you I admired. You were a crushed and broken thing, like a butterfly crumpled in the hand of a child, but I saw the beauty in you. I found you, Muse. I created you. Someone like Stefan, he will never understand what we have."

"I didn't believe him," I whispered. Placing both hands flat on his chest, I soaked up his warmth. "I just... I was afraid." It wasn't strictly a lie, but neither was it the truth.

"I know. Don't worry about him. He'll be dead soon."

I let Akil pull me against him, hiding my spike of fear behind the flush of desire. I couldn't ask what he meant, not without rousing suspicion, but I couldn't get away either. I would have to wait until morning before I could make my escape. Until then, the only action I could take was to convince Akil I had no doubts about him. I was a rather convincing liar when the situation demanded it. Lying to Akil with my body was easier than lying with words. A trait beaten into me to aid in my survival. It would serve me well now.

Chapter Eleven

The flame twisted on its wick like a tiny exotic dancer. In the gloom of the humble basement apartment, the candle barely penetrated the shadows loitering beyond the coffee table. Stefan's artwork still adorned the walls, and those marks were the reason I was back. They subdued elemental magic, and that's exactly what I needed if I was going to survive an encounter with my brother.

Stefan wasn't there. I hadn't really expected him to be, and yet my own disappointment surprised me. He could clearly look after himself. While Akil had hinted Stefan's number was up, I was quietly confident the so-called 'Enforcer' had dealt with such threats before. Besides, there was nothing I could do. I didn't know where Stefan was or what Akil planned. I could only look out for myself.

The flame spluttered. A dribble of wax spilled over the candle lip, dribbling down its side and onto the coffee table where it hardened. I straightened the kitchen knife beside the candle, going over the incantation in my mind. Summoning a demon isn't as difficult as you'd think. In fact, all you need to do is invite them by name, but you have to be careful. They're slippery bastards, and my brother was no exception.

I picked up the knife then put it down again, wiping my clammy palms on my jeans. "I can do this."

Outside the basement apartment, the city noises mingled in a cacophony of passing cars, high heels clicking on the sidewalk, and the occasional blaring horn. I found it all comforting. I always had. Silence made me nervous. I picked up the knife again, wrapping trembling fingers around the handle. My brother Val would sense my fear. He'd enjoy it. If I was uncomfortable, he was happy. It had always been that way, but he wouldn't be pleased I'd summoned him. At least the marks would keep him under control—hopefully.

"I must be mad," I muttered. The one demon I know without doubt wanted me dead, and I was summoning him. What part of that was sane? But Val would have answers.

Kneeling, I leaned forward over the table, my face close to the flame. Knife in my right hand, I clasped my left hand around the blade and tugged. The cut stung, but it was a necessary pain, part of the payment for the summoning. Squeezing my hand into a fist, I lifted it before the candle and watched a few droplets of blood trail down my pale skin.

"Valenti, first born of Asmodeus, Son of the Seven, Guardian of the Dark, Brother by Blood, I— your half-sister—summon you into this time and place. I invite you to share with me your presence." My throat constricted. The sudden grip of fear strangled me. "You will not harm me." My voice trembled, "I bid you heed my words. By this flame, our element, I welcome you."

Nothing happened.

I looked around me, expecting some sort of movement, but besides the little candle flame, nothing moved. There was the chance the marks might have prevented me from summoning him, although a summons itself was not elemental magic. It was just an invitation extended between two layers of reality.

"Sister," he hissed.

I twisted to face the source of his voice and scrambled backward, knocking an elbow against the table, making the candle wobble.

Val stood motionless by the door, head slightly dipped, gazing from under snow-white lashes. His storm gray eyes were beautiful. I'd always thought so. Hair as white as snow cascaded over one shoulder. A simple leather strip tied it together. The weathered leather coat, which hung from his shoulders to his grey lace-up boots, was more cloak than coat. Supple black leather trousers and a black leather vest completed the ensemble. I could pick out the close-set tubercles in the cuts of animal skin and might have placed the leather as shark, but there are no sharks in the netherworld. There are however plenty of vicious, saw-toothed demons. I didn't want to think about what demons might have died to satisfy my brother's leather fetish.

Nerves fluttered in my chest like butterflies in a jar. My element stirred within me, but the marks adorning the walls prevented it from manifesting. In fact, all I felt was cold. The trembling in my body completely betrayed the depth of fear my own brother roused in me.

He had a look of perpetual amusement, as though this world and its people were an infinite source of humor. His lips constantly flirted with a smile, and his eyes were alight with infinite knowledge. He might not have been one of the Seven Princes like our father or Akil, but you wouldn't know it from the sheer confidence he exuded. He lifted his head, finally detaching his powerful gaze from me and sweeping it around the room.

I fought not to sigh with relief, trying desperately to keep all of my emotions locked tightly away.

"Curious," he mused, approaching the kitchen to admire Stefan's hastily spray painted artwork on the cabinets. "These will be the reason I cannot shake off this mortal guise." Every word was a precise study in elocution.

He had wanted to arrive tooled up in his full demon guise as opposed to the man-suit he wore now. I was glad he hadn't been able to. When he looked human, I could at least pretend I might have a hope of talking with him. I silently thanked Stefan's ingenuous symbols.

As I rather clumsily got to my feet, Val swung his attention back to me, pinning me to the spot. I froze, giving him the typical deer-in-headlights expression because it was all I could do not to run through the door out in the street. I hadn't been this close to him in nearly a decade. I'd been a young girl then. He hadn't aged at all.

He very slowly tilted his head to the side. "I had hoped you'd be dead by now."

"Did you send Hellhounds after me?" I blurted. The less talk, the better. Neither of us wanted to be here, in each other's presence, so the sooner I could get the truth from him, the sooner we could go back to our lives.

"Hellhounds are so archaic..." He continued around the small room, admiring the markings. He was certainly more interested in those than he was my presence.

Hellhounds archaic? No more or less than he was.

"Did you paint these symbols?" He flicked his hand.

I didn't reply. He could think that I had. It might make him wonder what else I knew. He smiled at my silence, not in the least bothered whether I answered or not.

"No, I see not. This cage is beyond your rudimentary thought processes."

It wasn't an insult, not in his eyes. It was fact. I clamped my teeth together, refusing to react to his words. They were, after all, just words.

His tour of the lounge complete, he stood opposite me, mere feet between us. I had a fleeting thought that if Akil knew I was doing this, he'd never let me leave his side again. Val reached inside his coat and withdrew a rapier, the type of sword one might use to pierce one's opponent through the heart. The point would be needle sharp, the edges less so.

I smiled, an odd reaction, but I could appreciate a well-crafted weapon, and his rapier was indeed a work of art. The blade appeared to ripple. Light glanced off its mirror smooth surface. There was no elaborate flare about it, just ruthless efficiency. "Really? Swords? I mean, I'm unarmed, I'm half human, and I'm a female. Strapping guy like you, you don't need a sword to kill me."

He lowered the sword until the tip hovered a few inches from the floor. "Looks can be deceiving, especially in your case, Muse. You're wasting my time."

Right, time meant nothing to him. I slowly lifted both hands. "All I need to know is if you sent those hounds after me."

"You think your fleeting existence occupies my thoughts? You insult me, Muse." He didn't look particularly insulted, just amused. I imagined some cats have that expression, right before they bite the heads off their prey.

He hadn't approached me, so perhaps he didn't intend to use the sword. "Is that a no?"

"Tell me who crafted these symbols about the room, and I'll tell you the truth."

I remembered then how Stefan had told me he'd wanted my help to kill Val. They obviously had a history of some sort and here I was, caught in the middle of it. "His name is Stefan."

Val's level expression ticked. His fingers twitched on his sword. "He helped you?"

"Now answer my question. Did you send the Hellhounds?"

"No." He smiled, enjoying the fleeting emotion he saw skip across my face and my subsequent attempt to hide it.

Akil had sent those hounds. Nobody else was capable of summoning them. Nobody had enough power to control them. Akil had sent them. He meant to kill me. Had he set the explosion at the workshop? The demons at the party? Even the detective? No, not him. Akil had slain him to save me... No, not to save me, to save his own honor.

Val laughed as he read the panic in my eyes. Irony dripped from that laughter. Its menace unbalanced me, and a peculiar lightness swept over me. I swayed a little, reaching for the couch. Val lunged forward as I knew he would, stealing what he thought to be a moment of weakness on my part. I sprang back, snatching the kitchen knife from its snug little hiding spot, tucked into my jeans against my lower back.

Val slashed the sword toward me with a snarl. The kitchen knife wasn't the most appropriate weapon against a sword, but it was all I had. He kicked over the coffee table, toppling the candle onto the floor where it snuffed itself out.

Val immediately pulled back, realizing his mistake. With the tiny flame gone, he had no anchor to hold him there. With the summoning revoked, he could do nothing but let it happen. His human form began to dissolve before my eyes, blurring around the edges first. The white of his hair smudged against the shadows like a chalk drawing in the rain.

He peeled his lips back, those eyes as dark as thunder clouds. I'd escaped him this time, but I'd also reminded him I was still alive. If he hadn't been trying to kill me before, he might just step up his efforts now. I saw him casually slip the sword back into his scabbard before he fixed me once more with a threat-laden stare. He didn't need to say a word for me to know what he was thinking.

Only when every swirling speck of his image had vanished from the room did I breathe again. It took a few minutes of measured breathing to regain anything resembling composure, and it didn't last.

The front door of the stranger's apartment beckoned, but outside Akil would find me. Out of the frying pan and into the fire. How was I meant to stand next to Akil and not let him see how afraid I was? Just that morning, I'd believed he cared for me. He was right. He had never given me reason to distrust him, and yet here I was, going behind his back and summoning my brother to answer my suspicions. Val hadn't given me a name. He wouldn't have even if I'd asked. He'd rather see me suffer than tell me the whole truth. But he'd given me enough.

Thoughts rushed through my head as I attempted to clean up the apartment, working on auto-pilot and trying to think of a plan. I left a note for the owner, apologizing for the mess and left a few hundred dollars. It was all I could afford.

I had to find Stefan. He was the only person who appeared to have an interest in keeping me alive. If Akil realized what I'd done, how I'd summoned Val, I couldn't even imagine how he'd react. He'd been less than jovial when he'd demanded I tell him everything Stefan had told me. Stefan had proof. Akil knew it. That must have been why he'd demanded to know everything Stefan had told me.

I leaned back against the kitchen cupboards, folding my arms crossed and chewing on my bottom lip. The second I stepped out of that door, I'd be fighting for my life. I could run. I might even escape the city, but Akil would find me. I'd invited him in and when you invite a Prince of Hell in, they don't just get access to your home, but also your life. He would know where I was until the day I died. What an idiot I'd been.

Not all was lost though. There were ways of revoking an invite. I'd never looked into them because I was never going to be stupid enough to invite a Prince of Hell into my life, but it could be done. Stefan seemed like the type of guy to know how. In fact, Stefan's company looked mighty appealing, considering the alternative.

I noticed a phone propped up in its cradle at the end of the countertop and on the spur of the moment, picked it up and dialed Sam's number. He was the only person in my life who wasn't out to get me in one form or another. I needed that normality.

"Hi, this is Sam Harwood, Architect. Leave a message, and I'll call you back between the hours of nine and seven." Even the sound of his voice on his answering message lifted my mood.

"Hey." I sounded gruff in comparison. Glancing at the door, I wondered if I'd ever see him again. "I wanted to tell you I'm sorry. For everything. You're a good man, Sam. The best. You..." My vision blurred, forcing me to lift my head and blink. "We had some great times. I'm sorry if I hurt you. You didn't deserve that. But I'm not who you thought I was. I'm not a good woman, Sam, and the people around me, they're dangerous. I just... I just wanted to hear your voice again before..." The phone beeped, cutting me off.

I wanted to go to him. He was honest, and I'd meant what I'd said. He was a good man. Too good for me. He would wrap me in his arms and listen as I talked. We'd crack open a few beers, rent a movie, and I'd curl up beside him on the couch, head resting against his shoulder while his arm hooked around my waist.

I could no more go to him than I could go to the police and tell them I was being hunted by my demon boyfriend, not to mention the dozen bit-part demons that thought it was their duty to separate my head from my neck. I placed the phone back in its cradle and cast one last look around the basement apartment. The closed front door loomed in the corner of my eye.

"Here goes nothing." I shoved away from the countertop and left the apartment.

Chapter Twelve

It took all of about thirty minutes for Nica to arrive and sit herself in the comfy armchair across my table in Starbucks. I'd been sipping a grande latte while people-watching as I waited for her to arrive, hoping the safety in numbers theory applied to me. The coffee house buzzed with activity. Professionals tapped away on their laptops. Some teens sat engrossed in a game on an iPad beside a line out the door for coffee. It was exactly what I needed. Should Akil or Val show their faces, they weren't likely to try anything untoward in such a public place. That didn't mean they couldn't though.

"Thanks for coming." I smiled at Nica, hoping it reached my eyes.

"No problem." She crossed her legs, straightening her pencil skirt as she watched me sip my coffee. "I'm due about a dozen lunch breaks, so figured I was owed a little personal time." Her bright smile had already begun to lift my mood.

"You didn't tell Akil?"

She shrugged. "I doubt he'd be interested in the fact we're having coffee together. It's not exactly high on his agenda."

This time my smile hitched a little higher. I'd called her from a public phone and asked her to meet me. In all likelihood, Akil would have sent her after me as soon as I'd left the safety of the basement apartment, so I figured

I might as well preempt his move with one of my own. "You know that file you gave me on Stefan?"

"The assassin?" She tucked her short blond hair behind her ears and leaned an arm on the table.

"Yeah, whatever he is. Did you discover anything about where he lived?"

"No, he covers his tracks really well. But there was something... We had a lead on a guy who deals in guns. He's sold some ammunition to Stefan in the past. The gun Stefan uses, the one with the scorpion branding on it, it's a fifty caliber brushed chrome Desert Eagle. A gun like that gets noticed."

I wondered briefly if Stefan had retrieved the weapon from his car after it rolled. I hadn't seen it on him afterward, and I'd had an eyeful of him post-accident, but something told me he wouldn't leave a gun like that behind.

"Why?" Nica's smile teased across her lips, her eyes brightening with mischief. "What are you planning?"

"Who says I'm planning anything?" I placed my cup down on the table, licking my lips. I couldn't trust her; I barely knew her. She worked for Akil—spent every day with him from what I could gather. Whatever I told her, I could assume would go straight back to him.

"Okay." She tried to catch my eye. "I can get you the address of the dealer if you want." She plucked her phone from her bag, fingers tapping out the security code to unlock it. "Why do you want to find Stefan?"

I had to tread carefully. "I want to know what he knows."

"Even if he tries to kill you?" Her thumb navigated across the touchscreen of her phone.

"He won't."

Nica lifted her gaze over the phone to question me with her eyes. "What makes you so certain?"

He saved me from the Hellhounds, saved me from the explosion at my workshop, saved me from the demon in the stairwell. Right now, anywhere he occupied was the safest place for me. "I'm not that easy to kill."

Nica grinned and showed me a map on the screen. "If we take my car, we'll be there in less than fifteen minutes."

I nodded. "Won't Akil miss you if you don't return to work?"

Nica flicked her hair back, suddenly becoming animated with excitement. "No. He's out most of the day. I can catch up with paperwork tonight. I'd much rather be shaking down a back alley arms dealer than filing tax returns. Wouldn't you?"

I chuckled. "That's not what this is. I'm just going to ask some questions."

"Right, and he's going to tell two uptown girls what we want to know because he's a nice guy?"

"You're uptown. I, most certainly, am downtown. Trust me."

***

At least it wasn't night. The dead end street would have looked much less appealing draped in darkness. In full daylight beneath the winter sun, the dumpsters glistening wet from a recent rain shower, it didn't look quite as foreboding, but it still wasn't going to feature on a tourist map any time soon. Air conditioning units hummed from the mismatched buildings lining the narrow back street. An abused 70's Corvette sat beached unceremoniously on bricks outside a car workshop, its wheels gone. Either it was in a state of repair, or in the process of being picked-clean by local thieves.

A group of three young men loitered on the corner of a side street, hoods up, watching Nica and me climb from her silver Mercedes. I had to wonder if her car might resemble the Corvette on our return.

"I have mace." Nica said, not all that quietly, as she walked beside me, clutching her bag a little tighter.

I smiled. "Don't worry. Mace will be the least of their concerns." A tingle of energy trickled through me. My demon half stirred at the promise of violence. I shook the thrill of it from my hands, pushing back the thirst for chaos.

Nica gave me a sideways glance. She saw my smile and loosened her white-knuckled grip on her bag. "I forget what you are sometimes."

"Thanks." I took it as compliment as we approached a solid black back door in a three-story brick building. A scribble of unintelligible graffiti adorned the wall beside the door, but it was the small symbol etched into the painted wood beside the handle that caught my eye. The entwined scorpions stood out because they'd been painted white against the black of the door, but they were small, barely larger than a dime, not meant for the whole street to see. Just visitors. Nica saw it too. We shared a knowing glance before I knocked on the door.

Behind us, the three hoods watched our every move, muttering among themselves. They were unlikely to represent a threat, just curious as to why two young women were entering their neck of the woods. Nica and I probably weren't the usual type of client for these parts.

The door opened, revealing a man who looked as though he'd just rolled out of bed with creases everywhere. His jeans and shirt crumpled like waste paper. Even his face had creases, hiking my age estimate to late thirties. He peered through narrow eyes at us, chewing on a toothpick. In dire need of a shave, his bristly chin and short ruffled hair completed the 'disheveled and don't care' look.

He seemed to like what he saw in us because he grinned and draped an arm against the doorframe. "Hello ladies. Yah' lost?" He slipped his attention past us to Nica's car. The spotless paintwork gleamed like a beacon of temptation for any would-be thieves.

Plucking the toothpick from between his teeth, he pointed it at me. "He won't be happy you parked that hunk of German metal outside his shop."

"Are you David Ryder?" I asked, not in the least perturbed.

He tucked both thumbs over the waistband of his jeans. The last few buttons of his shirt were open. Evidently, he had problems dressing himself. I wasn't surprised.

"Ryder, sure. Whatever. What d'yah fine ladies want?"

"Can we come in?"

He took another long look at us then glanced over his shoulder into the dark hall. "Well, sure, why not."

Nica and I helped ourselves inside. The oppressive atmosphere of the hallway embraced us as she closed the door. I followed Ryder's quick retreat down the hall, passing several closed doors before we reached what had, at one time, been a kitchen but now resembled a workroom. Cardboard boxes were stacked high in one corner. Beside them on a small round table, two guns had been stripped and were in the process of being cleaned. Small rectangular ammunition boxes lined the countertops beside half-finished mugs of coffee. Some harbored islands of mold.

"'Scuse the mess. Wasn't expecting guests." He made a half-hearted attempt at cleaning a space on the countertop but quickly gave up.

Nica stood very still beside me, hands clasped in front of her, as though afraid to touch anything. "Those marks on the door?" she asked in a rather curt voice. "The scorpions..."

Ryder shrugged. "Previous owner of this place, I reckon. Why? You recognize them?"

"No." She smiled a little too sweetly to be convincing.

"Yes, actually." I intervened. "I want to ask you about a man who has that exact same mark on a gun, a Desert Eagle."

Ryder leaned back against the countertop, folding his arms crossed. His beady eyes assessed me. "Nice gun.

Don't get many of those 'round here. Too big, bulky. You can't stash 'em easily, if you know what I mean."

Not really. "The guy who owns that gun. He's a friend of mine, and I just need to find him."

Ryder suppressed a smile. "A friend, and you don't know where to find him, huh? Maybe he doesn't want to be your friend."

"He's tall. Blonde hair, about this long." I touched the corner of my jaw. "Has a thing for red leather. Drives an old Charger—well, used to."

Ryder's smile had begun to fade away, the laughter fleeing from his eyes. He knew Stefan alright, but I was getting a distinct angry vibe off this guy, so perhaps they didn't get along too well. Not surprising. Stefan appeared to have that effect on people.

"What did you say your name was?" he asked.

"Charlie. And this is my friend, Nica." I held out my hand only for Ryder to look at it as though I'd just offered him a dead rat.

He popped the toothpick between his teeth, chewed on it, then grabbed my hand in his and shook it hard. Only when I tensed to pull away, I realized he wasn't letting me go. I tugged, frowning, about to ask him what the hell he thought he was doing when he yanked me forward.

"I think you lost your way." He leered down at me. "Best you run along now. Wouldn't want anything to happen to you fine ladies, now would we?"

Perhaps he expected me to squeal and flee. His leering face certainly betrayed a confidence in himself. I couldn't blame him. I didn't look like much. Perhaps it was the way I held his stare and smiled a little, or he may even have sensed the temperature change in the room, but he was human, so he couldn't have seen the elemental magic spilling down my arm. It heated my hand. From the widening of his eyes, I knew he felt my grip tighten. The rising heat radiating from my palm must have been uncomfortable.

"You'd better leave," he warned.

I pulled him toward me. "Where is he?"

"I don't know who..." He yanked on my hand, trying to pull himself free, then growled when he realized I wasn't letting go. "What the hell are you?" He twisted, trying to writhe free, but I wasn't budging. The acrid smell of burning flesh permeated the air.

"Okay, okay!"

"Where?"

"I'll take you! He's right across the street."

I released his hand and watched with a little too much glee as he quickly turned toward the kitchen sink and plunged his hand under the cool water.

Nica arched an eyebrow. She had her hand in her bag, ready with her can of mace just in case.

"Holy crap." Ryder stepped around a knee-high tower of magazines and tugged open the rusted refrigerator. With his burnt hand, he reached inside and grabbed a can of beer, clasping it in his hand with an audible sigh of relief. "Remind me never to piss you off."

"That's nothing compared to what I can do, so don't get any ideas."

Ryder didn't look surprised by any of this. No flurry of questions about how I could heat my hand to those temperatures without burning myself. It made me wonder what he knew about demons. Despite appearances, he was not a typical gun dealer.

Nica and I followed Ryder back outside. The hoods had gone, and Nica's car had survived intact. Ryder jogged across the street to the workshop, and snatching the handle at the bottom of a garage door, he lifted it high above our heads to reveal another classic car in the throes of restoration, this one stripped back to bare metal and awaiting its body panels. Mechanic's tools hung on the walls. Every inch was covered with assorted equipment, from wrenches to jumper cables, hub caps to hood ornaments. The pungent odors of oil and metal reminded me of my lost workshop. A pang of sadness stabbed me in the chest, and a brief grimace touched my face.

I heard Stefan's voice coming from the back and nodded at Nica behind me.

"Yo, Stefan," Ryder called out.

I followed Ryder's path past the partially restored car into the back of the workshop and through a doorway.

Stefan sat behind a desk, rocking his chair back, boots up on the desktop, legs crossed at the ankle. He cradled a phone between his chin and shoulder. When he laid eyes on me, his conversation came to an abrupt end. He hung up on his caller and tossed the phone into a pile of papers strewn about the desk. Making no attempt to stand, he flicked his cool gaze across the three of us.

"Hell must have frozen over," he drawled, looking particularly pleased with himself.

"She fried my hand." Ryder lifted the beer as though that explained everything and then cracked it open and took a few gulps for good measure. "She made me bring her."

"S'okay. I've been expecting her." Stefan stared straight at me, waiting for me to speak. I deliberately stayed quiet, drawing out the silence. Nica shuffled behind me, her fingers tapping out a restless little tune on the side of her bag.

Ryder cleared his throat. "Anyway... As I've opened the beers, anyone else like to partake?"

Nica looked at me, saw my encouraging expression, and sighed. "He's an animal."

"You have mace." I grinned.

Ryder scowled at the both of us. "Standing right here."

With a grumble, Nica reluctantly followed Ryder back into the workshop. I heard him attempting to engage her in small talk, but she wisely avoided him. If he tried anything, I'd be out there in a shot, but given Stefan's reaction to Ryder, I was confident he wasn't going to cause any trouble.

Stefan on the other hand... He hadn't moved, and I wasn't entirely sure how he'd react to my being there. His office—if you could call it that —was surprisingly normal. I wasn't sure what I'd expected. Having seen him in action, perhaps I was hoping for something like my old workshop: weapons on the walls, maybe a demon head or two—not that I had those, but he might have.

"You're a mechanic?" I failed to keep the surprise from my voice.

"When I'm not working."

His half smile wasn't budging but if he wanted an apology, hell would indeed have to freeze over.

I absorbed the normality of the surroundings. Apart from the mess of papers on his desk, the room was tidy, sparsely furnished, with one metal filing cabinet in the corner with a plant in a plastic pot on top as though that would make all the difference. It was an office in which he didn't spend much time. That was clear.

He planted both boots on the floor and stood, moving out from behind the desk with a fluid stride. His blue jeans were worn threadbare in places with a few smudges of oil and grease across his thighs. His gray t-shirt sported the occasional oil stain, a trend which continued onto his face where a smudge of grease had been brushed across his forehead. He looked decidedly normal, and it completely threw me.

"How'd you find me?" He leaned back against the desk.

"Nica has a file on you." I listened, hearing her clipped voice respond to something Ryder had asked. "I don't trust her."

"What does she know?"

"They think you're an assassin, or a bounty-hunter, depending on the money at stake I guess. She'll tell Akil about this place."

He didn't look concerned. In fact, he still had that smug smile on his lips. Placing his hands on the edge of the desk, he dropped his head. "I told you to stay in that apartment."

"Yeah, I know." I snorted a laugh. "I'm not very good at following orders."

"This isn't a game, Muse." The smile had gone. In its place, he'd summoned concern from somewhere as though he actually cared.

"No?" I felt the power turning over inside me, roused by a little shiver of anger. "It feels like it is. Like some elaborate game and I'm the only one who doesn't know the rules."

"You're right. You don't know all the rules. They've been deliberately kept from you by a succession of owners, most recently Akil."

"So why don't you enlighten me?"

He shoved away from the desk and strode toward me. I straightened, refusing to give an inch. He stopped beside me and leaned in close. "I will, but first there's something you need to see."

Chapter Thirteen

Nica was enjoying a beer by the time we left the office. She appeared to be relaxing around Ryder, who had ditched his surly persona for a friendlier version. I'd been about to advise Nica to slow down on the beers when Stefan had stopped me. He surreptitiously extricated her phone from her bag and removed the battery, placing just the phone back in her bag. He didn't want her making calls, and quite honestly, neither did I.

Turning back toward me, Stefan ran a hand down the bare metal of the car that sat squarely in the middle of the workshop. "She'll eventually replace the Dodge I wrecked the other night."

I couldn't help feeling a little responsible for that, seeing as the hounds had been after me. "Akil sent those hounds," I blurted.

Stefan scratched at the smudge of grease on his forehead and nodded, for once avoiding the smug-son-of-a-bitch expression in favor of a sympathetic frown. "Follow me."

He squeezed by me. The car's bulk left little room to maneuver. A peculiar flutter of excitement flipped in my chest as he brushed against me. The fleeting reaction distracted me completely, briefly emptying my mind of rational thoughts while I watched him walk toward the back of his workshop.

"You coming?" he called, disappearing through a narrow doorway.

"Huh? Yeah."

Nica and Ryder were deep in conversation. Ryder tossed me a wave, apparently enjoying his babysitting task. Who'd have thought Nica would be so easily led astray? Maybe she had a hidden desire for bad boys. She was distracted, and that was all that mattered. I'd worry later how I was going to prevent her talking to Akil.

Following Stefan's path through the doorway, I found myself in a narrow hall. Bare bulbs flickered above, poorly illuminating unfinished, plywood walls and a bare concrete floor. A chill swept over me, snagging my thoughts. I glanced back, expecting to find someone watching me, but the doorway stood empty. I could still hear Nica's voice, but it felt oddly distant. A little hesitantly, I emerged through a second doorway into what could only be described as an armory.

Symbols covered every inch of the walls, similar but not identical to those Stefan had used to ward off elemental magic. They were likely the reason for the chills I'd just experienced. My human senses never failed to detect forces that didn't belong on this side of the veil.

Workbenches butted against the walls, stretching from one end of the room to the other, on them the array of weapons boggled the mind. Knives, daggers, swords, axes, guns. A deadly weapon for every occasion. Need a two-handed axe? A broadsword? A rifle? The room bristled with sharp edges like an underwater cave brimming with spiny urchins.

"That's quite a collection." I absently reached out to touch one sword in particular, a broadsword with substantial pitting on the blade. Before I realized I'd even touched the metal, a flood of images burst through my mind in such a flurry that the onslaught nearly floored me. It was only Stefan's sudden grip clamped around my arm that brought me back. Stumbling against the workbench, I sucked in a few deep breaths. Usually, it requires blood to secure a link between my mind and the metal, but not this time. That sword wanted its history told.

"Don't touch anything," he warned, his azure eyes brilliant in the subdued lighting.

The sword beckoned, even now, its secrets demanding to be told. "I saw..." I couldn't be sure what I'd seen. Blood, but that's normal. You don't read the history of a sword and see happy endings. It was almost always horrific and one of the reasons I didn't like to do it. I tried to isolate the images in my mind—horses foaming at the mouth—a woman cowering over her motionless child — but Stefan's voice pulled me back.

"You don't want to know. There's enough history in that sword to knock you out for a week." He touched my face, fingers lightly brushing my cheek. I gasped, not meaning to, but my mind was elsewhere, and his touch so unexpected that a brief flicker of heat bloomed defensively inside me, an instinctive reaction to a perceived threat. He must have sensed it because he turned his back on me, instantly severing the peculiar moment.

The ghost of his touch still brushed my cheek. I lifted my hand to my face where the cool imprint lingered. It hadn't hurt—quite the opposite. It was as though his ice element had briefly eased through my skin. It was a natural reaction for two demons, like an elemental handshake, but our opposite elements made for an interesting interaction. I found it quite intriguing and deeply confusing.

"This is the sword that's caused all the trouble." He lifted a katana from its cradle and presented it to me in such a formal manor that I didn't want to take it, especially after just having one sword download a gruesome fragment of its history into my head. The elaborate guard, unusual for a katana, confirmed it as the same sword he'd brought to my workshop.

Seeing my hesitation, he set the sword down on the workbench. "You need to read this."

In my workshop when I'd first laid eyes on the weapon, I'd instinctively touched it, sensing a connection with it. Now though, I recognized my hesitation as fear. The undulating ripples along the surface of the blade were the result of the metal being folded over and over during its forging process. Each fold strengthened the blade and made the weapon unique. Like a fingerprint, those marks could never be reproduced. Whatever secrets it contained were there forever.

Stefan stepped back, giving me room, but I didn't move. "It's not going to be easy," he warned.

"Why don't you just tell me?" I shivered and clutched my jacket tighter around me.

He hesitated, as though considering it. "You won't believe me."

I didn't like the sympathy in his eyes or the weight of his words. "This is the proof... About Akil?" I chewed on my lip.

"It's all in there."

"How far back do I have to go?" Old weapons have many memories. If I was going back more than a few years, it would take time and effort.

"Monday morning."

"A few days, not long. Good." I stalled. The recent event should be easy to pin down. All I need do was look for Akil. "Will I see you?"

"Possibly." He thought for a few beats. "Probably."

I stepped up against the workbench but kept my hands back, locking them against the edges of the bench. I had my suspicions about Akil. My brother had denied all involvement. In all likelihood, Akil was the one behind the Hellhounds, but I didn't have proof. Proof meant I'd have to believe it, and inside, I didn't want to. Without Akil, I was alone in a world that wanted me dead, and that was not somewhere I wanted to be. Sure, I'd tried to run away, but Akil had always been there, watching over me. If I had proof Akil was trying to kill me, I had no idea what I was supposed to do about it.

"Would you prefer I leave?" Stefan tried to catch my eye, but I couldn't look away from the sword. I flexed my fingers beside me.

"No. When I go under... I'll need you here." A quick glance told me he watched closely. "I don't know how I'll react."

Stefan nodded. "You won't be able to summon much of your element here. The marks you see on the walls, they'll prevent you drawing on the energy outside this building. Like at the basement apartment. The worst you can do here is blow a few bulbs."

His brief smile held more warmth than I'd seen from him all afternoon. Even those bitterly cold eyes had softened. It occurred to me that he might actually care until I realized what that must mean. Whatever was hidden in the blade, it wasn't going to have a happy ending.

I deliberately ran my left hand down the katana's edge. The blade was so sharp I hardly felt the cut at all, but the blood flowed freely. A few drops pooled together on the workbench. I wiped my hands together, smothering them in blood. It would seal the link to the past more easily if the blood was fresh. Wrapping my left hand around the cool metal, I immediately felt the weight of knowledge bear down on me.

"We have a problem." Ryder's gravelly voice penetrated my wandering thoughts. I'd have fallen into the past had Stefan not touched my hand. His warm fingers resting over mine tugged me back before I could slip further into the blade. He eased my left hand from the sword, fixing his eyes on mine before turning his attention to Ryder. It took a moment to clear my head. I'd only touched the blade for a few seconds, but the weight of its secrets had quickly tugged me under. Left any longer, I wouldn't have been roused so easily. Ryder showed Stefan the screen on his phone and dragged a hand down his bristly chin.

"Damnit. How did he find us?" Stefan and Ryder looked at me.

"What?"

Stefan presented the phone to me. On the screen, I clearly saw the black limo parked adjacent to Nica's Mercedes, blocking the street outside. I winced. "Yeah, I was going to ask you how to revoke an invitation..."

"You invited him into your life?" Stefan's gaze widened. "Are you insane?"

I clamped my jaw shut, grinding my teeth. "Hey, don't judge me. Okay? It's your fault."

"My fault?" He barked a laugh. "And how exactly did I force you into signing your life over to a Prince of Hell?"

"You wouldn't leave me alone." I clenched my hand around the cut in my palm. The slight sting of pain was oddly welcome. "When you showed up at my apartment, I had to reveal what I was, but after you fled, I couldn't control the energy." I frowned. "With no outlet, it turned on me. Akil was..." Stefan's stare bore into me. I felt the disappointment roll off him in waves. "He was there. Okay? When I needed him, he was there."

Stefan tossed the phone back to Ryder. With his back to me, he ran a hand through his hair and took a few moments to think. "He knows you're here." He faced me once more, his blue eyes crystalline. I felt the temperature in the room drop a few degrees. "Go to him. Lie to him. Whatever you have to do. You brought him here, Muse. You get rid of him."

It wasn't that simple. "I can't lie to him. He'll know."

Stefan scowled. The displeasure on his face darkened my mood even more. "There's no other option here," he said. "If you don't lie to him about why you're here, he'll tear you, me, and this place apart."

Ryder gave me a sympathetic glance. At least he seemed to realize exactly what Stefan was asking of me. "He only knows you're here, Muse. He doesn't know why, and he doesn't know Stefan's here. Just tell him the Merc died on you. I'll back you up."

"What about Nica? She'll tell him."

Stefan plucked a short sword from the workbench. "I'll talk to her. Just get out there, Muse, before he comes looking for you."

"Don't hurt her."

Stefan gave me a weary sigh. "I'll find you. Just keep Akil happy. I'll get to you."

Ryder beckoned to me, and I had no choice but to follow, my steps heavy with dread. After a quick stop in a washroom to clean the blood from my hands and stem the flow from the cut with a paper towel, we returned to the workshop. The shutters were closed, thankfully, so Akil couldn't see inside. It didn't stop me from sensing him though. My body trembled a little as the sheer weight of his power lingered in the air like the threat of an oncoming storm.

"I can't do this."

Ryder clutched my shoulders, all authoritative. "You get out there. You tell him what he wants to hear. It's not just your life that's at risk here. You've got to do this." He released me and beckoned Nica forward. She'd been watching quietly, aware that something was very wrong.

I nodded, indicating she should do as Ryder asked while wondering what Stefan would do to her. I didn't think he'd hurt her, but I couldn't be sure. She was Akil's personal assistant, a spy in our ranks and liable to reveal all.

As Ryder escorted Nica out the back door to the armory, I stood behind the personnel door in the front of the workshop, hand gripping the handle. Akil's elemental magic wrapped its explorative tendrils around me, calling to me. I was about to lie to a Prince of Hell, Mammon, the Prince of Greed. Had I been a full demon like my brother, I might have been able to pull it off, but half human, my emotions were my weakness. I wasn't capable of it.

I shoved open the door, shielding my eyes from the piercing brightness of the winter sun. Crossing in front of Nica's car toward the limo, I tried to plaster an easy smile across my lips, but it felt wooden, like trying to snap twigs. My hands trembled. I clutched them in front of me as the limo's rear door opened. *I can't do this... I can't do this...*

Akil emerged from the back of the car. The sunglasses shielding his eyes made it impossible for me to accurately read his expression. He wasn't smiling. His lips pulled thin. My heart did a little skip. *I can't do this.*

"Hey," I gushed, forcing too much glee into the single word in my desperation to appear innocent.

Akil stood behind the open door, a hand placed on the roof of the car. He turned his head to take in Nica's car beside us, and the closed shutters on the workshop. I smiled brightly, but figured it probably came off as a grimace.

"We—er—we had some car trouble."

"Where's Nica?"

His voice betrayed nothing, its tone flat. I assumed he was angry, and the stoic mask was there to cover the simmering rage. He hadn't called his element, but that only meant he wasn't concerned.

"She'll be out in a minute. She's talking to the mechanic... You didn't have to come all this way. We were having coffee." I shrugged. "A girls' afternoon out."

His gaze dropped a little. The direction of his attention was difficult for me to ascertain behind those dark glasses. Then I realized he was looking at my hands. I clasped them a little tighter together, shifting awkwardly from foot to foot. Akil slammed the car door and strode toward me. He took my hands in his and turned them over, revealing the two cuts across my left palm: one from summoning Val and the other from attempting to read the sword. He wouldn't know why the cuts were there, but there was no way I could disguise my sharp intake of breath.

"What did you do?"

I looked up at him. "I...I summoned Val."

Akil dropped my hands and snatched the sunglasses from his face. He slowly folded the sunglasses and tucked them over the waistband of his trousers, each movement precise and deliberate. I wasn't sure how long I could stand there waiting for him rage at me. My knees were about to give out.

"Why would you do such a foolish thing?" His voice still level, he fixed his dark eyes on me. I'd preferred him with the sunglasses on. Now I had the full weight of his stare on me. I refused to look away, knowing if I did, it would give him the hint of guilt he needed.

"I wanted to ask him why he sent the Hellhounds."

Ryder stepped from the door with Nica in tow. He swaggered up to Akil, thrusting out a grubby, grease-covered hand. "Nice car, but I wouldn't leave it around here for long." Ryder indicated across the street with a nod. The hoods were back—five this time, a veritable crowd. They watched us, hands tucked in their pockets, shoulders slouched, but I began to wonder if there was more to them than first met the eye. Perhaps the little collection of fine cars had brought them out, or Ryder knew them. Were they back-up?

Akil barely registered their presence. He regarded Ryder's hand with a slight curl of his lip. Once Ryder realized Akil had no intention of shaking his hand, he tucked his thumbs into the waistband of his jeans, not in the least bit bothered by Akil's brush off. "These ladies, huh? Can't live with 'em, can't live without 'em." He slapped a hand on the hood of Nica's car. "Ran out of fuel. Would you believe it? They're lucky I'm a nice guy. Especially as this little doll here has had a few too many beers."

Nica flicked her hair out of her face. "I'm fine. Thank you, but... Charlie, you should drive."

"Sure." I was all too happy to get in her car. The thought of riding back with Akil made me nauseous. She tossed me the keys. Grateful for the excuse to get away from Akil, I hurried around the car and ducked in the driver's side, acutely aware of Akil's stare burning into me. Nica climbed in beside me, and we both watched Akil say a few words to Ryder. Whatever they had been, it was enough to wipe Ryder's smile off his face. We drove back in virtual silence, the limo a constant presence in the rear view mirrors.

"I won't say anything," Nica said.

She wouldn't meet my glance and didn't say another word for the entire journey. I believed her, but I wondered what Stefan had said to her to guarantee her silence. I had more to worry about than Nica's silence. Akil would have questions, and he wasn't going to like my answers.

Chapter Fourteen

The superb surroundings of the Trade Restaurant bustled with Boston's elite. Glasses chinked while laughter tickled the air. An authentic décor hinted at its waterside location. Pieces of driftwood decorated the room like well-placed pieces of art while leather and glass gave the place an air of quality. It was delightful, but I was miserable.

Nica had called Akil's apartment to inform me that my presence was requested here at 7pm. Akil couldn't even be bothered to ask me himself. That annoyed me. Nica's cold shoulder annoyed me. The fact I had no idea how I was going to get myself out of this mess angered me. Frankly, I could barely contemplate surviving another night. I told myself it wasn't as bad as all that, and then remembered where I'd been before Akil had plucked me out of obscurity. There are things worse than death.

Akil was late. When he eventually arrived, someone accosted him in the doorway, shaking his hand as though he were royalty. Maybe they knew what he was. Maybe they didn't. It didn't really matter. Human or demon, he was untouchable. He had it all. Money. Respect. Anyone of the women in the restaurant would have gladly followed him home. All he needed do was catch their eyes. He was a force of nature. An elemental demon walking amongst men. A god.

How the hell was I supposed to beat that?

Akil noticed the half empty wine bottle on the table and suppressed a smile as he sat down opposite me.

"You're late," I grumbled.

"Traffic."

I snorted a laugh. Traffic? He could bend reality around him, and a few stop lights had prevented him from being on time. Right.

A waiter appeared and offered Akil a choice of wine. I glared at him through the brief exchange, watching him taste the wine and express his preference before the waiter poured him a glass. Once the waiter departed, Akil met my stare, his smile hitching up a little. "You're angry."

I shrugged. "No."

He leaned forward, swirling the wine in his glass. "You are angry with me." He, on the other hand, appeared to be in quite a good mood, as though my anger pleased him.

"Yes." I sat forward, planting an elbow on the table and picking up my wine. "Do you think I'm an idiot?"

"Sometimes."

I bit into my lip. A flicker of anger ignited inside me like a pilot light. From that one little light, an inferno could blaze, but right now it was controlled. "What are you doing, Akil?"

"What do you mean?" Oh, playing coy now was he?

"Let's cut the bullshit." A few of the other diners in the restaurant glanced our way. Akil also found that amusing. "What's going on? The workshop? The Hellhounds? Did you know a demon attacked me in the stairwell at your hotel? Damn thing nearly chewed my face off."

"You're surprised?"

That little flicker of anger, it flared brighter, my element stirring, awakening. "Are you doing this to me?"

"No." He said the word softly. Both of us leaned close enough that he didn't need to raise his voice. "How many times do you need me to say it?"

"It's not Val. I asked." I waved my left hand. The wounds from earlier in the day were scabbed over but still sore.

"That was idiotic." He pointed a finger at me, smile failing. "You're very lucky he didn't turn you inside out."

"He couldn't. I protected myself." Ha! See? Not so stupid. I decided not to mention how my brother had tried to skewer me. "He said he didn't send those hounds, so who else, Akil? There's only one other demon I know who has enough power to control those beasts."

"And this one demon you say you know, did he save you from an abusive owner, the very same owner that sheered a wing from your ethereal body and destroyed your mind? Did this demon give you the tools you needed to exact your revenge on your owner? Did he protect you from that day to this one? Has he ever hurt you? Ever?" Embers of heat briefly sparkled in Akil's dark eyes before vanishing as he blinked.

And that's where my argument always fell over. I sucked in a breath and closed my eyes, rubbing my hand over them. "No."

"I don't deserve your anger, Muse."

I opened my eyes to see him watching me. "So who does?"

"I don't know. Why does one demon have to be to blame? You've ruffled enough wings to infuriate a whole hoard of demons. Look at that detective; who I saved you from, in case you'd conveniently forgotten that as well. He was just one of many. What does it matter? If you did as I asked and stayed with me, none of this would happen."

He knew all the right words, but it wasn't enough anymore. "Why me? I'm just a half-blood. Why do they even care if I live or die?"

The waiter appeared with his pen and pad. "Are you ready to order?"

Akil glared at him with enough force to make the poor guy squirm in his shoes and slink off. Akil picked up his glass of wine and took a generous sip. "There is something I've... neglected to mention."

"Oh?"

He swept a pertinent gaze about the restaurant. "Not here."

"Then let's leave." I pushed my glass to the middle of the table, about to stand, when Akil's hand covered mine, his warm fingers closing, holding me tightly.

"No. We order. We eat. And we enjoy each other's company."

The heat from his hand wove its way up my arm, its sensuous touch rooting me to my seat. His words weren't a request. A part of me resented being told what to do, but the power in his words teased through my human barriers and did peculiar things to my demon half. There was no denying the control he had over me, over the demon inside of me. She would roll over and let him tickle her belly if she could, and I couldn't blame her. She was me, and there was a large part of me that desired everything about Akil. How else does a woman fall in love with a demon?

***

Once I'd shrugged off my anger, I'd actually enjoyed the meal. The food was fantastic and Akil all the right levels of charming with an undercurrent of wicked innuendo that had me nearly salivating with the thought of what we might get up to. He hadn't got to where he was by bullying his way to the top. His suave exterior, irresistible charm, and outright sexy demeanor were virtually impossible to deny. The evening air had a frosty bite when we left the restaurant, prompting me to pull my coat tighter around me as we walked along the waterfront. Yachts of all shapes and sizes bobbed in their moorings, rigging clinking against the masts. We leaned against the railing beside a vast yacht with a helicopter on its retracted top deck.

I took a deep breath of sea air. There was something pure about the sea, its endless ebb and flow, timeless and constant. It would be there long after I'd gone, maybe even outlast my brother. I hoped so. Akil hugged me against his side. His jacket was over my shoulders, keeping out the worst of the chill. We stood like that for a few minutes. I listened to his breathing, let the warmth of him soak into me. The sky above sparkled with diamond stars. The water below was a bottomless black darkness.

He turned me to face him. The press of his body, coupled with the lightheaded effects of the alcohol, conspired to rouse temptation in me. As he lifted a hand to my face, I leaned my cheek into his palm, closing my eyes and sighing.

His lips brushed mine. "Why did you leave me?" he whispered.

It was the only single question I could never answer in a way he would understand, and perhaps that was an answer in itself. He would never understand what it meant to be human. He could pretend, but he had none of the fragility of life. It wasn't even that though. He wouldn't know the joys of the simple things in life because he was always playing the grander game. We were like ants to him, milling back and forth, our destinations of no interest. I'd only caught his eye because I'd belonged to Damien.

Five years I'd been Charlie, and it had been the best five years of my otherwise wretched life.

"I didn't leave you." I rested my forehead against his, moistening my lips as a depth of sadness dragged my mood down. "I left behind the part of me that's demon."

"After everything I did for you." His hand pushed against my face. Only when I felt his touch tremble, did I open my eyes. I searched his eyes. Slivers of heat fragmented the dark irises. It had never really occurred to me that I could have hurt him. But standing beside him, my gaze lost in the maelstrom of emotion in his eyes, I realized I had. I'd walked away from him after everything he had done for me. I'd turned my back on him.

I stood on my tiptoes and pressed my lips against his. When he didn't immediately respond, I pulled back a little. "Akil?" The way he held my gaze, his eyes ablaze with heat, told me something was wrong. I caught a glimmer of emotion like nothing I'd seen from him. Before I could process it, his lips met mine with a ferocious hunger. I immediately succumbed, but a fragment of uncertainty had splintered in the back of my mind. I'd seen something in Akil that struck fear through my heart like the piercing jab of a rapier. Hatred.

"You want to know why they seek your demise?" he breathed, pinning me back against the railing. His hand roamed down my waist, over my hip, and gripped my thigh, hitching my leg up, enabling me to hook it around him and pull him tighter against me. I couldn't think clearly. His kisses burned on my cheek, my neck, branding my trembling skin.

"Yes," I hissed.

"You're not half a demon."

He let his element roll over me. The warm flush of it across my skin aroused my element. My demon woke from her slumber, summoned like a cobra at the beckoning call of her charmer. I struggled to pull her back, fearing she might spill over my skin and reveal herself right here by the marina.

He smothered my mouth with his, blunt teeth nipping gently at my lip. "There is no such thing as half a demon. Inside..." He splayed a hand across my chest. "You are whole."

His hand roamed higher, fingers easing behind my neck. "You're entirely human and demon, and they despise you for it." His grip tightened around my neck while the demon inside me rode higher, fighting to be free. I tried to rein her back in, but Akil's hardened grip distracted me. I couldn't breathe. I dug my fingers in behind his, trying to pry his hand free as my demon burst out of my flesh, enveloping me.

Akil took a few steps back to admire his handiwork. I stood bathed in my demon form and tried to consider my actions, tried to think clearly about what I was doing, but the chaos spiraled out of control. I couldn't reason with chaos. It wanted the madness, the hunger, the glory of destruction. He could see me battling for control but wasn't preventing me from manifesting. If anything, he was enjoying his personal freak show and my outright failure.

"What are you doing?" I panted. My wing sprouted from my back, tugging at my flesh as it unfurled. My right side slumped. The weight of the one wing pushed me down, while the opposite stump protruded uselessly.

"You're beautiful."

I was dangerous, not beautiful. He was calling my element, luring all of it out of me but with nowhere for it to channel, I would fall victim to its wrath.

"Stop." Another wave of heat washed over me, its receding edge dragging the last vestiges of power out of me. I dropped to my knees, giving myself over to her completely because it was inevitable. I couldn't control her, not like this, not with a demon of Akil's lineage pulling my strings.

"Akil, please... Don't do this. I can't..." I slumped over, one hand on the ground. "I can't control it." Heat from the earth pooled about me. I felt the residual warmth from the city shoring me up, an unending supply of chaos to fuel my lust for destruction. I didn't want to hurt anyone, but before long I wouldn't have a choice.

Akil stood over me. "This is what you are." He took my hand and pulled me to my feet, apparently impervious to the tendrils of my power lashing around him.

"How dare you?" A snarl rippled across my lips. "You think I won't use this? You think I can't? You have no idea what you've done." My voice no longer sounded like mine. My demon spoke through me. The words echoed in on themselves.

Akil reached a hand through the shimmering veil surrounding me, as if to stroke my face, but the thought of his invasive touch only angered me further. How dare he play me like this? I batted his hand away with a growl. When he tried again, I planted both hands on his shoulders and shoved him back.

He just smiled. I peered through my demon guise and watched his demon form emerge, framing his human vessel so that both man and demon existed, one layered over the other. Mammon leered at me, his leathery wings held aloft. Embers fizzed along their ragged edges. I cocked my head to the side, closing the fingers of my right hand into a fist while pooling energy into my arm. It came willingly, like an eager pet, rushing into me. I flung the blast of heat outward, feeling it peel over my arm and spill from my fingers. Akil staggered back, lifting a hand, palm out. He laughed.

By that point, I'd had enough of the games. I summoned everything I could call, pulling heat from every surface, teasing it from the tiniest of molecules and drawing it into my very being. I drew the lingering heat from the metal of the engine of the boat behind me. The lights, central heating systems, electricity cables, even the residual warmth inside the walls of the nearby buildings, the ground beneath our feet. It came freely to me, rushing from every crevice to bolster my strength.

"Nobody uses me, Akil," my demon snarled. "And you're a fool if you think you can."

He backed up and gleefully shook off his mortal appearance. His truly demonic being appeared before me. He smiled, betraying rows of pointed teeth behind black lips. A chuckle rumbled through him like distant thunder. I lashed out, cracking a whip-like tendril of fire in the air before thrashing it across his chest. He flinched but opened his arms, his muscles quivering as the wound I'd opened instantly resealed itself.

I lashed the tendril of heat at him again, catching him across the face. A gash smoldered across his cheek before the leathery skin stitched itself back together. My demon roared her frustration, not just at him, but at everything. The torture we'd endured, and then my attempt to forget she even existed and now these numerous attempts on our life ignited a molten river of rage. I lifted both hands, holding them in front of me and balling the free-flowing energy between them. My fingers, blackened like coal, framed the pulsating sphere. Its heat rippled in the air around me.

"You can't hurt me, Muse." Mammon's voice resounded in my head.

"I already did." I saw him falter. Even with him in his demon state, I could see his features pitch into a frown. I launched the radiating sphere at him, cast with it every ounce of anger and frustration in me. I funneled it all into that attack with a scream of rage that shattered the glass in the buildings behind him. Alarms shrilled in the air as the flow of energy slammed into Mammon. He deflected it with ease at first, but as the flow strengthened, its blanching heat flooded over him, forcing him to stumble back. Seeing him hesitate only drove me forward. I called more power into me, letting it flow through me and blast outward, taking with it a lifetime worth of fury.

Mammon found his back against the wall, wings pinned flush against the granite blocks, and still I poured everything through me, channeling it all down my arms so it could spill from my hands. Suddenly he lunged, plowing a shoulder right into my stomach to drive me back. I hadn't seen him conjure the ethereal blade, but I saw it now, right before he lifted it above his head. I had a moment to appreciate the beauty of its shimmering blade before falling. Mammon's demon face sneered down at me as I reached for him, but I was fast falling away from him. A cool breeze brushed against my smoldering flesh right before the water engulfed me, quenching the blazing rage within a few breathless seconds. My demon retreated inside me so quickly that she knocked the air from my lungs. I gulped water, a current of bubbles fluttering in front of my eyes. My lungs burned for air. My head pounded.

I didn't know which way was up. I kicked out and twisted, desperately seeking the surface but saw only darkness. My demon cowered inside me. The water completely robbed her of any helpful input. My attempts to summon my element were met with spluttering denials.

I'm drowning...

That wasn't quite how I'd envisaged bowing out of this life and certainly not by Akil's hand. Quiet descended over me. I still thrashed, my limbs desperately seeking purchase in the endless black. My chest heaved, lungs flooded with water, but I didn't mind so much. I could watch it all from afar, as though it were happening to another poor soul, not me. It was okay. I'd be okay. It no longer hurt.

Chapter Fifteen

Salt water bubbled up my throat. I bucked against the wooden boards beneath me and coughed water from my lungs. My stomach heaved up water and the remains of my meal, dumping it unceremoniously on the decking beside me. I spluttered and spat, my throat burning, eyes watering, but I was alive.

"She's okay!"

I didn't recognize the voice, or the people looming over me. Someone rushed in and wrapped a blanket around me, saying the paramedics were on the way. I might have muttered something about being fine, which of course I clearly was not. It took a few minutes before I could stand. Flashing blue lights danced off the yachts around me. Police cars and fire trucks lined the marina. Glass glistened on the roadway. An ambulance peeled its way through the crowd. Someone asked me if I knew what had happened. I shook my head quickly, wet hair clinging to my cheeks. The marina looked as though it had survived a bomb blast. I began to tremble, shock rattling my bones. I couldn't quite breathe. My head spun. I had to stop walking and clutch hold of the stranger who'd been helping me. When the paramedics finally got to me, I needed them.

***

By the time I arrived at the city hospital, I'd regained some of my wits. I couldn't stay there, not without them asking too many questions. I still had the death of a detective hanging over me not to mention a Prince of Hell trying to kill me. At the first opportunity, I found the washrooms and attempted to clean myself up. My reflection didn't look like me at all. The woman in the mirror looked like death warmed up—literally. I ignored her terrified eyes, her bruised flesh, and dozens of cuts and tried to gather my thoughts into a coherent order.

"He tried to kill me." My wide-eyed reflection peered back at me. The demon inside me twisted anxiously, knotting a ball of pain. I could argue I'd brought it on myself, but Akil had been the one poking the sleeping tiger with a stick. He should have left well alone.

There was nothing I could do with my appearance. I tried to comb my fingers through my tangled hair, but the knots refused to give in. I'd have to walk out of the hospital and hope I didn't get stopped. Outside the washroom door, a hand gripped my arm. I turned, armed with a stock response about being fine, only to find Stefan frowning at me. I snatched my arm free of his grip and brushed my hair back, preferring to watch the people flow through the corridor around us than see the concern on his face. He was going to be nice, and if he did that, I'd likely cry. I sure as hell was not crying in front of him, or anyone.

"I'm sorry." He stepped into me as someone briskly brushed by him. I backed up, finding the wall to lean against as he bowed his head, searching my expression. "Are you alright?"

I nodded curtly, avoiding his stare.

Stefan hesitated as if searching for the right words. "I didn't think he'd..."

"Drown me?" I shrugged. "Me neither."

Stefan looked as though he had a few hundred questions, but my general washed out appearance must have shocked him into silence because he stayed quiet.

130

"Can we..." I tried to swallow and winced. My throat felt as though I'd attempted to drink shattered glass. "Can we get out of here?" I couldn't look at him. I wasn't ready for questions or any of the answers. I didn't want to think at all and almost wished I could hide like my demon, just curl up in a ball and pretend it never happened.

Stefan's car looked like a rental and smelled like one too, but the quiet comfort inside immediately lulled me into a sense of security that I hadn't had since, well—forever. I twisted in the front seat, pulling my legs up to my chest and wedged myself there, chin resting on my knees as I watched the city blur past. The shivering wouldn't stop, and my throat burned, constantly reminding me how close I'd come.

"Are you okay?"

"Stop asking me that."

After twenty minutes, I noticed we were in the suburbs. The houses were sparsely scattered along the tree-lined streets. Then Stefan pulled the rental car onto Route 95 North. We joined the four lanes of traffic, and before long, Boston was little more than an orange glow against the night sky in the rear view mirrors. The drone of the wheels on the road eventually lulled me to sleep.

***

We arrived at a lakeside house. Its whiteboard timber-clad façade and wrap-around porch did a grand job of declaring it a New England character house. The interior looked as though it had once undergone some modernization —in the seventies—but it was clean, functional, and had some of those wonderful anti-elemental-markings on every wall. Stefan let me wander as he retrieved a duffle bag from the car and dumped it in the middle of the lounge.

"This where you bring all your girls before you bury them in the woods?" I broke the silence we'd harbored since Boston.

He chuckled. "This is—was my father's house."

I remembered that Nica had told me his father was dead, but I wasn't comfortable enough with Stefan to ask about him.

"I don't suppose you have a change of clothes in that bag?" I smelled the salt water on me, combined with the delightful odor of diesel, vomit, and my own burnt-out smoky residue.

Stefan hefted the bag onto the coffee table and unzipped it to reveal a selection of guns and swords. It made for an interesting overnight bag but was not exactly packed with home comforts.

I screwed up my face. "Is there a shower here?"

"Sure. It'll be lukewarm... Take a right up the stairs. It's on your left. Check for spiders."

He looked deadpan serious until I began to climb the stairs and saw him enjoy a little smile as he busied himself checking the contents of the bag. He looked up suddenly, catching me watching him.

"You're safe here."

I nodded, afraid my voice might betray exactly how much that meant to me and then hurried upstairs.

Chapter Sixteen

I slept the remainder of the night on the patterned couch with the weapons strewn about the coffee table within reach should Akil burst through the door. Without an invite from the owner of the house, Akil couldn't enter, but that didn't stop me from waiting anxiously for his arrival. Borrowing one of Stefan's shirts to sleep in had been a good idea in the middle of the night when I was exhausted and didn't care. Now it was early morning, and I wasn't entirely comfortable walking around the house with only his shirt covering my dignity, and not much dignity at that.

The smell of coffee lured me into the kitchen where the panoramic lakeside view immediately beckoned me toward the windows. The land below the house swept down to the water's edge. The lake stretched to either side of the expanse of windows and beyond, hidden behind towering pine and birch trees. I couldn't see another house in the isolated landscape, let alone another person. I'd never been so detached from the city and wondered if I should feel isolated. I didn't. I felt safe.

"Hey."

Stefan's sudden appearance made me jump. I tugged self-consciously on the edges of the shirt I'd borrowed, pulling it down as far as it would go—not very. If he noticed, he didn't show it. Points for him for keeping his eyes to himself.

"That's some view..." I gazed out the window again.

"In the winter, it's breathtaking."

I skewed a smile at him. Of course he'd like the White Mountains in the winter. He would literally be in his element. He'd dressed casually in jeans and a black shirt, the dark color brightening his astonishing eyes. I had to wonder how he passed for human at all. Those eyes were compelling to the point of distraction.

"Coffee?" He gestured at the percolator already working its magic.

"Definitely."

Watching him breeze about the kitchen, it occurred to me that I hadn't really considered his part in all of this. He continued to show up and help me out of sticky situations, and yet he hadn't really asked anything of me. He'd mentioned in passing how he wanted my help to kill Val, but the subject hadn't been broached since. It wasn't as though we'd actually sat and talked. We could now though.

"Are you going to ask me what happened?" I watched him pour the black coffee into two chunky mugs.

"I know. Half the demon population of Boston knows." He flicked his gaze to me. "Muse, you practically drained the city center of heat and threw it all at Akil. I didn't need to be there to feel that." That was a fair assessment, although I was still trying to figure out how exactly it had happened. "But I was there...at the end."

He passed me the mug of coffee and a box of sugar cubes. "I saw what you were doing—what he did. You were in the water for five minutes. At least."

I sipped the coffee, letting it scald my lips. Five minutes was a long time. I remembered the dark and the cold. So damn cold. The water had snuffed out my element in one gut-wrenching blow. Had I not been drowning, the sudden quenching of the inferno raging through me could easily have sundered my soul in two. It would be like pouring ice water into a roaring forge. Anything caught between those two opposing forces could easily succumb. Had Akil known that when he'd pushed me over the edge?

"You didn't think to help?" I'd meant to ask lightly, but a quiver undermined the confidence of my words.

Stefan gave me a hint of a smile, making it seem sympathetic. "And get between you two? I'd rather face the Hellhounds again."

I couldn't blame him for that. If Akil hadn't have killed him, I might have. My thoughts hadn't exactly been my own.

"Akil waited for you to resurface."

"How long?" I blinked too quickly and leaned against the kitchen cupboards, needing a little more support than my legs could offer.

"A few minutes. Some people showed up. Someone called the cops. He didn't hang around after that. I couldn't see you in the water, let alone save you. You were lucky, really lucky. The two of you had managed to wake the entire marina. Someone saw you..." He averted his gaze to the windows. "They pulled you out the water..." He paused, and I had to wonder what I'd looked like. Limp. Cold. Pale skin. Blue lips. "I thought you were dead."

"I've been dead before. Several times. It's nothing to write home about," I said. He mirrored my smile, but he wasn't buying my bravado. It was, however, true. Damien had enjoyed bringing me back from the brink of death, nursing me back to health so he could start all over again. The unwanted memories vied for attention, forcing my eyes closed. I rubbed at my aching forehead.

"How are you holding up?" Stefan asked.

Considering my on-off again boyfriend had almost succeeded in killing me, and how my demon-self had attempted to summon the molten rock from beneath her feet... Yeah, I was doing fine. "I'm okay." It was a lie, but what else was I supposed to say? "I think you were right...about Akil. What you didn't see last night... He..." I rested the coffee on the countertop and admired the view of the lake. The serenity beyond the windows helped level my fragmented thoughts. "I hurt him. I mean, when I left a few years ago."

Stefan sat at the pine kitchen table, leaning back a little in the seat. "You walked away from the Prince of Greed."

I skewed a sideways glance at him, but his habitual smugness had evaporated. If anything, he looked weary.

"That sealed your fate, right there."

"But..." I didn't need to say it again... *but you don't know Akil like I do.* "He's never hurt me. Not once."

Stefan sighed. "He tried to kill you."

"No, he didn't. He was deliberately baiting me. That's all. He summoned my demon, and I lost control. He wasn't trying to kill me. He wanted... it − her." I tapped my chest.

"Muse, listen to yourself. You're defending a demon, and not any demon, a Prince of Hell. They aren't known for their patience and understanding."

I shook my head. Akil was right about one thing. Stefan would never understand. He spent his life killing demons. He had it simple. I'd spent my life among them. I might despise the majority of them, but I knew them. They were family. Twisted, bitter, dangerous, slippery, back-stabbing, but family all the same.

I held Stefan's sorry expression. He pitied me. I knew that. We weren't ever going to agree.

Stefan finally broke the standoff. "There are some things we need to do. Are you up to it?"

"Depends what it is."

"We need to revoke that invitation. It's easily done, but we need to do that soon, before he realizes you're alive and missing."

"Okay." I was up to that. "And?"

"The sword."

Ah, the sword. "I don't know." Stefan stood so suddenly I jumped. The cool clarity in his eyes had returned, scolding me with a frosty glare as he passed by me. Apparently, I didn't have a choice.

***

Revoking the invitation was easy enough, as it turns out. A bowl of warm water to house my pale reflection, and a few utterances later, it was over. I didn't feel any different, but Stefan assured me it was enough. As with anything demon-related, it was the intention behind the symbolism that held the power.

He left me alone for an hour while he went into the nearest town for groceries. I took the opportunity to be nosey and gave myself a little tour of the lakeside house. Stefan had said it was his father's. If that was the case, Stefan's father had been an avid reader because the books lining the wall beneath the stairs were all old, leather-bound editions. The majority focused on the subject of demons. I plucked a few from the tight rows and thumbed through them. Much was already known about demons, but not nearly enough. The demons kept it that way, preferring to flit through the veil without the hindrance of worshippers and scholars tripping them up.

Many myths were forged on truth. Christianity had attempted to reveal the veil, but they'd mixed the message up with too much of the divine. There is no divine entity, no good versus evil, no heaven or hell. It's all part of the netherworld, hidden just out of sight in the corners of your vision. That flicker of movement at the end of a poorly lit street, the tingling across your flesh as you sense you're being watched. The demons are right there, with us, and yet just out of reach. Some tinkered on this side of the veil, some preferred the netherworld. Akil liked it here. He enjoyed walking among the people, playing their games, feeding off their greed. If there's one thing we mortals have a lot of, it's greed. Other demons hop back and forth, preferring quick visits. Val despises it here. To him, we're worthless bags of flesh and bone.

Wandering about the house, I found a framed photograph of a grizzled man in his early forties standing by the water's edge, fishing rod in one hand, the catch of the day—a salmon—on the grass at his feet. He had a substantial grin on his weathered face. On a second glance, I recognized a fierce glint of pride in his eye. Just like his son. He had to be Stefan's father. Stefan had his mother's eyes but his father's mischievous grin.

Returning to the bag of weapons on the coffee table, I noticed the katana protruding from among the other swords. The damned thing was haunting me. I wrapped my hand around the handle and lifted it out. A new scabbard covered the blade, made of carbon fiber by the looks of the interwoven sheen. The sword felt light in my hand, with a perfect balance between the handle and blade. I could never forge something so labor intensive. The process took months and involved upward of four swordsmiths. Of all the weapons in Stefan's bag of tricks, this one was priceless.

I closed my left hand around the scabbard and pulled it a few inches free of the guard, exposing a hypnotic swirl of light on the tempered edge of the blade. I'd revealed just a hint of metal, just a little tease, but I couldn't resist freeing the entire length of the sword before laying the scabbard on the couch behind me. I tipped the blade up, watching the sunlight from the window drape across the carbon-steel. The cross-cross pattern of leather around the handle had been cut from shark skin, tough, light, and durable.

It felt good in the hand, weighty with potential. I turned my left hand up and lay the blade across my palm. Almost immediately, a snap of energy danced up my arm, just enough to release a tickle of excitement inside me. My element simmered but didn't wake. I should have left it alone, should have put it back in its scabbard and tucked it away safely in the bag. The horror in that blade might have stayed there for a little while longer, but my old friend, curiosity, lead me astray.

I sat on the edge of the couch with the sword across my lap. I was safe here. Stefan would be back soon. Why not get it over with? I ran my finger down the sharp edge, watching a bright red droplet of blood gather at my fingertip before dripping freely on to the floor. I curled my fingers into my palm and waited for the blood to pool, then smeared it over both hands. When I placed my hands gently on the blade, the images rushed me so suddenly I jerked rigid, sucking in a gasp.

The lakeside house and its comfortable decor vanished. The lake and mountains beyond became a distant dream. I could see, hear and smell the city. The noise, the lights, the colors. The images printed themselves on my thoughts, stamping over one another in their rush to be seen. I struggled to keep up, my breathless panting and the rush of blood in my ears all that anchored me to my body. The sword plunged through flesh. I cried out, then, now, in my head. I couldn't see who it was, but I heard his liquescent gasps, lungs bubbling with blood.

Voices, male. The room spun. The city lights behind the windows swirled like fireflies in the air. Red coat, a smiling face. *Use this,* Akil said, tossing the sword at the man in the red coat. He caught the sword, snatching it from the air with one hand, a half-smile pulling at his lips. The image shattered, fragmenting into hundreds of pieces before each sliver rushed back together, pulled as if by a magnetic force. I saw the blade sink into a man's chest again, felt the metal carve precisely through muscle and lung tissue. He choked on the rising blood, spluttering it over his lips as he fell forward. I saw his face.

I knew him.

Sam.

The sheer wave of horror tore me from the vision, thrusting me back into my trembling body like an unwelcome visitor. My stomach lurched. A disorientating pain sliced through my skull. I couldn't breathe, couldn't think, could barely remember where I was. All I saw was Sam's face and the fear and confusion in his eyes. Hunched over, I sunk my fingers into the rug beneath me, digging my nails in as a wretched groan escaped from my lips.

"Muse..."

Stefan's hand rested on my back. His touch ignited the fury within me. I snapped my head up, snarling at him. "Get away from me."

He lifted his hands in surrender, leaning back on his knees, a muscle jumping in his jaw as he gritted his teeth. "I was there, but I had no hand in what he did."

A sob bubbled up my throat, followed by another. I tried to keep it all inside, to blockade the rush of grief, but sorrow swept aside what little strength I had left. Collapsing back against the couch, I covered my eyes with my bloodied hand, not wanting to witness or believe what I'd seen. "Not Sam..." I choked on the words as cool tears trickled over my cheeks. "Not him."

Stefan's hand pressed lightly on my shoulders. His grip tightened as I trembled.

"Don't." I shoved at him, pushing him away. "Don't touch me." But he caught my hand, then my arm. I tried to tug free, needing to retreat, but his grip tightened, preventing me from fighting him and then his arms closed around me, holding me close to his chest. Trapped against him, listening to the sound of his steady heartbeat, the fight in me evaporated, and I couldn't hold back any longer. I cried so hard the sobs wracked my shivering body. I clutched his shirt and buried my head against him, welcoming the embrace as though it could block out the truth, shut out all the anguish and pain. My element thrashed inside me, but the demon slunk back, cowering at my core. Perhaps it was Stefan's embrace that held her back, or the symbols on the walls, because I didn't feel the raging heat that I should have. I just felt fragile and alone.

Chapter Seventeen

I sat at the end of the jetty with the shimmering water of the lake all around me. The cold wind teased through my hair and nipped at my face, forcing me to hunker down and tug Stefan's heavy leather coat around me, pulling my legs against my chest. But I wasn't going inside. I couldn't. Not yet. Stefan had known. He'd known Sam was dead days ago, and he hadn't said a word, preferring instead to force me to witness it firsthand.

Akil had killed Sam. There was no denying it. No amount of lies could refute it. I'd seen it.

I remembered the message Sam had left me. A job, he's said, one he couldn't refuse. Akil. Phoenix Developments. The biggest property development firm in the city had invited Sam with the promise of a contract, and he'd gone willingly, walked right into Akil's office with no idea he was meeting with one of the Seven Princes of Hell. I could imagine Akil's charming greeting, his easy-going mannerisms, and all the while he was playing Sam for a fool.

I should have told Sam the truth about me. If I'd been straight with him, told him everything about me, he might still be alive. In trying to protect him, I'd left him exposed, like a lone sheep in a pack of wolves. Tears moistened my cheeks, but the sobs had died. I hugged my knees against me and watched the ripples on the lake. The wind hissed through the trees behind me. I felt Stefan watching me from inside, probably wondering whether he should leave me or intervene. He had better leave me.

Not a single word. He'd swaggered into my workshop. *I want you to read this blade...* Why didn't he just say, "Akil killed Sam and he's coming after you?" What was so hard about that?

I thought of the phone messages I'd left for Sam. I'd said I was sorry, that I was wrong, that I was afraid. He would never hear those messages. I should never have got involved with him. He was a good man, one of the best. I wasn't meant to have someone like that, tainted as I was. I should have stayed away. He'd died because of me. It didn't matter how you looked at it. The blood was on my hands.

"Come inside." Stefan stood behind me. I hadn't even heard him approach.

"Screw you." I sniffed. The wind whipped my hair across my face and in front of my eyes so that I had to raise a trembling hand to sweep it back.

"Please. Just come inside."

"You're no better than Akil." I rested my chin on my knee, teeth chattering against the cold. "For all I know, you're working for him."

"I am."

I tensed and turned my head to look up at him.

Stefan crouched behind me. "At least, that's what he believes." He held out a hand, fingers curled lightly into his palm. His gentle smile tried to reassure me. "Come inside."

I watched the wind tease his hair about his face. His brilliant eyes locked unblinking on mine.

"How do you think I knew about your workshop?" he asked. "Knew what your demon name was, knew about your talent for reading metal? Akil hired me, Muse. He believes he hired an assassin. I was to play with you before killing you, and his involvement would never be revealed. But he's been deliberately misled. I'm an

Enforcer. I protect people like you, caught in the crossfire."
He paused, offering his hand again. "Come inside."

***

It felt good to wear properly fitting clothes again,
even if they weren't mine. Stefan had picked some up on
his visit to town, guessing my size surprisingly well. Boot
cut jeans and a white V-neck long-sleeved top. Simple, but
comfortable, and that's what I needed. I was a long way
from home, and my life old was life torn to shreds. I had
nothing to my name, literally nothing to call my own. Even
the clothes on my back had been bought for me. I couldn't
go back to my apartment, and I dared not go back to Akil.
There was no one else. Even Stefan's motives were
dubious. I had begun to trust him; why wouldn't I? He'd
been the one ray of light in this whole wretched nightmare,
but I could no more trust him than I could Akil. By his
own admission, he was working for Akil—hired to play
with me and execute me.

Stefan planted a tub of chocolate ice cream on
the kitchen table and handed me a spoon. We hadn't
spoken since his confession on the jetty, and in that time,
the silence had begun to drag like a trawler net between us.
Unspoken words weighed us down.

He saw me frowning at the ice cream. "What?
Don't tell me you don't like ice cream?" He looked
shocked enough that I had to smile.

"Sure." Ice cream before lunch? It was just a bit
odd. That was all. I sat across the table from him and
watched as he popped open the lid. "I gather you like ice
cream?"

An eyebrow twitched comically. "Snow demon."
He shrugged.

His oddly placed humor made it difficult for me
to stay angry with him. Leaning forward, I sunk my spoon
in into the ice cream, cracking the hard chocolate layer

before scooping out a bite-sized chunk. It did taste pretty good.

"I meant what I said." He flicked those dazzling eyes to me before scooping out some ice cream for himself. "You're safe here."

My smile fell short of meaningful. "I've never been safe. You think you being here makes me safe? Or the remote location? He'll find me. Nobody escapes Akil. If he doesn't... some other demon will. I've only survived this long because he protected me. I've always belonged to one demon or another. On my own... I'm vulnerable."

He bowed his head, pressing his lips as though struggling to find the right words. When he looked up, he leaned on the table, closing the distance between us. "They lied to you. You're not vulnerable. You're powerful." Pointing the spoon at me, he said in all seriousness, "They want us dead because we have it all."

"What do you mean?" I jabbed at the ice cream with my spoon, chipping off frozen chunks.

"They kill half-bloods because we're dangerous, preferring to scrub us from existence rather than regret it later."

I licked my lips, twisting the spoon in my fingers. Akil had said something by the marina, right before he'd dragged my demon out of me. *There's no such thing as half a demon.* I looked up at Stefan, meeting his eyes. A flicker of understanding passed between us.

"They've lied to you since birth, Muse. It was that or kill you."

I laughed. "Okay, say I believe you. What makes us so terrifying?"

"We exist in both worlds. The veil means nothing to us. You and I, we can pass freely between realities. We have the ability to call upon a vast amount of power, not just in this world, but from across the veil too. Full-bloods can't do that. Not even a Prince of Hell can do that."

I grunted disbelievingly. "Right. Even if that were true, I could never contain that much power. It'd tear me open..." He looked at me in such a way that I felt a tickle of excitement dance across my skin. Those eyes peered through his lashes. A crooked smile lifted his lips at one corner. "You've done it... Haven't you?" I whispered.

"Twice." He jabbed his spoon into the ice cream. "It's not easy to control, but I can show you. I need to show you if we're going to stop Akil."

A flicker of hope skittered through me, a fleeting dash of possibility. "You're not lying?"

"No."

My demon shifted inside me, a curious resettling as though she were satisfied. I was not yet convinced. "No? Then why did you keep the truth from me?" I dropped my gaze. "About Sam."

"I couldn't trust you. If you cared for Akil as much as I thought you did and I told you he'd killed Sam, you wouldn't have believed me. I tried to call you after it had happened. To warn you... but you'd have gone straight to Akil. I'm sorry I kept it from you—I am. But the only way you would believe me was to see it for yourself."

The white noise on my answering machine—the silent messages from Monday morning. They'd been from Stefan. That didn't explain why Stefan had been there, in my vision. Why he had smiled when Akil had tossed him the sword. "I saw your expression. When I looked into that blade... You were there, right by Akil, when he killed Sam."

Stefan stabbed the spoon into the ice cream and left it there, leaning back in his chair. "I didn't know who Sam was. I'd been about to leave—our business transaction was over with—when Sam arrived. I was late—he was early—whatever. Akil thought it would make the ideal opportunity to test my allegiance. I had no idea he was going to kill him in front of me." Stefan rubbed a hand across his face. "The plan was to infiltrate Akil's operation.

We'd set up the assassin identity and put the word out, knowing he'd eventually bite."

"You and Ryder did this? You set Akil up from your garage and Ryder's kitchen? I find that hard to believe. Akil's got people everywhere. He'd have checked you out."

Stefan crossed his arms and leaned back. "It's not just Ryder and me. There are others. The Enforcers don't stop with me. You think Akil's got people everywhere? You don't know the half of it."

It was a great deal to take in, and I wasn't entirely sure I believed any of it. I set my spoon down on the table, wondering what other secrets were out there. I'd been sheltered by my demon owners—I knew that—and later by Akil. Frankly, I hadn't gone looking for trouble.

"Why me?" I asked. "Akil hired you to kill me, right? So... Would you have done it? How far were you meant to go?"

"When he told me you were a half-blood... I knew—I knew I couldn't hurt you." Stefan's chair scraped back as he stood. He moved to the kitchen cupboards where the view captured his attention and held onto it. "I had no intention of hurting anyone. It was a ruse to get in..."

I waited, sensing he had more to say. He turned and rested back against the countertop, facing me. "I've not met a half-blood before—someone like me." The perpetual smile had vanished, and I realized he felt the loneliness as keenly as I did. A lifetime of persecution. I had no idea what he'd been through, but being different was never going to be easy. He might not have suffered as I had, at least not physically, but that didn't mean he wasn't hurting.

I'd spent so long believing him to be a pillar of strength that I hadn't even considered the cost to him. He'd become tangled in a battle between a Prince of Hell and little old me, and yet he'd stayed. He could have walked away. He should have.

"Do you see now why I had to know I could trust you?"

I nodded slowly. "You're taking a big risk, telling me all this. We don't know one another, not really. I could go to Akil and try to use this information to save my own ass."

"True." His smile was back. "But I think you'll find your ass is beyond saving."

He was right about that. "Well then." I replaced the lid on the ice cream. "You'd best teach me how to raise hell because we're going to need it."

Chapter Eighteen

Stefan stood in front of me, just within reach. The pine trees surrounding us blotted out most of the dense gray sky. Pine needles blanketed the forest floor. The rich smell of wood sap and pine permeated the air, cleansing the city smog from my lungs. It was cold, the breeze bitter, but all that was about to change.

Apparently the lack of heat in our surroundings would restrict how much of my element I could summon, rendering this experience fairly safe. Or so Stefan assured me. It wasn't my element we wanted to call. It was my demon. In theory, she would need to manifest, and I would learn to maintain control. From there, the two of us combined, sharing the same space, time, and reality could draw upon the heat—my element —beyond the veil. I had never attempted such a thing and wasn't entirely convinced it was even possible. To draw power from beyond the veil would mean stabilizing a link between the two realities. Demons could hop through, but the journey was static. A to B. I was going to summon my element through the veil while keeping the link open: destination B coming to me.

"Don't look so worried." Stefan grinned.

He wore his infamous red coat with the buckles strapped closed, pulling his coat tight across his chest. The breeze teased his hair across his face, whipping it in front of his dazzling eyes. Whether he knew it or not, his presence alone made my demon restless. I didn't know if it was the cool surroundings or just the nerves getting to me, but I felt the chill of him even at arm's length. From the eager smile, the glint of mischief in his eyes, and the quiver of excitement in his voice, he clearly thrived in this wilderness. Some of that enthusiasm must have rubbed off on me. A trickle of delight shivered down my spine.

"They lied to you, Muse. You've spent so long hating half of yourself that you've stifled your abilities." The words rushed from his lips.

"I don't hate that part of me." From the twitch of his smile, I knew he saw through my lie. I'd spent my entire life holding her back. She was a part of me, but she'd always been the darkest part, the shadows in the back of my mind, the horror in my depths. I summoned her when I had no other choice because I was afraid of her, scared of the chaos, the undeniable desire for the madness that overwhelmed me every time she broke my surface. Stefan had told me I needed to embrace her, to let her have all of me, to drop the reins and trust her entirely. He made it sound easy.

He nodded once, my cue, and I relaxed the mental barriers that held her back. I closed my eyes, shaking out my hands. There was nothing I could do about the trembling. She would know I was afraid no matter how hard I tried to hide it. This wasn't about hiding. I had to reveal everything to welcome her in.

A flicker of panic snatched at my breath. What we were doing was dangerous. She could easily smother me, swat my attempts at control aside, and do whatever the hell she pleased. Hence the uninhabited location. She could also turn my efforts against me. Without a specific outlet, the result was always the same. She'd drown me in my element, my punishment for calling her and not releasing her.

So many things could go wrong.

"It's going to be okay." Stefan's voice was laced with a confidence I didn't share.

The breeze filtered through the branches of the trees. The sound of the wind rose and fell like waves caressing a beach. Slowing my breathing, calming my mind, I called to her. She immediately stretched inside of me, her power flexing beneath my skin. A ripple of heat rode over me, chasing away the bitter mountain air and flooding my body with warmth. Cocooned by her touch, I felt her crawl into my skin, layering her existence over mine. I smiled. With no rage, no resentment, only curiosity fuelling us, her explorative approach felt almost welcome, like an unexpected hug at a family reunion. It felt as though she too was surprised, and it occurred to me that I'd never really been alone.

I tilted my head, eyes still closed, as I felt her fill out my body. Then her warmth broke over my skin and explored. Curious tendrils sought an elemental source. The trees fencing us in, the ground beneath my feet, all held residual warmth but nothing like the potential we found in the city.

"How do you feel?" Stefan asked.

I opened my eyes, fixing him in the center of my gaze. "Good."

"Okay. Take her to the next level." His broad grin mirrored the thrill strumming through me.

This was where it got tricky. Usually by now, I'd be experiencing some sort of emotional burst. Rage often sparked the next level, but resentment, fear, and desire all served as triggers. I had none of those things. I would need to invite her to manifest.

I closed my eyes again, shutting out all exterior stimuli. Stefan hadn't said exactly how I was meant to invite her, but I figured it was like anything when it came to Demons. Intention was enough. I simply focused on relaxing, chasing away every ounce of fear and dread, leaving my mind clear of the resentment I'd harbored for my demon half.

She laughed, the sweet chuckle spilling from my lips as though it were mine.

The only chance you have of defeating Akil is to wield every ounce—every fragment of power you have, and to do that, you must have full control of your demon. Stefan had made it sound so simple.

I snapped open my eyes, fixing my stare back on Stefan. His image shimmered in the heat rolling off me in a haze. She was coming, and my doubts about my own capabilities were beginning to undermine my confidence. My control wavered. I staggered a little as my demon breeched my physical form. She became me. Her ethereal form superimposed itself over my human flesh. Lifting a hand, I saw her blackened skin stretched over mine, her fingers tipped with sharp obsidian claws. My wing opened behind me, stretching upward with a refreshing flick.

Stefan's expression had hardened. A slight smile still played across his lips, but he'd wisely adopted caution. Once manifested, I am a wild and unpredictable force of nature. Chaos personified. Chaos spiraled at my core. Blazing heat radiated through my chest.

"Summon your element," Stefan said. "All of it. Reach beyond the veil, and call it to you." He took a step back, then another, but he kept his eyes on me.

My demon watched his retreat keenly. I felt her measuring him, trying to decide if he was friend or foe. I lifted a hand, letting her trail an explorative ribbon of power from my fingers in his direction. It shimmered in the air with intangible heat. He wouldn't react well, of that I was sure, but curiosity prevented me from pulling it back. Stance rigid, Stefan let the ribbon of heat twist around his ankle. His opposing chill spilled over my fingers as though my hand touched him. The cool bite of it felt sharp, but it didn't hurt.

"Muse..." he growled my name, eyes narrowing.

I got the message: stop getting distracted and get on with it. As the power spooled into me, I breathed in, summoning the warmth from everything around us. I called it all forth, gathering it against me, but it wasn't nearly enough. There was only one other source. The veil.

Beyond it lies the netherworld, a place of extremes, a home I'd run from long ago. My brother would sense me the second I breached the veil.

Thoughts of Val turned to niggling doubts and became obstacles. My demon reared up, sensing my weakness, and then she plunged forth, her will overriding mine. The veil tore open between Stefan and me, a ragged wound in the fabric of reality. Beyond it, the heat was immeasurable. My element flooded through the veil into this reality, spiraling around me. I couldn't catch my breath, let alone control the rush of raw energy spilling into me. The wild element whipped around me, searing nearby branches and burning the ground at my feet. I stood in the center of a molten maelstrom, in the eye of a firestorm, my body alight with heat and flame. It just kept coming, gushing through the veil, over and into me.

I threw open my arms, back arched, wing held high behind me, and summoned it all. Swelling with power, my blackened skin simmering with energy, I heard my laughter twist in the madness. My physical body shone like the center of a star. The tumultuous heat built, fire rushed like liquid through my fingers, my hair, and across my flesh. Limitless power dripped from my flesh. A nuclear reaction charged my demonic core. I felt alive, connected to the source of creation. My humanity melted away. The demon rode high.

The veil began to shatter. The wound broke and disintegrated, its edges flaying, peeling away. I sensed the change. I wanted more. All of it. I wanted to taste the chaos, to swallow it whole and let it consume me.

The gap in the veil failed, collapsing in on itself. Immediately, my source of power vanished. I felt the break like a sword through the chest. Bathed in flame, I raged at the world and flung the heat away from me. Fire rushed outward in a tumbling blast, flattening everything in its path. A whoosh in the negative space behind the tidal wave of flame dropped me to my knees.

It took a few breathless moments for me to ground myself back in reality. Perspiration hissed against my demon skin. Steam rose from my flesh. Wood smoke twisted in the air around me. The ground beneath my feet was scorched to cinders. Hunched over, my wing hanging limp against my back, both my demon and I were spent. I barely had enough energy to lift my head and see Stefan crouch in front of me, drenched from head to toe. His hair clung to his face. His multifaceted ice-wings streamed with rivulets of water. He mustered a smile, but it barely reached the corners of his lips. As he reached out, I saw ice sparkle on his fingers. His face where the heat had melted his ice began to sparkle. He shook his head and swept a hand back through his hair, fracturing the ice that accumulated in the wet strands.

I took his hand firmly in mine and gasped. Power lanced up my arm, a fizzling, darting, pins-and-needles kind of power. Instinct told me to pull away, but he leaned in close, capturing my surprised stare with his iridescent eyes. As I clutched hold of his hand, the curious touch of ice laced its way up my arm, threading through and around the wavering ripples of heat. It should have hurt—in a way it did—but such was the mischievous intensity in Stefan's expression that I wanted the brittle ice against my sweltering flesh. I wanted to know how it would feel to have those quenching chills writhe over me. It was wrong. Our opposing elements clashed, but it felt so right.

He stood and tugged me to my feet. I stumbled against him, sucking in a gasp as his chill wrapped around me. Shivers sped down my body. I lifted my gaze to his as my demon slipped away, satisfied and exhausted on so many levels. Stefan fought back a smile. He opened his mouth to say something, then thought better of it and looked away. Following his gaze, I saw the destruction I'd wrought upon the forest. The pine trees stood naked, their bark black against the gray sky, needles scorched from the branches.

Stefan extricated himself from my grip, taking with him the cool wrappings of power. He rolled his shoulders, and the glorious sculpted wings dissipated into flakes of snow before fizzling against the hot earth. He glanced back at me. "You are capable of great things," he said with conviction.

If by great things, he meant complete destruction, then yes, it would seem so.

***

I couldn't sleep. Not surprising considering how I'd torn a hole in the veil and sucked heat out the very fabric of the netherworld. The remnants of adrenalin chased through my veins. My mind buzzed from the overdose of power. Sleep was the last thing on my mind as I lay in the dark, watching the moonlight cast swaying shadows across the walls. My demon sat smug and satisfied inside of me, I felt her languishing in the afterglow of the power she'd tasted.

I tossed aside the sheets and tugged on Stefan's shirt. The clothes I'd worn in the forest were in the wash. They'd survived, in the same way that my human flesh survived the blistering heat whenever my demon manifested. I can only put it down to the fact that, when my demon stepped into my skin, she protected my fragile human flesh, protecting herself in the process. That didn't stop her from tearing into me mentally when she didn't get her way.

I padded barefoot downstairs, startled to find Stefan seated on the couch in near darkness. He saw me and leaned forward to place the photo-frame he'd been holding on the coffee table. When he looked up, the smile didn't lessen the distant look in his eyes. I lingered on the bottom step of the stairs, hand resting on the banister.

"I couldn't sleep." I explained awkwardly, getting the distinct impression I'd intruded on a personal moment.

Elbows on his knees, shirt sleeves rolled up, he bowed his head, rubbing his hands together as if he sought to regain some composure. When he looked up, a few locks of hair had fallen over his face, forcing him to sweep them back. "It's okay."

I contemplated returning to the guest bedroom. Half-dressed and intruding on his personal time, I felt a little awkward and out of place. "Erm... are you okay?"

"Sure."

Clearly, he wasn't. I'd been expecting some sort of witty comeback making light of our situation. A 'sure' wouldn't cut it. Now I was concerned. It wasn't like I knew him well, but up until then, he'd pretty much made it all look like a breeze. As though this sort of crap was his day job. His unrelenting confidence had shored-up my complete lack of it. I sat on the edge of the couch across the coffee table from him, tugging the edge of the shirt over my thighs.

"I was wondering something..." I hesitated as his gaze followed my efforts to cover my legs. He quickly flicked his attention back to my face, then elsewhere, anywhere but my eyes. "You're the same as me, right? I mean. We're different elements, but you're powerful too?"

He nodded and settled back in the couch, draping an arm across the back.

"So why do you need me? You started this to get to Akil... Set it all up to get close to him before you even knew who I was. You must have had a plan. An end game?"

"The end game was to catch Akil out. We know he's overstepping the boundaries here, breaking the laws. We just need to catch him in the act. Hiring me, among other things, was part of that. But you're right... We didn't know about you—although I'd heard of a half-blood that Akil 'kept'."

I winced a little at the word 'kept' and saw Stefan flinch in return. "It became clear, early on, that I'd need your help."

"Why? What can I do to him that you can't?"

"You're his weakness."

I didn't understand. Akil was a Prince of Hell. They don't have weaknesses, at least none that I was aware of. "What does that even mean?"

"He's obsessed with you, Muse. I don't know why—no offense, you're easy on the eye, but he's a pure-blood demon, a Prince, and you're what they class as... filth."

I frowned at the last word. It was true, and yet knowing it, hearing it, always summoned horrid memories.

His smile chanced a return, but it didn't linger. "Anything to do with you, and he's distracted. Even hiring an assassin, he's sloppy. He can't see straight when it comes to you. Maybe it's because he's full-demon. He can't fathom why he's drawn to you. Either way, you're the key to stopping him."

I sighed and let my stare wander about the room. "I think it's a power thing. After what you helped me do today, I'm pretty sure it's not me he wants—or wanted. It's my demon. Now... Now I just think he wants me gone. I walked away from him, and nobody does that, especially not a half-blood. My brush-off would have slighted his honor."

Stefan smiled softly. "No doubt. His ego too."

"What about you?" I leaned forward to turn the picture frame toward me. The photo was the same one I'd seen earlier: the handsome fifty-something man with the catch-of-the-day at his feet. "What's your story?"

Stefan averted his gaze once more, dipping his chin before blinking slowly.

"I'm sorry." I said. The quiet became a little too awkward. "It's none of my business." If it was anything like my past then I could understand why he didn't want to tell me. "We survived though, right?" Barely, in my case, but barely was enough.

"Against the odds."

Something in those three words, perhaps the weary tone or their implied meaning, whatever it was, it made me feel such a depth of compassion for him that a stubborn lump formed in my throat. On impulse, I shifted off the couch and moved to the cushion beside him. Perched awkwardly on the edge, I clasped my hands in my lap with a nervous smile ticking across my lips. "I had no idea there were people like you out there. I just thought it was demon or be damned. Then, Akil taught me how to summon my demon with intent, not just by accident. He woke her in me, and together we killed my owner. It was the best day of my life. My owner, Damien...he was a sick son-of-a-bitch. Vile in many ways. Akil taught me...that it didn't have to be like that."

"You were lucky," Stefan said softly. I caught an undertone of sadness and knew he understood.

I was lucky. If Damien hadn't paraded me in front of Akil, I might not have survived much longer. Had Akil not taken it upon himself to free me... Had Akil been worse than Damien... Had I not been strong enough to maintain my sanity through all of the pain and degradation...

"My point is." I cleared my throat. "We're the products of our past. Without those experiences, as horrid as they were, I wouldn't be the person I am today."

Stefan moved so quickly I barely saw him move at all. He was suddenly very close. His hand hovered beside my cheek as though he'd lost his nerve at the last second. I froze. For a few moments, I didn't breathe, didn't move. Then he eased a little nearer, his lips so close all it would take was a little give on my part, and we'd kiss. As his hand lightly touched my cheek, a sliver of power snapped between us. Its dart-like flicker forced a hiss through my teeth. He laid his hand against my cheek, and the chill of his element slid over me, a shivery tremor following in its wake as a traitorous muffled groan slipped from my lips. I could have kissed him, should have... He was there, so close, but I knew if I did, it wouldn't stop there. My heart fluttered nervously. The urge to close that tiny distance between us was so intense that I had to grip the couch to stop myself. He took a breath just as his lips brushed mine, so lightly, like the gentle flutter of snowflakes.

I sprang back, hand clasped over my mouth, the other pulling the shirt down to cover my thighs. "I er..." I waved a hand in the air, gesturing wildly. "I should um...you know, get back—get some sleep. Not that I... Erm... Yeah." *Stop waffling before you say something you'll regret,* I thought. The tease of desire had ignited inside of me at his touch. My element bloomed quickly, spilling heat though me. My heat and his cold, fire and ice, it was wrong on so many levels. And I wanted it.

He grinned wickedly, his demeanor as cool as ice. Damn him.

I clamped my mouth closed, afraid I might tell him what I really wanted, although he probably read it all on my face. His eyes in the dark held all manner of tempting promises. The gape of his collar betrayed a hint of his sculpted body. I could so easily have sat back down and undone those shirt buttons, one little button at a time. Hot lips on his cool mouth, tasting, exploring. I'd lay him back. Slip my hands beneath his shirt and let my heated touch ease across the rippled plain of his sculpted chest, across the scorpion tattoo, lower... Hot, flustered, and within a few heartbeats of giving in to temptation, I turned quickly and headed for the stairs.

A howl fractured the serenity of the night. The hollow sound of the beast sliced through the heat of desire and dashed my wanton thoughts. Stefan was on his feet. He plucked the katana from the bag of weapons and tugged off the scabbard. He flicked the light off in the kitchen and then returned, snatching a gun from the bag before joining me at the foot of the stairs. "It can't know we're here. Not yet," he whispered. "But this isn't the city, and we're the only things out here."

In other words, we're screwed.

Another howl echoed outside, closer this time. A chilling fear swept through me. I tried to summon my element, but the preventative marks on the wall snuffed it out before it could breach my flesh. Stefan shook his head, sensing the stirring of my power, then handed me the gun. I noticed it was the gun I thought he'd lost when I felt its familiar weight in my hand.

"You have seven rounds in the magazine," he said. "Use them."

"What if we go outside? Use our elements."

"Only if it finds us." He planted a hand on my shoulder and forced me to sit, my back against the wall. "There's a chance it may not... Call enough of your power to see it."

I flexed my elemental muscles, calling just enough to spill a veil of power in front of my eyes. The last time we'd dealt with the hounds, we'd only escaped by hiding. This time, hiding was all we had. I cupped the gun in my left hand, right hand around the grip, finger off the trigger but ready against the trigger guard.

Stefan did a double-take, then grinned. "Flick the safety off."

"You enjoy this crap way too much," I grumbled, doing as he'd advised.

"Slide the chamber back."

I skewed a scowl in his direction, catching that glint of humor in his eyes. "I have fired this gun before—" The kitchen windows exploded inward.

Glass blasted through the kitchen doorway, showering the spot on the couch where we'd been seated moments before.

"Go!" Stefan shoved me up the stairs as the thunderous crash of splintered glass and wood filled the air. I stumbled on the steps, clambering up on all fours as the heaving bulk of hairless hound slammed its way through the kitchen doorway, taking out half the wall with it. I got a glimpse of its blood-red eyes as it swung its head around before I finally found my feet and dashed up the remaining steps and down the hallway.

Stefan flung open a bedroom door. "The window. Go. Get outside."

I was inside the room before I realized he wasn't following. "What are you doing?"

"Go. I'll keep it here. Run. Don't stop. Just run." He was gone.

I headed for the window and yanked open the lower section enough so I could duck outside. The wind blasted into the room, whipping around my bare legs as I stood frozen. I couldn't leave him. Gun in hand, I turned and darted back out into the hall. The massive hound had clawed its way up the staircase, knocking the banister out in its furious attempt to get to Stefan. I saw the beast snap its jaws together, lunging at Stefan as he swung the sword across its snout. Its whimpers sliced through my skull. Teeth gritted, I raised the gun, steadied it in my left hand, and aimed down the barrel. As the hound lunged at Stefan again, I fired. The gun jumped in my hand. The casing ejected. The hound jerked and swung its crimson glare on me. I fired again. The bullet sliced down the right side of its hideous face. Again, and this time, the bullet hit the Hellhound right between the eyes, blasting through its skull. The beast jerked back and collapsed, slipping from the landing to land with a dull thud on the living room floor.

Stefan lunged at me, grabbed my left hand, and tugged me forward, back down what remained of the stairs. The hound's breathing snuffled from its wet jaws. It wasn't dead. They don't die.

"Quickly." Stefan pulled me toward the door. He yanked it open. And froze.

I plowed into the back of him, about to ask why he'd stopped when I saw the mountainous bulk of Hellhound blocking his path. The beast hunched forward, fat paws splayed on the path. Pools of glistening drool gathered below its rippling lips. I reeled back. The hound behind us snarled and shook its head, snapping its jaws together as it regained its senses. Instinct tugged on my demon, but she couldn't break through whatever magic those marks on the walls performed. Backing into Stefan, I slipped my left hand into his. The Hellhound beneath the stairs stamped its feet, steadying itself. It ducked down, legs ready to spring.

I lifted the gun, not entirely sure how many bullets I had left. My arm trembled, aim all over the place. Then I heard an all too familiar voice.

"Invite me in, and I'll call them off."

Flinging my stare over my shoulder, I watched in horror as Akil walked around the hound outside, running a hand down its quivering, hairless flank. The beast jerked its snout, sniffing the air and chomping its jaws. There could be no doubt who controlled them. Stefan stepped back into me, then glanced behind him at the hound beneath the stairs. His eyes found mine, a brutal honesty raw on his face. We were in trouble. I tightened my hand in his, saw the fleeting smile on his lips, and then he let go to face Akil.

"Come in, make yourself at home." Stefan stepped aside, sweeping a gesture into the house. "Sorry about the mess. Unexpected guests."

Akil stepped across the threshold. He slid his gaze over the chaos in the room before straightening his shirt cuffs. His stoic expression gave nothing away. Dressed immaculately in a dinner jacket and black trousers, right down to his polished Oxford shoes, he looked every inch the city tycoon. Silver cufflinks caught the moonlight seeping in through the back windows. The same light danced in his dark eyes when they settled on me. Instinct told me to shirk back. I might have done, had I not learned what he'd done. The suave son-of-a-bitch had murdered Sam—my friend—in cold blood. I was under no illusions about Akil.

I stood there in my underwear, wearing Stefan's shirt and glared back at Akil, my chin up, shoulders straight. I was not backing down.

He humphed a laugh and said, "Amitto," with a flurry of his hand. The Hellhounds slumped in unison. Their leathery hides began to dissolve. Fizzling embers devoured them, spiraling dust into the air until nothing remained.

With the hounds gone, I became aware of the wind flowing through the open door and through the house, into the kitchen where the panoramic windows had been smashed. I heard the trees outside creaking against the weight of the wind, branches snapping. The forest groaned as though it recognized the ageless forces of chaos inside the house. I lifted the gun, my aim surprisingly steady.

Akil glared back at me and smiled. "Shoot me."

Finger on the trigger, I wanted to. It would take just a twitch, the smallest of movements to blow him away. "You killed Sam."

Akil looked away, blinking slowly. His smile widened. "Is that what Stefan told you?"

"No." My hand began to tremble. "I saw it in the sword."

He met my glare once more. "Did you? You're sure? Because... from what you've told me in the past... The images can be difficult to define. Blurry. Inconsistent."

No, he wasn't going to do this. I knew what I'd seen. I had felt the sword plunge through Sam's chest. It was real. "Why?" I hissed through gritted teeth.

"Put the gun down, Muse." The growl beneath his words offered a clear warning.

Stefan stood beside me. He reached up and closed his hand around the top of the gun, bringing the weapon down, so it pointed toward the floor in front of Akil. "You don't want to do that."

He eased the gun from my hand and flicked the safety back on. Frowning, I watched him toss the gun onto the couch and then hand the sword to Akil. Unease crawled across my skin as Akil lifted the katana in his right hand, his heated gaze admiring the blade. "A fine weapon, don't you agree, Muse?"

Stefan stood to Akil's left, hand tucked casually into his jeans pocket.

I frowned, eyes narrowing on Stefan. What was going on here? I searched his face for any sign to indicate this was wrong, but he just stood there, cold.

Akil ran a hand down the flat plain of the blade. "Your little stunt earlier, drawing your element from beyond the veil... That was... astonishing. I knew the moment you called the heat to you. Even in Boston, I felt the shift in power. It's how I found you."

My hands clenched into fists. "I'm not the pathetic half-human girl you think I am."

"I know that. Why do you think I've kept you all these years? I even had Stefan test you, to see whether you were capable."

I clamped my teeth together. Anger trembled through my muscles. My demon twisted, eager to break free but unable to do so. Stefan didn't deny Akil's words. Even under the weight of my stare, he didn't flinch. He just met my gaze as though none of this mattered to him.

Akil's lips hitched up at the corner as he glanced from Stefan to me. "Stefan's working for me, Muse. Always was."

I knew that, well sort of, but was I meant to know it? If I revealed I knew, would that put Stefan in danger? "What—what do you mean?" Was Stefan still working for him? Even now?

Akil closed the distance between us in a few strides. I stumbled back, bumping against the wall as he invaded my personal space. "You don't get to walk away from me, Muse. Ever," he said with a snarl.

I sneered up at him. "I got that when you tried to kill me at the marina."

He slid a hand over my shoulder and laced his fingers around my throat, but the tightening of his grip didn't come. His thumb rubbed lightly against my neck. "That was...a mistake."

"A mistake? I nearly died, Akil."

"That was not my intention..." He bowed his head, bumping his forehead against mine as he brought his hand higher, cupping my face. "I just meant to... I wanted you to react. To see your demon. She's quite remarkable."

I turned my head away, fighting to breathe beneath his overbearing presence.

"That's what this has all been about," he whispered in my ear.

Hands on his chest, I pushed against him, trying to force him back, but I might as well have been pushing against stone.

He breathed in through my hair, his chin brushing my forehead. "It's her I want. Not your weak human shell."

"Akil...Please." I shoved again, pushing hard enough to force him back a step, but that only gave him the room he needed to bring the sword up between us and press the blade against my throat.

The sharp edge nicked my skin. A warm trickle of blood dribbled down my neck. I pleaded with wide-eyes, snatching breaths where I could without worsening the dig of the sword against my flesh.

"Your previous owner had no notion of the creature he kept in chains." Akil slid his left hand over my hip.

I couldn't stop the shivering. As the demon thrashed inside me, my human body had become riddled with fear. My heart galloped, thudding in my ears. "You don't own me," I growled.

"No?" He leaned into me, pushing the blade against my neck, forcing my head back. "I beg to differ."

I heard the metallic chink-chink of a gun slider being pulled back. "Step away from her." Stefan had pressed the gun against the back of Akil's head. From my awkward angle, I peered down my nose and over Akil's shoulder at Stefan. His element swirled in his arctic eyes, their intense blue fracturing deep, revealing his ice-bound soul.

Akil chuckled. The lurid ripples of his laughter rode over me. My head was light and my legs weak. Fear robbed me of my will. "I'll cut her throat," he snarled.

"Do it. But know I'll blow your skull apart. Immortal or not, that's gotta hurt."

Akil raked his gaze across me, almost as though his glare alone could slice through me. He measured his options. Indecision narrowed his eyes and then, reluctantly, he pulled back. Stefan countered behind him. Only when Akil withdrew the sword from my throat did I slump against the wall, able to breathe again. After dabbing at my neck, my trembling hand came away slick with blood.

I looked up at Akil in time to catch a twisted smile lashing across his lips. He didn't resemble the man I could have loved, didn't even look like the demon that inhabited his body. He was a stranger to me. The darkness had corrupted him, creating a monster, or had he always been that way?

"You fell for her, didn't you?" I noticed Akil's fingers flexing around the sword's grip. "I killed the last man who touched her."

Stefan couldn't help looking at me. I may have seen some acknowledgement in his eyes, right before Akil twisted around, knocking Stefan's gun-arm up before plunging the katana deep into Stefan's left shoulder, driving him to his knees.

Instinct lurched me forward as Stefan cried out. He fought to bring the gun around, but Akil twisted the sword deeper into his flesh, wrenching a strangled cry from Stefan's lips.

"Stop!" I yelled.

Akil swung his head around, yanking the blade free from Stefan's flesh. He rounded on me, bringing the bloodied sword around to point the tip at me. "You are mine," he growled. "And I'm taking you home."

"No!" He didn't mean home to Boston, he meant the netherworld, and the thought flushed my veins with white-hot terror, wrenching my strength out from under me. I dropped to my knees. "No, please." I shook my head from side to side, and tears blurred my vision. Panic tightened my chest. I clenched my fist over my heart. I couldn't go back home.

Akil's face twisted into a hideous mask of disgust. "I will tear that demon from your human flesh if I have to peel your skin off piece by piece." The venom behind those words severed the last vestiges of hope I might have had that, somewhere deep inside, he still cared for me.

A gunshot cracked through the air.

Blinking rapidly, I watched the curious bloom of blood spread across Akil's white shirt. He looked down, as though wondering where the blood had come from. Another shot, and his torso jerked. Another, and I felt a warm spray of blood mist across my face. The forth gunshot rang out, its deafening retort causing me to flinch. Akil sank to his knees, his face white with shock and then he collapsed forward, motionless.

Stefan had propped himself up on an elbow, gun quivering in his right hand. His aim wavered with his labored breathing. He gritted his teeth as he pulled himself up onto his knees. "Go," he grunted. "He won't stay down... for long."

Adrenalin ousted my fear. Self-preservation kicked in. I rushed to Stefan and hooked an arm under his, helping him to his feet. I staggered as he fell against me. "Can we kill him? While he's out?"

"No. He'll come back no matter what we do."

I glanced back at Akil's motionless body, expecting him to twitch awake at any moment.

"Go. Take my car—just go, Muse."

I felt Stefan's element stirring, it's chilling touch snapping at my flesh, lashing out protectively. "Where exactly?"

Stefan pried himself from my grip and stumbled toward the door. "Ryder."

"Ryder?" He was the least likely go-to guy to get me out of this. I stole one last fleeting look at Akil's body, tremors rattling my bones, then followed Stefan outside. The bitterly cold night air nipped at my face. My trembling intensified. If I could hold myself together a little while longer, just long enough to get away...

Stefan had slumped against the driver's door, his left arm limp at his side. Blood dripped from his fingers, creating bright red rivulets down the car's paint until it pooled along the door seal.

"Stefan, please. Let me help you."

"I'm okay." He forced every word through clenched teeth. "Ryder will know what to do. Go."

"I'm not leaving you here."

"Just go." He grimaced, pain wracking his body. He tucked the gun into his waistband and pressed his right hand against the wound in his shoulder, struggling to hide how his fingers shook. It didn't take long for the blood to swell and spill over the back of his hand.

I placed my hand over his. His shivering seemed all the worse now that I could feel it. He allowed me to ease his hand away, then dropped his head back as I stripped his shirt away from the wound. He snatched breaths between spasms of pain. Akil had stabbed him low in the shoulder. The blade had passed right through. The jagged wound oozed dark blood and showed no sign of stopping. "Get in the car. I'm taking you to a hospital."

"No, Muse." He sighed, eyelids flickering closed.

"Stop being stubborn, and do as I say." I opened the rear passenger door and gave him a warning look. "Get in, or we both stay here."

"You're impossible," he muttered, clutching the open door and moving gingerly to climb inside.

I drove us out of there as fast as the rental car could bump along the dirt track to the main route. Stefan sat slumped in the back seat, teeth clenched. I glanced in the mirrors, watching him battle the pain. Every pothole, even the slightest ridge in the road, tugged a restrained groan from him.

"No hospitals," he said when we hit the smooth main route and I planted the throttle to the floor. "Get to Ryder."

Chapter Nineteen

I screeched the car to a halt outside Ryder's premises, bumping it up the curb as close to the door as I could get. Early morning air wrapped around me as soon as I stepped from the car, stealing the warmth from my bones. The brilliant blue sky only made the desperate situation feel all the more dire. I banged on Ryder's door. The car's engine ticked behind me as it cooled.

Stefan was sprawled across the back seat, asleep or unconscious. The milky pallor of his skin was pale enough to frighten me.

"C'mon Ryder." I hammered a fist against the door. "Open up!" My shout echoed down the empty street.

What is he wasn't home? Where was I supposed to go?

The door finally opened. Ryder rubbed his eyes, yawning. Wearing the same clothes I'd seen him in days before, he scowled at me. "What the..."

His wide-eyed stare took in my blood soaked shirt, bare legs, and blood-splattered face. Then he noticed Stefan's motionless body in the back of the car. "What happened?" Ryder shoved by me and flung open the car door. Climbing inside, he pressed his fingers against Stefan's neck, checking for a pulse.

"Akil." The tremor in my voice barely registered against the swirl of dark thoughts in my head.

Ryder climbed out and nodded. "Get in. I'll drive."

I climbed into the back with Stefan's head resting in my lap as Ryder took control. I was grateful for it. The hours it had taken us to get back to Boston—the constant checking the mirrors for any sign of being followed—the worry that Stefan would die in the backseat—had left me beyond drained; numbed. I rarely felt properly cold, but I felt it then, a deep soul-weary chill. I had no idea what Ryder was going to do, but he seemed to have a plan because he swung the car around and sped out of there as quickly as I'd screeched in.

Stefan breathed lightly. The rise and fall of his chest reassured me a little. He felt cold, but I chose to take that as a good sign. However, the pool of congealed pool of blood on the back seat told another story. "Akil will be after us," I warned Ryder.

"Okay. It'll be okay." Ryder assured, and, bizarrely, I believed him. "Where we're going, Akil can't follow."

***

After no more than ten minutes, Ryder pulled the rental car into a narrow industrial street dominated by a vast warehouse at its end. Graffiti plastered every inch of the red brick walls. Scrawling letters and gang symbols wound their way around a steel door.

"Ryder?" I peered out of the car windows, not seeing anything in the street that could possibly help. If anything, we were in a worse neighborhood than the one we'd just left.

He rolled the car to a halt outside the steel door and cut the engine. Twisting in the driver's seat, he said, "When inside, do as they say."

"What?" I hadn't heard him right. What did he mean? My thoughts dragged through molasses. Exhaustion wrapped me in a woolly cocoon.

Ryder climbed out. I followed suit, too tired to argue. We managed to pull Stefan from the car, hitching his arms over our shoulders. Stefan barely registered us at all. He was just a dead weight against me. As we shuffled Stefan to the door, I noticed the huge scorpion spray-painted over the doorway, its pincers embracing the top of the doorframe. "What is this place?" I grunted, heaving Stefan's limp arm into a better position behind my neck.

The door rumbled sideways, and we were met by an armed guard. He ushered us into an antechamber and closed the door behind us. The small room couldn't have been more different to the exterior of the warehouse. White walls gleamed beneath harsh fluorescent lights. A second steel door had a small reinforced glass window, revealing hints of a white corridor beyond.

The guard buzzed a button beside the door which opened with a whoosh of antiseptic-scented air. Two guards bore down on us, one female, the other a stocky male with a scar below his right eye, both armed with assault rifles.

"We'll take him from here." The guard beside me said, extracting Stefan's arm from around my neck. He handed him over to two waiting white-coat-clad men. I managed to catch sight of a gurney but as I stepped forward to follow, the scarred guard shot his hand out, shoving me. "Stay back," he warned.

"Hey." I instinctively lifted my hands. I wasn't a threat to them; couldn't they see that?

His scarred face held a determined grimace as he shoved me again. "Against the wall," he barked.

"What?"

He grabbed my upper arm and twisted me around, slamming me face first against the wall, then proceeded to frisk me. His female companion stood back, rifle clutched across her chest, face empty.

"Get off me. I came here to help." I winced as his hands rode roughly over my bruised skin. "Get your hands off me," I snarled, summoning enough of my element to cause him a nasty burn. My demon woke eagerly, answering my call. An alarm sounded. The rapid chirps accompanied the sound of locks automatically bolting.

"She's demon." The female guard declared matter-of-factly.

Scarface drove an elbow into my back. The impact wrenched a cry from me. I snarled and twisted, balling my hand into a fist and driving it into his cheek. Considering all the crap I'd had to deal with in the last few days, he was lucky I didn't incinerate him where he stood.

My first cracked across his jaw, just as female-guard strode forward, clutched my right arm, and stamped a branding of some sort on the back of my hand. A jagged dart of pain thrust up my arm and struck me in the chest. I fell forward, doubling over against the ball of agony in my gut. My demon suddenly fell back from me, as though something tugged her out of reach. Her rapid retreat arched my back, jerking the air from my lungs. She didn't go easily and sunk her claws into my metaphysical insides, but it was no use. I felt her tear from within me, and then there was silence; a quiet like I've never known. An empty pit had opened inside of me, a void where my demon had existed. She was gone.

"What have you done?" I wheezed, before collapsing.

Chapter Twenty

I woke in a bright white room. A fresh pile of clothes sat neatly beside the door. The bed beneath me was bare but surprisingly comfortable. I couldn't hear anything outside the room, just the buzz of the lights above and my own raspy breathing. The air smelled of disinfectant, the scent so strong it tickled my nose and scratched my throat.

I shivered and collected the clothes before peeling off Stefan's ruined shirt and dressing in a gray jump suit. I did all of this without thought, my mind peculiarly numb. Once dressed, I tried to run my hands through my hair, but found it in desperate need of a shower to wash out the blood. Akil's blood. I couldn't think about him, about the threat he'd cast at me. *I'm taking you home.*

Standing on tiptoes at the door, I peeked through the glass. A single empty chair sat against the opposite wall, but otherwise the place was empty. Shivers rippled up and down my back. Why was I so cold? I hugged my arms across my chest and noticed the mark on the back of my hand. An angry red welt indicated exactly where the female guard had stabbed me with something. Whatever it had been, the effects had chased away my demon. She'd gone. I couldn't call her, couldn't feel her. There was nothing of her left inside of me but a cavernous void.

I began to pace from one side of the tiny room to the other, flexing my hands into fists. What was this place?

They'd known I was part demon as soon as I'd tried to summon my element. They'd been prepared. The scorpion over the door couldn't be a coincidence. Ryder had breezed in, while they'd abruptly stopped me. Were these the Enforcers Stefan had spoken of? He'd said there were others. The guards though, they looked like military. They hadn't hesitated when dealing with me, although I had managed to swing at one. I had the bruises on my knuckles to vouch for that.

The door rattled and opened. Another armed guard regarded me coolly. "Come with me."

I narrowed my eyes at him and crossed my arms. "I want to see Stefan. Is he okay?"

He stepped back and gestured for me to leave the room. He was taller than me, stockier, with a swagger borne of rigorous training. He carried the gun firmly, his grip one of confidence, as though the gun were just an extension of him. I could have lunged at him, but what good would it do me? I might have gotten out the room, but there would be other guards. This wasn't a holiday camp. It would make more sense to gauge the lay of the land before I lashed out.

"Are you taking me to Stefan?" I asked.

"No." He blinked, eyes disarmingly warm. "I'm taking you to Adam."

"Who's he?" I rubbed at my arms, desperately trying to warm myself.

"Come with me, and you'll see."

If I didn't, I got the distinct impression from his military-grade stare that he'd force me. I'd already been on the receiving end of their greeting and didn't relish the thought of repeating it. So I followed him through the rats-maze of corridors, passing a few casually dressed people who didn't give me or my armed guard a second glance. We climbed a few steps and entered a level far more conducive to comfort, like a busy office floor, no... like a hospital ward but where you'd expect to see beds, there were desks. Dozens of people milled back and forth, chatting animatedly. Phones rang. A bubble of laughter sounded somewhere behind me. I caught glimpses of people in white coats and saw various curved ultra-thin televisions suspended on the walls, showing what looked like newsfeed from around the world.

We arrived at an office. The blinds were closed, so I couldn't see in. My guard rapped on the door, and a sharp voice inside said, "Enter." I came face to face with an older version of the man in the photograph at Stefan's house. I tried to hide my surprise by watching the guard leave. If this man was Stefan's father, how come he was alive and well?

Standing against a chair, my hands resting on the back, I flicked my gaze about the comfortable office space. A bookcase brimmed with books along the whole of the left wall. A couple of comfy chairs, glass-topped coffee table, antique ball and claw footed desk rounded out the space.

"I apologize for the harsh treatment." The man, who I assumed to be Adam, stood behind his desk, a steaming cup of coffee in his right hand. I smelled the blend and wondered if he'd offer me a mug. I needed it.

He pinched the bridge of his nose, dislodging rimless glasses before taking them off and rubbing his eyes. "I wanted to thank you personally for bringing Stefan back to us."

"Is he okay?"

He nodded slowly and replaced the glasses. "He's fine. Exhausted, but recovering well." He pulled out his chair and sat down, gesturing that I should do the same. When I didn't move, he smiled. "My name is Adam."

He could play nice. The niceties might even be genuine. He did have a warmth about him that slightly disarmed me, but I wasn't buying whatever he was selling. "You tore my demon from me."

"Yes. A precautionary measure. Don't worry. We'll give you the antidote when you leave."

How could he appear so flippant about tearing out a part of me? "I didn't come here to hurt anyone. I don't even know what this place is. Ryder brought us here. Stefan's safe... so I'd like to leave. Can I leave?"

He took a sip of coffee then leaned back. His chair creaked at the shift in weight. Brushing absently at his deep green sweater, he sucked in a deep breath before exhaling slowly. "You could, but I suspect Akil will be looking for you."

My fingers dug into the back of the seat. "How much do you know?"

"Everything." He brushed a hand across his stubbled chin. "You're safer here."

"Says you. So far, you've violated me and tossed me in a cell." I didn't like him. He appeared to be a fatherly-figure, the caring type, but I stood before him with a chasm inside of me where my other-half was missing, and I couldn't forgive him that. "I don't know you. I don't trust you."

"We mean you no harm," he said but his nonchalant tone wasn't sincere.

"I want to see Stefan."

"He's resting." He must have caught a glean of frustration in my eyes because he tried to soothe me with a soft smile. "Very well. You can see Stefan and then perhaps we can have a candid discussion about the options available to you."

I tossed him a worthless smile. Until I spoke to Stefan, I wasn't trusting anyone.

***

A guard deposited me outside a numbered apartment door. As far as I was aware, we were still in the warehouse, but without any windows, and after ascending and descending so many different staircases, I'd completely lost my bearings. I knocked on the door, watching the guard get himself comfortable in a chair a few strides from me. Either they were worried I was going to do something, or I was a prisoner here. I'd yet to figure out which. Maybe it was both.

Stefan opened the door. For a few fleeting seconds, he didn't smile, didn't react at all. His navy blue shirt hung open, revealing the corner of a bandage plastered over his left shoulder. A spot of blood had oozed through the gauze, but otherwise he looked remarkably well.

The smallest hint of a smile finally twitched across his lips as he stepped aside, then acknowledged the guard outside with a nod. His room was small. A bed, desk, TV, no windows. Functional, like a hotel room, but with the locks on the outside. Once Stefan had closed the door behind him, I opened my mouth to ask one of the hundred or so questions I needed answered. He pressed a finger to my lips. He shook his head and beckoned me toward the desk. On a piece of paper, he scrawled: *They're listening.*

Oh crap. The frown on his face confirmed my suspicions. All was not well.

I cleared my throat, glancing around me as though I might actually see the microphones. "How come you got the guest suite, and I got a prison cell?

"They don't trust you." He caught sight of the angry mark on my hand and must have known what it meant because his eyes narrowed. His lips set in a terse line. "Are you alright?"

Folding my arms, I hugged them against me. "Yeah, I'm okay. Feel a bit... peculiar without my demon."

"She's still there; they've just repressed her." He sighed then made a frustrated noise in the back of his throat. "I'm sorry."

I shrugged. Sorry wasn't going to bring her back. "How are you?"

"Good." He brightened. "Thanks to you."

"And you wanted me to leave you there." I grinned. "After everything you've done for me, that wasn't going to happen."

He tried not to smile, then gestured at the bandage on his shoulder. "Could have been worse."

"You're lucky he missed. He never misses."

"He won't again, especially now that he believes we're lovers."

I snorted a laugh as though such an idea was ludicrous. Fire and ice? Impossible. I must have done a good job at dismissing the idea because Stefan's smile fell short before he turned away and buttoned up his shirt. "Did they introduce you to my father?"

The man in the photo. I was right to guess he was Stefan's father. "Adam? Yeah..." I stopped short of telling him what I thought. "I was told he was dead."

"He likes the world to think so. I often wish he was. He and I... We don't get along..." Stefan slid a glance my way. "Ever."

Oh. "Good, 'cuz I don't like him." I looked at the door, wondering whether the guard was still outside, then searched the generic landscape pictures on the wall and the cheap ornaments for any sign of cameras or microphones. I couldn't see anything, but that was the point of hidden surveillance. I had so many questions burning right on the tip of my tongue and couldn't ask a single one.

"Am I a prisoner here?" The weary undertone in my voice surprised me. I hadn't realized how exhausted I was, not just physically but mentally too. It had been one hell of a week.

"No." But he nodded contrarily, which threw me. He gave me a sheepish smile, as though he were responsible.

Clearly there was more going on here than I had any hope of understanding on my own. "What is this place?"

"The Institute. The human response to demon occupation."

Never heard of them. "Since when are demons occupying this realm?"

He gave a slight shake of his head, implying he couldn't explain. Then without a word, he took my hand and opened the door, startling the guard outside. As the guard moved to stand, Stefan waved him off. "We're good."

"My orders are to watch her," the guard grumbled.

Stefan, a head taller, straightened up to him. "I said I've got this."

"You can strut all you want, but I've got orders, and I'm following those orders, *Demon.*"

Stefan was on him in one swift lunge. Hand twisted in the guard's jacket, he rammed his arm under the guard's chin and slammed him back against the wall. "Call me that again, and I'll show you exactly how *demon* I can be."

My breath misted in front of me as the temperature plummeted. Stefan was calling his element, and if the guard reacted like they had with me, then Stefan was better off backing down. I lightly touched his wounded shoulder, briefly feeling the full force of his arctic glare on me before he blinked and loosened his grip on the guard.

"Fine." Stefan backed off, striding down the hall, so I had to jog to keep up. I gathered his reaction hadn't been personal and suspected he was as frustrated at the whole situation as I was. We walked in silence. The guard lagged behind.

Only after it felt as though we'd walked the length of the warehouse four or five times, through various corridors, passing through a cafeteria, did Stefan slow. A little out of breath, I stopped beside him, catching sight of the guard weaving his way through people loitering in the hall behind us. Stefan opened the door into what I assumed was the Institute's library but felt more like a storeroom. Freestanding metal book shelves created a dozen or so rows dividing up the windowless room. As we entered, the lights above flickered on, detecting our presence. We were the only two visitors, besides the guard who followed dutifully behind us.

Stefan left me beside a bookcase. He returned to the guard and muttered a few words. They both glanced my way, sharing a conspiring smile. I frowned, wondering what they were up to and then ran my finger down the spines of the books. They weren't like any books I'd seen at the local library. Some were stained, their foreign titles barely decipherable. Some were the size of concrete blocks, great tomes that I'd struggle to lift. I'd recognized latin, but couldn't speak or read it. Another had been written in what I assumed was Cyrillic.

Stefan slipped an arm around my waist, startling a gasp from me. I twisted around to face him, surprised to find him so close. He leaned into me, backing me up against the books. "Go with it..." he whispered, a seriousness on his face where I'd expected to see mischief.

The guard had dropped into a chair, facing the opposite direction while absently thumbing through a book. Stefan bowed his head. I felt the abrasive stubble of his chin brush against my cheekbone and his cool breath teasing through my hair. I could blame surprise for my racing heart, but it would've been a lie. I rested a hand on his lower back, then moved it awkwardly to his hip. A deep chuckle rumbled through him. He took my hand and placed it on his lower back.

"You could at least make it believable," he whispered.

That wasn't my problem; the wicked thoughts running through my distracted mind were. Without my demon, my element didn't flush through my skin, but a different kind of heat had begun to pool inside me. Without realizing it, I'd blamed the demon part of me for the attraction I'd felt toward Stefan ever since he'd first walked into my workshop. I'd told myself she'd wanted the opposing power coiled inside of him, but it hadn't been just that. Now my demon was trapped, out of reach, and yet as he stood close against me, I couldn't think clearly through the rising thrill of desire.

"This place, the Institute, is where I trained." Stefan's whispered words tickled my ear. "They deliberately created me as a weapon. That's all I've ever been in my father's eyes. If you ask him, he'll tell you I'm not his son, I'm an experiment. They'll use anyone, exploit everything, to get what they want."

I shivered. "What do they want?"

"They protect this side of the veil, our reality. They're the reason there aren't more demons on this side. They monitor all demon activity. If one steps out of line, they're quick to dish out their idea of justice."

I swallowed, flushed and light-headed. "Why did Ryder bring us here?"

"Because this is the only place Akil can't get to us. The graffiti on the walls outside —you must have seen it—creates a void. This place is a demon blind-spot. No full demon can pass those symbols." Stefan teased my hair back from my cheek. "Like you, I've spent much of my life trying to escape my past—this place."

"They aren't the Enforcers you spoke of?" I was following the conversation. Barely.

"Yes and no, the Enforcers are the soldiers on the front line. We're trained to kill demons. Ironic, considering I'm half demon. The irony is lost on my father."

I could see the guard from where we stood. He'd picked up a magazine, not in the least bit interested in what we were doing.

"Why are they watching us? Why don't they trust me?"

"You belong to a Prince of Hell. You're powerful, volatile, and ill-informed. I'm not sure I trust you." He pulled back just enough to look down at me.

"The feeling's mutual." I pressed my lips together. "At the house by the lake... For a minute there, I thought you were going to hand me back to Akil."

He tilted his head, and a curious smile betrayed a wicked flicker of mischief. His eyes narrowed. Those eyes had a magic that held me spellbound every time I met his gaze. If an ice-demon could have a heated gaze, he had one.

I dropped my head back and closed my eyes, trying to escape his intensity without succumbing to the building urge to grab him with both hands and devour him. My world was falling apart around me, and I could do with the distraction. A distraction; yes, I could tell myself that lie. Stefan was a welcome distraction. That's all.

"You're trembling."

"I'm cold," I lied, then added with a sigh. "I want my demon back. I don't feel... right, without her."

"I can take your mind off her," he said softly, "off everything."

Opening my eyes, I found him watching me, lips slightly parted, raw hunger in his gaze. I could pull him against me and drown in desire. I glanced at the guard, who now rested his head on a propped up hand, bored and probably dozing. Stefan turned my face toward him, his fingers trailing down my cheek to skip across my mouth. I parted my lips a little, breaths coming too quickly to hide. He knew what he was doing to me, but the smug humor had vanished. The severity in his expression only served to further enflame the hunger inside me. He leaned in, and I closed my eyes, expecting the kiss to come, but he deliberately avoided my lips and brushed his cheek against mine. I groaned, left hand clutching his shirt.

His rapid breathing tickled my neck as he bowed his head. Had my demon been present, I was sure I'd already have lost myself to desire. I felt the crawl of his element, the explorative touch of it, but it was gentle, nothing like the bold approaches of before, as though he knew I was lacking half of myself and was holding back.

The door to the library opened. Adam strode in. Just a few moments more, and I'd have had Stefan against the bookcase, shirt open, and been trailing kisses down his chest.

On Adam's arrival, Stefan tensed. The growl that rumbled from him perversely further aroused my already overly sensitive body, but the desire I'd seen in him had quickly been replaced by anger.

"Stefan, you and Muse need to join me in the prep room," Adam announced, oblivious to the moment he'd destroyed. "Now."

The guard had found some enthusiasm and was on his feet, acting the part of model sentry.

I didn't want to let Stefan go. He moved away so that I had no choice but to release him. I wanted to gather up that shirt in my fists and pull him into a kiss so hungry he wouldn't be able to escape. Neither of us would. But that moment had been dashed. It was only when he'd moved away that I'd realized how much I'd ached to have him. My legs were weak, and it took me a few moments to find my strength.

Stefan flung a knowing glance over his shoulder, eyebrow arched. The promise to finish what we'd started rested silently on his lips.

Chapter Twenty One

The Prep Room—or Preparation Room as the sign on the door read—appeared to be a room bristling with flat screen TV monitors. Behind the bank of monitors, each showing a different news channel, CCTV feed, or webcam footage, sat an empty meeting table with enough places for fifteen or more people. Ryder was already in the room, leaning against the far wall, arms crossed over his chest, hands gripping his upper arms. He wore the same un-tucked crumpled shirt, same threadbare black jeans. He grunted a hello, back to his surly self. Tufts of unkempt hair stuck out at all angles. He made the fell-out-of-bed look all his own.

"Your man is lighting up the town," Ryder grumbled, nodding toward the monitors.

I followed his gaze and saw several TV screens showing news footage of South Boston, or Southie as my neighbors fondly refered to it. I recognized my home neighborhood from the eclectic mix of terraced houses, cream clapboard facades, and leafy streets. The footage showed the same brownstone building on fire from different angles. Then I recognized the street, the buildings opposite bathed in fire-light, the same buildings I'd woken to each morning. The blazing building was my old apartment building. My heart sank. "Were there people in there?"

"No, but it's lost. The fire department is letting it run its course—too dangerous," Ryder explained. "That's your apartment building, right? One damned coincidence, Muse."

It wasn't a coincidence.

Stefan stepped forward, concern etched across his face. His father hung back by the meeting table, watching our reactions. "It's a warning. Akil can't find you, so he's sending a message."

I scratched at my arm, grimacing. "He could have killed someone." I had a moment of panic as I wondered if my cat Jonesy was okay, but there was nothing I could do. On the screens, flames licked from the arched windows, and black smoke bellowed skyward. The last part of my normal life—Charlie Henderson's life—had just gone up in smoke.

Ryder watched my reaction. "He will kill if you don't go to him."

"I can't." They were all looking at me, waiting for me to make the call on what to do. "I can't go to him. He wants to take me home, to the netherworld. I can't... I won't go back there." The thought alone turned my stomach. The world works differently there. My human half wasn't cut out to survive among the demons, especially considering what Akil had planned. I looked at each of them, my frown deepening with each disapproving stare. "He wants my demon. He wants her out of me..."

Adam shook his head as he perched on the edge of the meeting table. "It can't be done." Briefly, he flicked a glance at Stefan who ignored him. "Half-bloods are irrevocably one and the same, demon and human. He can't separate your demon from you."

I grinned and threw a hand in the air. "Right. Are you going to tell him that? Because he's going to try. If he takes me back there... Either he'll kill me, or Val will. The second I step through the veil, I'm demon-bait."

Stefan spoke up. "You have the strength to fight them."

Sure, if this were fantasy land. "Not all of them, Stefan. I've barely begun to experiment with what I'm capable of. I could maybe fight off one or two, but..." I didn't need to finish the sentence. I was as good as dead if I stepped through the veil, and everyone in the room knew it.

I glared at Adam. "You need to give me my demon back."

"I can't do that. Not while you're under our roof. You're too dangerous."

"And he isn't?" I flicked a gesture at Stefan.

"Stefan has control," Adam said calmly. "You do not."

Maybe he was right, but without my demon, I was vulnerable. "You have to give her back to me." I crossed the room and stopped in front of Adam. He looked back at me without an ounce of fear, so complacent in fact that he just about dared me to lash out at him. "Please." I didn't want to beg, but I needed her back in my skin. She was my strength, my soul, my fire.

"There is a way."

"Please. Anything." I despised the desperation in my voice.

"You stay here. Work for us."

I blinked, as taken aback as though he'd struck me. He noted my reaction and smiled. "We can always use half-bloods like you. Properly trained, you're valuable assets."

Stefan stepped between us at about the right time. He eased me back a few steps, perhaps sensing I was about to leap at Adam to try and shake the antidote out of him.

"I'm not working for you," I snarled. Stefan held me back. "Give me my demon back! You had no right to take her! Who do you think you are?"

"Muse," Stefan warned.

"I don't care." I tried to step around him, and he caught my arms. "Let go of me. He's putting this right. He has to give her back. I need her." An unexpected sob choked me, and with a sneer, I broke free of Stefan's grip and lunged for Adam. He lashed out before I could reach him, the back of his hand striking me across the face with enough force to fling me down against the table. Blood pooled in my mouth.

I pushed down on the table and flicked my hair out of my face, pinning him with my stare. His expression had barely changed at all. Stefan saw me tense and grabbed me from behind, pulling my arms behind my back as I struggled to get free.

I spat blood at Adam's feet, fighting against Stefan's vice-like grip. "If you don't give her back, I'll tell the world where this place is. I'll tell Akil."

Adam sighed and removed his glasses, rubbing at his closed eyes. "Take her away."

Stefan swung me around and shoved me toward the door and then rounded on his father. "This is all your doing." He jabbed a finger at Adam. "Don't make an enemy of her."

Adam stood slowly. "Like I did you?"

Stefan clenched his right hand. His knuckles whitened, and then he spun around to escort me out of the room. In the hall outside, I shook off Stefan's grip. "I need her back, Stefan. They don't understand. You don't understand..." A few passing employees gave us a wide berth.

Stefan pulled me along a few steps until I managed to yank my hand free again. He glared at me. "How do you think they came up with the poison they injected you with? Who do you think they tested it on?" He saw the horror on my face. "I understand more than you know, but lashing out at him won't get you anywhere. We're prisoners here until he says otherwise."

I sunk a hand in my hair. Panic began to steal away my rational thoughts. I needed my demon back. With every hour that passed, her absence damaged me. An ache had begun to spread outward, a terrible heartfelt ache, like grief. On top of everything else, it was almost enough to flip me over the edge toward insanity.

Ryder emerged from the Prep Room and froze midstride. Stefan waved him back. I darted my gaze between them. A sickly wave of fear washed over me. I had to get out of this prison, get away from these people. I wanted to go home, to my apartment, to my cat, to Sam. None of those things existed anymore, and besides, the Institute wouldn't let me go. If they did, I'd be walking straight Akil's arms. Oh god, I didn't want to do this anymore.

Bumping against the wall behind me, I slid down to the floor, pulling my knees up and scrunching myself into a ball. "He's going to kill me."

I heard Ryder tell someone to keep walking and felt Stefan's warm touch on my back.

"Akil..." I lifted my head. "He won't stop. I can't escape him, and I can't stay here. What am I supposed to do?"

"We can stop him." Stefan slid his hand down my arm and took my hand, lifting me back onto unsteady legs. "There is a way."

***

We were back in the little-used library with books strewn across a coffee table. I sat in one of the comfy armchairs, knees drawn up, hands clasped around a Styrofoam cup. I listened to Ryder and Stefan talking. Ryder sat on the arm of a chair while Stefan paced. He collected and deposited books as he voiced various plans. I hadn't said a word in at least twenty minutes. My coffee was cold, but I didn't notice. The shock of the events over the past week had finally caught up with me. I'd showered, thinking it might help me feel half way to human again, but not even the hot water could banish my trembling.

188

"There is a way. Muse can drain him of power," Ryder was saying. "Akil can't summon from the veil like she can. He has to draw his element from the city, and that's a limited resource. If she drains him, he'll be vulnerable."

"But still immortal," Stefan said.

Ryder shrugged. "Well, yeah. There ain't no way around that."

"We can trap him though. I've trapped demons before using the glyphs. Once inside, he's contained. He can't summon his true self. If there was a way to keep him like that..."

I ran my tongue across dry lips. "What about the drug they put in me?" They both looked a little surprised that I'd spoken. "What would it do to him?"

"PC-thirty-four," Stefan replied. "The Institute uses it to knock out lesser demons. It represses the demon aspect. To Mammon, Akil's true form, it'd probably give him a headache."

"What if I could administer it while he's in his human form? Would it prevent him from manifesting his true self?"

"It might." Stefan nodded. "If you then summoned your element, you could render him weak enough to trap him."

"How do we trap him?" I asked.

Ryder grinned and nudged an elbow into Stefan beside him. "You remember that time we sent Barbatos back to Hell? The look on his pig-ugly face when he realized what was happening... Man, that was priceless." Ryder chuckled. "Good times."

Stefan fought not to smile, then gave in and grinned. "Yeah, that was something..." He realized I was waiting for the two of them to get over their male-bonding moment and cleared his throat. "We can either send him back through the veil to the netherworld or trap him here, on this side. Sending a Prince back won't be easy. They're too powerful. It would require a blood sacrifice." Stefan hesitated, seeing my confusion. "A human sacrifice. Someone mortal has to go with him, but it's a one-way trip."

Ryder nodded. "That's a death sentence. Nobody is going to volunteer for that." We all silently agreed. "So we have to trap him here."

Shoving some books aside, I set my coffee down on the table. "How long does the drug last?"

"It's uncertain. At least..." Stefan's pause held more weight for what he didn't say. "We know it can last years." He tried to hide the tremor in his voice while avoiding my gaze. He swallowed and dragged a hand across his chin.

I thought I'd had it bad, but at least I'd always had my demon with me. Through the beatings, the torture, she'd always been there. The Institute had taken that strength from Stefan; his own father had torn out half of Stefan's soul. No wonder Stefan had control. He'd had it conditioned into him. The pain he'd endured—I'd spent less than a day without my demon and already felt her absence like the loss of a limb. What would the drug do to Akil? Would it even affect him?

"I suppose they've never tested it on a Prince before?" I said, halting the approach of an awkward silence.

"No. It may not even work. Lesser demons are weaker here than across the veil. Princes... They're different. His vessel is little more than a mask. The drug may have no effect at all; in which case, he's gonna to be pretty damn pissed when you try and inject him with it."

I nodded slowly. Akil would kill me if he figured out what I was planning, but I was as good as dead anyway.

"You're going to have to get close to him, Muse, without him realizing what you're doing, otherwise he'll manifest and then...then he'll likely kill you without hesitation." Stefan crouched in front of me, searching my expression. I let him see the resignation on my face. Hiding from the truth was pointless.

"I can get close to him." I closed my eyes and dipped my chin. Getting close to Akil would be the easy part. I knew exactly how to distract him while keeping him tied to his human vessel. A little black dress and a bottle of red wine should do it. Getting the drug in him would be more difficult.

Stefan's touch on my cheek roused me, bringing me back to the present. The concern on his face wasn't particularly encouraging. I smiled, more for his sake more than mine. "What happens once I've injected him?"

"Hopefully, if it works and he's trapped, he won't be able to summon his true self. He'll be virtually human."

The idea twisted a knot of regret inside me. It felt wrong. What I was planning, it was worse than death for Akil. To trap him in his human form, unable to return to his home, unable to summon his true manifestation. Killing him would be kinder.

"Is there another way?"

Stefan glanced at Ryder, who gave him his usual non-committal shrug. "Had he been anything else but Mammon we could have warned him off, but he won't respond kindly to threats."

"Can't you just tell him about this place, tell him what they can do? He might walk away." It sounded as hopeless as it was. I was clutching at straws. Akil wasn't going to walk away. That wasn't his style. He wanted it all. If he knew about the Institute, he'd tear it wide open. Threats wouldn't deter him.

Stefan didn't even bother answering my half-hearted question. He stood and sucked in a deep breath before weaving both hands through his hair, hissing sharply as his shoulder twinged. "We had originally hoped to reason with him, to stack his crimes against him, and persuade him to go home." He sat on the edge of a chair, leaning forward to rub his hands together before facing me.

"That was before he killed Sam. Before I realized how far gone he is."

I couldn't help wondering if I was somehow responsible for Akil's unhinged behavior. I hadn't known any of this would happen when I'd left him. It had been a simple case of just leaving. I'd told him I never wanted to see him again and turned my back on him. He hadn't called, didn't show up outside my apartment, so I'd thought it was over. Easy.

Ryder dropped into his chair. Hooking a leg over the arm, he slouched at an angle, crossing him arms. "It's not just you, Muse. Nica's caught in the middle of it too."

"Nica?" Seeing Stefan slice a glance at Ryder, I immediately knew he'd said something wrong. "What is it?" Stefan struggled to meet my eyes, muscle jumping in his jaw.

"Nica was the one who put us onto Akil in the first place," Stefan said. "She set everything up from the inside. Akil voiced his... displeasure with you. She knew he was preparing some sort of retaliation, so she planted the idea of hiring an assassin and then steered Akil in my direction. She's been playing him from the inside and feeding us the information."

She was a braver woman than me, that was for sure, and not even half-demon. "She works for the Institute?"

"Yes and no."

Ryder let out an exasperated sigh. "Just tell her." When Stefan still didn't elaborate, Ryder said, "Nica is Adam's daughter. There. That didn't hurt. Jeez."

"She's your sister?" I asked Stefan, voice pitched with surprise.

"Half-sister." He cast a dismayed glare at Ryder who shrugged.

"Why didn't you tell me? How... Wha–Why didn't she?" All this time, she'd been working against Akil. Sourcing the 'file' on Stefan, chatting with me at the party.

She'd been right beside me, and I didn't have a clue. "At your workshop, you removed the battery on her phone... You didn't trust her."

"You didn't trust her." Stefan leaned back, becoming increasingly restless. "I removed the battery because I didn't want Akil tracking her cell. I didn't know you'd invited him in to your life, leading him right to us. It doesn't matter. What matters is that her safety is paramount. Her life is at risk."

"No shit." What kind of father lets their daughter go undercover as the PA to a Prince of Hell? Adam had a lot to answer for. "She's there now..."

Ryder arched an eyebrow. "Yup, and Adam won't pull her out. Says her intel is too valuable."

"I hate that man." I fingered the bruise on my cheek where he'd struck me. I was beginning to realize what kind of man Adam was, the kind who would indeed use and extort anything and anyone to get what he wanted, even his own children. At least the creatures that were trying to hurt me were demon; they couldn't help themselves. Adam was meant to be human. I'd seen demons behave more humanely.

"Nica's involvement shouldn't matter," Stefan said. "If Muse can carry out the plan, she'll be safe soon enough."

"Okay." If Nica was there, in the middle of all of this then I could certainly find it in myself to back her up. "Then let's do this." But first I needed my demon back.

Chapter Twenty Two

Stefan held up a small cylindrical device, no larger than spool of thread. "It's a jet injector. Fifteen times smaller than the mass market varieties. No needles. A quick jab to the skin and it'll administer the drug into Akil's system via a near sub-sonic blast. Within a few seconds, he should feel the effects."

Such a small thing could deliver such a debilitating drug. I absently rubbed at the back of my hand where I'd been jabbed the day before. We were in Stefan's apartment, where I'd waited for him to return with the antidote for me. Every second I'd waited seemed like a lifetime. How on earth Stefan had endured months— years—without his demon, I couldn't even imagine.

He placed the injector on the desk next to its twin, which was marked with a plus symbol. That was my antidote. He reached for it, but didn't pick it up. Instead, he curled his fingers into his palm and looked back at me. "You're as close to normal now as you're ever going to be." I must have frowned because he leaned back against the desk with the injectors sitting neatly beside him. "If you ever wondered what it would be like to be human, you're feeling it now."

It hadn't occurred to me that, without my demon, I was essentially normal. I lowered myself onto the edge of the bed. Of course I had wondered what it would be like to be human. I'd tried to imitate a normal life and might even have succeeded had I kept running, but I was never going to actually feel normal.

Tucking my hair behind an ear, I lifted my gaze to Stefan. He might have gotten away with the neutral expression if his eyes hadn't betrayed an intensity that belied his calm exterior. He had dressed impeccably for him. His black shirt with ultra-fine vertical white lines emphasized the brilliance of his eyes while his jeans bunched in all the right places. And there I was, dressed in an unflattering Institute jump suit.

I wasn't sure what I was supposed to say. Maybe if I didn't have half the netherworld trying to kill me, I could flirt with the idea of repressing my demon—maybe. But it wouldn't feel right. It wouldn't *be* right. I couldn't hide from what I was; the events of the past week had taught me that. Besides, the thing inside me, my demon, she deserved more.

Without a word, Stefan shoved off the desk and strode into the bathroom. The door swung behind him. A few seconds later, I heard the hiss of the shower. He leaned around the doorframe and beckoned me inside. My gaze lingered on the injector.

The bathroom gleamed with stainless steel fittings while a waterfall shower bellowed steam behind glass doors. Its relentless hiss was the only noise I could hear. I opened my mouth to ask why we were in the bathroom, but Stefan pressed a finger to my lips. He leaned in closely and said, "The noise from the shower will prevent them from hearing everything."

I closed my eyes, taking a deep breath. I'd had enough of this place.

"You don't have to go back to being a half-blood," he said.

Opening my eyes, I saw what almost looked like hope on his face and smiled. "I want to."

"Don't take the antidote. Walk out of here, and make a life for yourself somewhere else, in another city. Get out of this, Muse. You can."

"Even if I could, he'd find me." It was an impossible dream. Without my demon, Akil might struggle to locate me, but it would happen eventually. He had resources beyond mine, means by which he could find me anywhere. I could change my name, flee halfway around the world, and he'd still find me. Then there was Val. If my brother discovered I was essentially human, he'd gut me the second he found me.

"Isn't it worth trying?" He looked almost pained. I wondered if this was his dream.

My smile twitched. "What you don't seem to understand is that I want the demon, Stefan." I licked my lips and leaned a hip against the counter. "In the five years I hid, there was one thing I missed more than anything else."

From the way he tore his gaze away, I could tell that he knew what I was about to say.

"You can't tell me you don't enjoy the chaos." Suddenly, I was grateful for the hiss of shower smothering our conversation. This was not a discussion we'd want the Institute to hear. "Five years, I kept it hidden inside. I played at being normal, but it was never going to last because I want the destruction. It's a part of me..." His lips turned up with a fragment of a smile, but he was fighting it. "When you walked into my workshop, you were the first demon I'd been close to in years. I knew you weren't human. I felt the power coiled in you and I... I wanted it."

His fingers danced across the granite countertop.

"And you can't tell me it was the demon because it wasn't. It's me. The lust for chaos is a part of me. I can't shut half of me out and live like that. My demon is half of what makes me whole."

"Even if it gets you killed?" His sudden gaze pierced right through me, sending what felt like a trickle of ice water down my spine.

"That's not going to happen." I faced him, sensing the weight of unspoken words. I'd thought him to be as

clear as the winter sky: the confident demon-slayer, all
bravado and no substance. But I'd been wrong. Beneath the
swagger, the smug smile, and complacent attitude pooled a
dark reservoir of emotion; its ice-covered surface had
begun to crack. I'd been naïve to think I knew him at all.

He abruptly pushed away from the counter, intent
on leaving. Without thinking, I caught his hand, pulling
him up short. He looked back at me with such a weighty
sadness that I sensed that he knew something I didn't. He
stepped against me, hands tilting my face up, his lips on
mine. Repressed hunger broke through my defenses, and I
fell completely into that kiss. I hooked my arms around his
neck and locked him in an embrace neither of us could
escape. My own hunger might have surprised me if I'd
cared to think about it, but the overwhelming need to have
him close left no room for doubts.

As he pulled back, I felt him tremble. His short,
ragged breaths fluttered against my cheek. His hands rode
over my hips, then sought the zipper at the front of my
jump suit, sliding it open so he could slip his hands inside
and ease the it off my shoulders. Where his light touch
brushed against my shoulders, the heat of desire flushed
my skin. I had expected his touch to be cold, but it wasn't.

He drew back with liquid ice in his eyes as he
watched me tug my arms free of the suit. I peered through
my half-closed lashes at him, a wicked grin on my face. He
responded with a throaty growl that pooled wanton heat
inside me. He hitched me up onto the counter and trailed
the most frustratingly light kisses across the rise of my
breasts. Leaning back, I let him tease those snowflake
kisses further down. I gasped as his lips tickled the curve
of my waist.

When his mouth found mine again, I hooked my
legs around him, refusing to let him go. Fumbling with his
shirt buttons, I popped them open one by one, feeling him
smile against my mouth. I sunk my hands inside his shirt
and heard him snatch a gasp as I grazed the wound on his
shoulder.

"Oh, sorry...!" I pulled my hands back, but he grabbed them.

"Don't stop," he breathed, shrugging the shirt from his shoulders and dropping it to the floor.

Despite the angry red wound on his left side, the light played across his chest in such a way that I wanted to touch—to taste—every inch of that divine masculine body so much so that I briefly froze, biting my lip, breaths coming fast and untamed. I held the tide of desire in my hands and could still pull it back. Doubts nibbled around the edges of my runaway thoughts. My needs, hungers, desires, all conspired to push me toward the precipice of surrender; if I fell for Stefan, I'd fall hard.

He gathered my face in his hands, drawing me up, so all I could see were those dazzling eyes. His lips brushed mine, but he pulled back when I tried to turn those teasing kisses into something hungry and all-consuming. He teased, luring me close with promises upon his lips, and then easing back when I answered. I groaned low in my throat, he'd be the death of me if he kept this up. When I couldn't stand the game any longer; when he'd tugged on the strings of desire until my thoughts had blurred and my body burned, he sunk his hands down my back and pulled me against him. I hooked my legs around his waist, molding myself against every inch of him, breath and body ebbing and flowing. He hitched me up, lifting me off the countertop, and carried me into the shower, still partially dressed. Hot jets of water pummeled us. I laughed and watched the warmest, most genuine smile lighten his lips.

He swept a hand through his hair, pulling it back from his face, lending his features an intensity I'd not appreciated before. The streaming water quickly drenched him. Rivulets ran down his face, across the shadow of stubble darkening his chin. He leaned me back against the cool tiles and slipped his hands inside the jumpsuit to ease it over my hips. The garment dropped. I kicked it away; consumed by the need to let me hands wander. A curious stir of power tickled my touch as I slid my hands up his chest. I could feel his element rippling around him; an aura of energy he kept restrained. The heat from the water likely helped with his control. I considered whether I should take the antidote and let my demon out of the bag but wasn't entirely sure I could control her. I could barely control myself.

I tugged at the waist of his jeans and popped the buttons, laughing into a kiss. He swept an arm around my waist and nuzzled my neck. I turned my head away, sinking my free hand into his wet hair as he planted frostbitten kisses on my neck and shoulder, deliberately summoning a little of his element into each touch. The pierce of ice through the heat shivered a primal need through me. "You're lucky I'm only half of me," I growled.

He dragged his gaze back to mine, and the unadulterated look of need he gave sent a quivering wave of desire pulsing through me. Panting, drowning in the urge to have him, all of him, I knew there was more to this than just a distraction. There always had been. I slid an arm around his neck and pulled him down into a kiss that came straight from my heart, my soul. It was the sort of kiss that defines moments, seals destinies, the kiss you remember forever. Whether he knew it or not, I'd fallen for him.

I shoved him back up against the tiles. He responded with a husky growl, the sound deep enough to be part demon. It was my turn to tease. I stepped back, even though every inch of my body ached to be near him. As the scolding water streamed over me, rushing through my hair, over my face and shoulders and down the plain of my stomach, his eyes drank me, devouring every inch of me. His smile said enough without words. He reached for me but I batted his hand away and quirked an eyebrow. Stefan lifted his chin, smile turning wicked. I scattered fleeting kisses across his chest. He muttered my name under rapid breaths. When I nipped at the tight flanks of muscle, he twitched and gasped. Wandering lower, I traced the tip of my tongue over the scorpion tattoo. His sharp intake of breath heightened my own maddening desire. Looking up the length of his body, he looked down at me, his smile interrupted as I tugged the jeans over his hips. He dropped his head back against the tiles, eyes closed, giving himself to me completely.

***

Stefan had hooked a leg over mine. The naked length of his body lay against me, his head propped up on a hand. He watched me while I stared at the ceiling. I occurred to me that the Institute had probably heard everything. Someone somewhere had been listening to one hell of a show, but I didn't care. Let them listen. His fingers skipped a haphazard path across my chest, deliberately tickling. I batted his hand away with a chuckle. He responded by summoning a small ball of ice into the palm of his hand. Pinching the ball between his fingers he traced lazy circles across my midriff. I giggled and closed my eyes, enjoying the sensation. Our time together, it felt wonderful in ways I didn't know were even possible and there was so much more we could do. If I had my demon, if we both embraced our elements and came together like we had then... The thought alone snatched my breath away and fluttered my heart in my chest. The resulting pleasure ride would be a primal thing; beyond words and likely dangerous, but imagine the thrill, the ecstasy, our elements entwined like the two scorpions in Stefan's tattoo. But our time was coming to an end, and we both knew it. In a few hours, I'd be with Akil and there was no guarantee I'd ever see Stefan again.

He sat up on the edge of the bed and rolled his left shoulder, wincing a little. I knelt behind him and kissed around the stitches. He watched me over his shoulder. I took that as an invitation to continue and teased fluttery kisses across his shoulder. "You held back..." I said.

He closed his eyes, leaning his head back. "Of course. You're vulnerable without your demon. I didn't want to hur—" He flinched as I nipped at his shoulder, and then twisted with a grin, and pinned me down on the bed.

I'd known he was holding back. His control was faultless. He was right. Without my demon, I was essentially human and vulnerable. Had he lost control of his element, he could easily have hurt me, but I'd sensed more hesitation than that. Looking up at him now, nothing of that hesitance remained. There was a chance I'd imagined it...

He kissed me slowly, languishing in the moment. I rose up into that kiss. I didn't want to let him go and pulled him close, slipping my hands down the curve of his back. The things we could do together with more time—but he pulled away.

"They'll be asking for us soon," Stefan said. I pulled him back down into one last, lingering kiss and then let him go. His roaming gaze slid over my body. A magnetic pull attempted to drag us back together, but he resisted with a sigh and stood to retrieve the injector from the desk.

Returning to the bedside, he asked, "Ready?"

I sat up, nodded and let him take my hand. A trickle of shivers surprised me, as though fear was trying to warn me. Stefan's words came back to me; *'If you've ever wondered what it would be like to be entirely human; you're feeling it now.'*

He noticed the goose bumps prickling my skin. "Sure?"

He might pine after normality, but I did not.

He jabbed the injector against my hand. A slight hiss and it was done. I closed my eyes. Within a few seconds, I felt my demon rush toward me, building inside me. Her weight, the elemental force, rolled over me, washing through me, wave after wave, pouring its strength—its energy—back into my flesh, my muscles and bones. I cried out, back arching, the power blazing white hot beneath my skin. Only when the force of her return passed, could Stefan close his arms around me. My fire inched outward, inspecting him, invisible tendrils threading around him, through him, curiously seeking his demon. I felt the cool touch of his ice element respond like the meeting of old friends.

He brushed my hair back and kissed the top of my head. "It's going to be okay."

I don't know who he was trying to convince, me or himself. Either way, I didn't reply.

Chapter Twenty Three

My high heels tapped out a beat as I walked beside Ryder down the hall toward Adam's office. He continued to grin at me, making no attempt to hide his smirk. I wore a short black dress. Knee high boots clashed somewhat with the dainty little dress. I'd asked for a 'sexy' black dress and boots since I didn't have a single item of clothing to my name. It was all for Akil's benefit, of course, but the boots were my indulgence.

We stopped at Adam's office. Ryder knocked, his tongue poking into his cheek as he arched an eyebrow at me. His wandering gaze had gone beyond irritating and into humorous. As much as Ryder grated on me, I was beginning to appreciate his honesty in a world filled with lies. "Will I see Stefan before I leave?"

Ryder shrugged. "Not bored of him yet then?"

I smiled. "Careful. Too hot to handle."

He lifted his hand. "I remember."

We shared a chuckle just as Adam called from beyond the closed door. Ryder opened the door, gave me a loose farewell salute and closed it behind me. Adam plucked his glasses from his face and stood behind his desk. He wasn't sneering, too proud for that, but he wasn't going to tolerate my presence any longer than necessary.

"Are you ready?" He stayed on his feet.

He had a commanding presence. Perhaps that's where Stefan got his innate confidence. Clearly, Adam was not a man to be trifled with.

"Why did you want to see me?" I avoided his question because I could.

"I wanted to thank you, for doing this."

A frown touched my face. "I'm not doing it for you or this place."

"Nevertheless, we have the same goals." He lifted his chin, raising his gaze to look down his nose at me. "My offer stands. We could use something—someone like you."

His choice of words dragged a smile across my lips. "*Use* being the operative word." I stepped closer. "I've known demons more human than you. I never want to see you or your people again."

"Good. Then I suggest you never mention any of this to Akil. We wouldn't want anything to happen to you... if you manage to survive him."

I snorted a laugh. This man was a waste of my time. I had bigger fish to fry. "Stefan was right when he said you don't want to make an enemy of me. If I can kill my demon owner, I can certainly kill you."

A smile cracked his otherwise impassive face. "Then we're on the same page." He sat down and picked up the file in front of him, replacing his glasses. "Good luck, Muse." I got the distinct impression he didn't mean it.

Chapter Twenty Four

It was snowing when I reached Akil's waterfront hotel. The sun, little more than a dull orb, hung low in the sky behind the skyscrapers of the financial district, its radiance smothered by a heavy blanket of gray clouds. I pulled my leather jacket tighter around me, flicked the collar up, and jogged up the steps into the Atlantic Hotel.

Walking into the opulent foyer, I felt a little like Julia Roberts, and not in a good way. My dress was too short and my boots too close to the knee. The bottle of red wine in my left hand finished off the rock chic don't-give-a-damn attitude. I'd buried my right hand in a jacket pocket. The injector nestled safely in my closed fist.

Catching the empty elevator before the doors pinged shut, I turned and saw Nica running toward me. I jammed my foot in the door, and she slipped inside, barely meeting my querying glance until the doors closed.

She faced me, suddenly animated, hands skittish. "Don't talk. Just listen. Stefan is lying to you—"

"I know."

"No, you really don't." She gripped my arms, her face pale and eyes wide. "I don't have enough time to explain everything. He knows you're here. Listen. Stefan is working for Akil."

"I know." I said again. She needed to calm down and listen to me. None of this was headline news.

She bit her lip hard enough to draw blood, then stepped back and chewed on a nail. "You don't."

We were running out of time. The elevator chimed its floors, fast approaching the penthouse suite.

"Nica." I tried to give her a reassuring smile. "It's okay. He told me everything."

The sheer depth of her pained expression trickled a rivulet of fear down my spine.

"You're in danger, Muse." Her hand went to her throat. "We all are."

The elevator chimed, and the doors opened, revealing the vast penthouse entrance hall with its opulent fitments and gleaming white walls. We stood looking at one another, no words, just confusion and fear bouncing between us. Then I stepped off the elevator and turned to watch the doors close between us. The expression of terror on her face had unsettled me, to say the least. Already nervous and afraid, I really hadn't needed her panicked, last minute pep talk. I shook myself, trying to chase away the renewed fear. Sucking in a deep breath, rolling my shoulders back, and keeping my head up, I strode forward into the lounge.

Akil stood by the windows, his back to me, but he saw my reflection in the glass like a ghost, hovering just out of reach. Fat snowflakes twirled in the air outside, bumping against the window. Occasionally, the wind would sweep them up and hurry them along, only for more to return. He wore a blood red shirt complimented by charcoal trousers, and even after everything he'd done, my shallow heart did a little traitorous flip at the sight of him. The mahogany color of his hair, the bronze glow to his skin, all seemed surreal after how I'd left him, face down on the ground, body riddled with bullet holes.

He looked over his shoulder at me. "You owe me an apology."

A spark of anger ignited inside me, quickly combining with fear to create a heady concoction of emotion that conspired to undermine my resolve. I couldn't mess this up. If I reacted in a way he found suspicious, it would all be over, but how exactly was I meant to react? The things he'd done. The things he had yet to do... Threatening to tear my demon out of me, literally peel my skin from my bones. How was I supposed to process all that?

"I'm not apologizing to you." I settled resolutely on anger and moved to the leather couch where I dumped the bottle of wine on the glass coffee table with enough careless force to rattle the glass.

"Then why did you come here?"

"Where else could I go?" I threw my glare over the back of the couch at him. "You burned my apartment."

He tilted his head to the side, assessing me, reading everything. The way I sat, my quickness of breath, the race of my heart, how I tucked my hair back behind my ear. I moistened my lips. He'd see it all, searching for any inconsistency. Maybe I was being paranoid, but I doubted it. His curious eyes drank me in, absorbing everything, making my skin crawl.

"I..." I faced forward, feeling the weight of his gaze burn into the back of my head. "I know I can't get away from you. So, I thought, why bother?" I needed to tone down the tight note of fear in my voice and hide the shake in my hands if this was going to work. "So...I'm ready."

He was suddenly behind me. I swallowed as his hands rested on my shoulders. His fingers squeezed, and for a moment, I wondered if he might try to strangle me, as he had at the marina. What was I doing here? I couldn't do this.

His thumbs rubbed against my back in undulating circular motions, massaging the tightness from my muscles. I tilted my head back a little, finding his touch bizarrely comforting. "Before you take me... home...I wanted to ask something," I whispered.

"Yes."

I jumped at his whisper against my ear.

"I wanted us to spend the night together. I mean, like this. We talk. We maybe... y'know. I brought wine." I was rambling, but that was okay, wasn't it? It was acceptable to be terrified of him. His hands vanished from my shoulders. I waited. He could break my neck without missing a heartbeat or stab me in the back, and I would never see it coming. No, no he wouldn't. He wanted me alive. If I died, my demon died too. To get to her, he had to keep my human half safe.

He moved around the couch and placed two wine glasses down on the table. I held back my sigh of relief and sunk my trembling hands between my thighs.

"You left me there, Muse." His level tone made it impossible for me to gauge his mood.

I blinked, my nervous smile flickering across the surface of my tight expression. My skin flushed with a clammy heat. Panic skittered at the edges of my thoughts, desperate to break through.

He caught my hesitation, my confusion. "At the house by the lake." He poured the wine. The swirl of the alcohol against the clear glass distracted me.

I laced a hand through my hair, tucking it back, out of my eyes. "You did set the hounds on me."

He handed me a glass, and I eagerly gulped back a few generous mouthfuls. I spluttered a little, lifting a quivering hand to my lips. Akil sat neatly next to me, draping his left arm over the back of the couch toward me, swirling his wine in his right hand. He appeared to be amused by my obvious anxiety and my failed attempts at concealing it. I might even have said he was savoring the moment, deliberately dragging every hesitation out of me, hanging on every stuttered word as though he knew what I was planning. He couldn't know, but that didn't stop me from fearing he did.

"The Hellhounds make for unbiased sparing partners, don't you think?" When I didn't reply, he said, "It was for your own good." His hazel eyes never left me, testing me, probing me, delving into my soul.

"How exactly does sending the hounds after me do me good?" My anger flared a little brighter, finding fuel. Anger, I could use. Fear, I could not.

"I wanted to know how strong you are. Think of it as a series of trials. To see if you're worthy."

I pinched my lips closed and placed my glass back on the table, unable to look at him. Heat seeped from my skin. Anger smoldered inside me, emotions fueling the summoning of my element, just as Akil had taught me. *Channel all of the hatred, all of the abuse, the fury and fear. Funnel every instance of pain into your center, and release it to your demon.* He had told me that. Stop fighting it, he'd said. Let her in, and I could do anything.

"You saved me." I said, surprised by my own words and the tremble of my voice. Tears pooled in my eyes. "You saved me from Damien and every day thereafter. You kept me safe... all this time. Kept Val away from me..." When I faced him, the tears skipped unbidden down my cheeks. "I thought..." I gritted my teeth, forcing the painful truth out. "I thought you loved me."

"No, you didn't," he calmly replied.

"Fuck you, Akil. Of course I did. Maybe not in the beginning. But... what we had... The way you—" Damnit, the words wouldn't come. I shot to my feet and walked a few strides away from him, heels clicking on the marble tiles. "When we were—when we *are* together, I feel as though there is nothing else in this world. Nothing else matters, just you. You let me think that. All these years, you played me." He set his glass down and moved around the couch. I couldn't stand to look at him. Hand on my hip, I bowed my head, hiding my face behind my hair.

"You. Left. Me."

I recognized his anger and felt a quiver of terror ripple through my already tense muscles. I straightened. He came toward me, lips pulled tight in a grimace. I fought the urge to turn and run. Planting my feet firmly, I stood my ground, summoning a little more of my element.

"You left me, Muse," he hissed. "You walked away." He stood too close against me. His power reached out to embrace me.

"Don't pull that shit, Akil. So, I walked away? Big deal. It's not like you couldn't find me. This isn't about me leaving you; it's about you playing me from the first time you saw me." He lifted a hand to touch my face, but I batted it away. "You must have thought it was your lucky day. Here was some lesser demon with a half-blood as a pet. Beaten, abused, one wing missing. I bet that ticked all your boxes. Didn't it?"

This time, he lifted a hand to strike me, but stopped short as our eyes met. He would see the fury broiling in my irises.

"Go on," I sneered. "Do it. You're no better than he was. You've been working me, biding your time, watching me squirm like a worm on a hook, ready for you to take the last bite. You make me sick."

He stepped back, his perfect face set in a frown. "I did all of that for you."

I laughed. The maniacal sound of it reverberated around the room. "Is that what you tell yourself? Did you kill Sam for me?"

Akil's lips twitched in a snarl. "Sam was nothing. An obstacle. A distraction. He didn't deserve you."

"He was a good man, and you murdered him in cold blood." I called the warmth of the room into me. The lights flickered. My demon purred her pleasure at the flood of heat shoring up my rage. "If I could kill you for that alone, I would."

His threatening snarl turned into a smile. He stepped closer, and this time, I did move back, but he didn't stop. He was on me, shoving me back against the windows hard enough to startle a cry out of me. His hand splayed aggressively across my cheek then dragged down my neck. I tried to turn my face away. Disgust turned my stomach over. He knew what I felt, saw it on my face, and with another snarl, he pinned both my wrists back against the glass. I didn't struggle. There was little point, but I did call more of the fire element out of the building, sucking the power of the city into my flesh, bolstering my rage and lust for revenge.

He chuckled into my ear. "I find it amusing that you think you can say these things to me and escape my wrath."

"Why?" I hissed. "Because it's the truth?"

"The truth..." He seemed to taste the words, let them play on his lips. "Do you even know what the truth is?"

He stood so close against me that the heat between us shimmered. We teetered on the edge of losing control. I couldn't, not yet. If I could get my arm free and pluck the injector from my pocket, it would all be over.

His lips brushed mine. I clamped my mouth shut, trying to pull away. I couldn't help the pull of hunger for him. My element sought his great well of energy. My demon wanted him, but I could damn well fight her. The human part of me held the reins, and neither she nor Akil were going to win.

He released my right arm. Now was the time. I could just...

He sunk his hand into the right pocket of my jacket. There was no hesitation. He knew what was in there, and sure enough, he lifted out the jet-injector. Horror doused my anger and spilled a cooling wash of doubt over the inferno within me. He knew. All long. He knew I'd come here to trap him.

His crooked smile and arched eyebrow confirmed it.

Turning the injector over in his hand, he admired the compact device for a few moments as though intrigued, then slammed it against the window beside my head, cracking the glass. When he lifted his hand away, the injector—what was left of it—fell away in pieces that tinkled against the marble floor.

He met my horrified stare, and I knew my time was up. He would kill me now.

"You think I don't know about the Institute?" he hissed through bared teeth. "That I didn't know what you came here to do?" He leaned in closer, pressing his entire body up against me. The intense heat rippled an aura of power around him. "You dress yourself like a whore and believe I can be fooled by such petty things?" He buried his face in my hair and took a deep breath. "I can smell him on you." He nuzzled my cheek. "Your half-blood savior."

Panic chased away all rational thought. I tried to push against him, but he barely moved. I moved to strike him with my free hand, but he slammed my wrist back against the cracked glass, holding me there like a sacrifice.

"Let me go," I growled, kicking out, but he jammed a knee between my legs. His body smothered mine. "Akil. Please." My voice trembled. "You didn't leave me any other choice. I can't go back home. I won't. I'd rather die."

"As you wish." He released my left arm and clamped a hand around my neck, constricting my throat. I wheezed in what air I could and clawed at his hand, but nothing even came close to stopping him. I thrashed, throwing my head from side to side, chest heaving. My demon rushed through my skin, flooding into muscle, but he responded in kind. Fire blazed in his eyes.

"Akil!" Nica yelled.

He turned his head and received a face full of mace. He roared, flinging himself away from me as he clawed at his face.

Slumped over on my hands and knees, I gulped in precious air, choking and coughing it back up again. Stars dashed my vision. Incoherent thoughts reeled around my head. Nica snatched my hand and dragged me to my feet, pulling me stumbling after her, down the hall before veering into Aki's study.

"Not here..." I wheezed. No exit.

Too late. As I stole a glance out the door, I saw Akil's silhouette bearing down on us. We were trapped.

Nica backed up against the wall of books. "Oh Jesus, he's going to kill us." She pressed herself back into the books as if hoping they could somehow swallow her up.

I crossed the room and snatched a very familiar katana from its brackets. The same sword he'd killed Sam with. He must have brought it back from Stefan's lakeside house. I plucked a lighter short sword from a bracket and tossed it at Nica. She caught it, but from the look of utter terror on her face, I could see I wasn't going to be getting any back-up.

"Stay behind me." I stepped in front of her as Akil rounded the doorway. He stopped a few strides into the room, regarding us both as we readied for the inevitable attack. He blinked slowly before looking away. A muscle pulsed in his jaw. When he faced me, sizzling embers danced in his dark eyes. He could call his true form at any time. If he did, Nica and I would be toast.

"Don't do this." All I could manage was a croaking growl, but it was enough. "You don't need to do this."

"I'll admit this is not what I wanted." He took a few languishing steps toward us, drawing out the inevitable.

I heard Nica whimper from behind me and raised the sword in both hands, sending a surge of element through my arms and down the blade. Flames licked up the steel, twisting unnaturally around the sword as my element embraced it. The blade would cut human flesh, while my element would slice through ethereal flesh.

"There's still hope for you, Muse." He reached the desk and danced his fingertips across its surface, leaving sizzling singe marks in the wood. "Give me that bitch, and I'll let you live."

"You're a liar."

"I'm the liar?" He slid his powerful stare over my shoulder to Nica. "She thought she could come into my home, my business, and my life and lie to me." His human image shimmered before settling again as anger undermined his control. "The insolence of the Institute astounds me."

I flexed my grip on the sword, never taking my eyes off him. "Blame them, not her."

"Oh, I do." He grinned.

My thoughts fragmented, vision blurring at the same time as Akil's human form rippled. I flung every drop of power inside of me into play and summoned my demon. She came eagerly, enveloping me in a burst of heat. My lone wing burst from my back. Its leathery flesh flapped in the air.

Akil laughed as I spread my stance. His molten eyes drilled into mine. Lips parting, he said softly, "There you are."

A snarl rippled across my lips. My blackened talons clenched around the flaming sword. "You think you know me." My wing flexed. "You don't."

A cool trickle of air teased into the room, like the promise of frost on a winter's morning and then Stefan sauntered into the room without breaking stride. He'd retrieved his leather coat and looked exactly as he had the night he'd entered my workshop and turned my world upside down.

"Akil," he said with an obscene tone of authority that both bemused and startled me. "This isn't part of the deal."

Akil slung a glare over his shoulder at Stefan, not at all concerned about his arrival. In fact, Stefan stopped next to Akil and stood beside him with as much confidence as I'd ever seen him wield.

I straightened, feeling a deep scowl cut into my features. A horrific idea planted itself firmly in my thoughts, Nica's words coming back to me. *Stefan's working for Akil.*

I pinned my stare on Stefan, hoping to see something like regret or sadness on his face. I searched those winter-sky eyes for any sign he was playing both sides: a wink, a twitch, anything. Any. Damn. Thing. But there was nothing for me in those eyes. He glared back at me, as cold and hard as glacial ice. Dread twisted a knot in my gut, turning my stomach over and tugging my strength out from under me. "Stefan...?"

Akil fought back a smile. "I admire your work, half-blood." He acknowledged Stefan with an appreciative nod. "And I upheld my end of the bargain. Nica is safe. In fact, the sooner you get her out of my sight, the better. Muse and I have much to discuss."

Nica gave me a wide berth and skirted the room, moving around to stand behind her brother. At least she had the decency to look sorry. She had tried to warn me.

I must have been quite a sight: a one-winged half-demon-half-human with her emotions raw on her face for all to see. I couldn't find my voice, let alone consider how I was going to get away. Stefan was working for Akil. Not in a let's-pretend-I'm-an-assassin way, more of a lying-the-entire-time kind of way.

"How long?" I rasped.

Stefan blinked, but otherwise stood motionless. "Since the explosion at your workshop."

Oh god. I staggered, my element briefly stuttering like a dying flame, its fuel burning out. "You set the explosion," I whispered. I even glanced at him to see if he'd deny it. Nothing. His skin held a delicate shimmer, like a touch of frost on the ground in the morning. I'd once thought him glorious. I'd seen him fight off Hellhounds for me. Watched Akil stab him...

"Akil never misses." I muttered. I should have known. Akil had plunged the very sword I was holding right through Sam's chest. He wouldn't have missed. It had all been an act. I lifted my head, and a growl bubbled up from my depths at the two of them, dark and light, standing together in their victory over me. I lifted my hand, dragging with it the latent heat-energy in the room to gather together in a tight ball of white hot heat in the palm of my hand. It pulsated, cracked, and fizzled. I flung the sphere at Stefan, but he easily sidestepped its arc, and it sailed past and splashed against the wall.

Nica backed up. "Muse—no!"

I breathed in energy, summoning every degree of heat from the building. It swept in from all sides, mostly from below, funneling through my legs and spooling at my heart.

Ice sparkled all over Stefan, as though he'd been powdered with diamond dust. He ordered Nica to leave and moved away from Akil. He held out a hand, briefly halting the proceedings, and checked Akil's mildly-amused expression, asking for permission. *As though Akil owned me.* It was the last straw. I sprang for Stefan, bursting forward, intent on plunging the sword right through him, but he batted the katana aside. I barreled on, slamming into him, driving him back against the wall beside the fireplace. Fire flowed from me, spilling over him. Its licking tendrils spat and hissed against his coating of ice. He snarled down at me and with both hands, shoved me back.

"You wanna test me?" I lifted a hand, talons glinting like daggers, and called upon the veil. "Because that's what this is. A trial, right? You've been testing me, preparing me for Akil." I laughed, and my demon laughed. Our voices mingled.

"Wait." He shoved away from the wall, ice wings cracking and snapping behind him.

The veil was there. I could see it, like a layer of flesh pulsating between worlds. I could slice it open and reach beyond, thrusting a world's worth of energy into my demon.

"I..." He bowed his head, as though he might finally have an explanation for me, but it was a ruse. He summoned a shard of ice and launched it at my face. I jerked an arm up, gasping as the dagger of ice plunged into my arm before boiling into nothing but steam.

Stefan plowed into me, slamming me down against Akil's desk. He drove his arm under my chin, forcing my head back. Ice cracked against spluttering fire. Steam and sparks hissed in the air. Ice cracked off his demon visage, quickly replaced by more as his demon repaired its shield in seconds. He snarled down at me, driving his arm harder against my throat.

"That's enough." Akil's voice boomed.

Stefan didn't eased off, if anything he leaned closer over me. Glacial-blue eyes were all I could see. "Trust me," he whispered and then the weight of him was gone.

I lay on my back, wing crushed beneath me, staring up at the ceiling. Trust him? No. I was done with trusting anyone. The bastard had lied to me over and over. He'd stolen my life from me, given me hope, and then torn it out from under me. He may even have captured my heart in ice, and he'd done it all with a crooked smile and glint of mischief in his eye. Damien, Akil, Stefan, the Institute— they could all go to hell.

Akil tugged me upright. His fiery gaze unashamedly devoured my demon. I hissed at him and shoved him back. He stumbled, narrowing his eyes, control wearing thin.

"You can't have her!" I screamed.

Stefan stood off to my left, multifaceted wings relaxed. Water dripped from their icicle tips. He moved around the room, flanking me. I growled at them both, snapping my teeth together and lunged for Akil. He'd seen me tense and dodged aside in time to avoid me. I twisted around in time to realize what I'd done.

Akil's human guise peeled away, and the Prince of Hell stepped forth. Fire danced in the air as his muscular bulk filled the space between the floor and ceiling. Wings of embers and ashes butted up against the ceiling, fire tracing through the veins like fireworks igniting the night sky.

Stefan's cold grip shoved me toward the door. "Go!"

I sneered at him, but I knew when it was time to leave. I made it to as far as the lounge before Mammon parted reality in front of me, stepping through the ragged tear in the fabric of this realm. He reared up, wings spread behind him, black lips pulled back over rows of curved fangs. Stefan skidded to a halt beside me. He must have seen something in Mammon that I didn't because he dropped to a knee and threw a shield of ice up around us like a brittle umbrella. I ducked behind the shield as a blast of pure energy slammed into it. The wave of heat flowed over us, but Stefan's shield cocooned us from the blistering tsunami.

Stefan leaned into the shield, holding it firm against the onslaught. He shuddered, teeth clenched, eyes closed as he poured all of his element into our defenses. Steam bellowed around us, water droplets instantly vaporized by the barrage of heat.

He was losing. He hunched lower with an anguished cry. It was no good. He couldn't draw enough of his element from the world around us. The city was heat. It was my world.

"Mammon, stop!" I yelled.

The blast of heat ceased. I peeked over the top of the rapidly melting shield and saw Mammon eyeing me with blank look on his demonic face. He snorted, lips rippling, wings ruffling behind him, dusting the floor with ashes.

I stepped out from behind the shield. "You were testing me, yes." Each step, I recalled the heat in the room, catching sight of Stefan slumped against the wall beneath the windows, drenched and struggling to gather his element. "Testing to see if I'm worthy... You want to take me home." I deliberately let my demon speak through me, over me. "To extract me from this human vessel."

"Yes," Mammon grunted.

"Then take me." My gravelly voice echoed back on itself. "Open the veil, and take me."

"Muse..." Stefan panted, "no."

"Shut up." I glared at Stefan. "You don't get a say in this."

Mammon snarled. He wasn't a fool. He sensed I was playing with him. But what was I to him? Just a lesser demon, and half of one at that. What harm could I possibly cause a Prince of Hell?

He shifted, slick muscles rippling, and then tossed a glance to my left where a tear opened in the veil. The thin skin separating the worlds peeled apart like flesh beneath a surgeon's knife. The edges frayed, and angry remnants of energy snapped about the mouth of the wound. I didn't hesitate. Reaching beyond the veil, I called the heat of the netherworld to me, channeling the unending reservoir of power. A huge swell of energy tore through the veil and into me, lifting me off my feet. I flung a hand out and directed the force of it at Mammon, but all he did was laugh.

He lifted a hand, capturing the flow of energy in his palm and tossed it back at me as easily as throwing a soccer ball. I heard the sound of glass shattering and had an odd moment to recall how Akil had cracked the window earlier, and then I felt the cool embrace of the night air wrap itself around me. I saw the dark above, and snowflakes danced in the air around my reaching hands, but they fled, rushing away from me.

The bitter wind tore at my blackened flesh, whipping my hair around my face. I was falling. Instinctively, I flung my wing out, but all it did was twist me in the air, tumbling me over and over. I tried to claw at anything, desperate to find purchase, but there was nothing except the relentless assault of the wind and the harsh patter of snowflakes against my face.

Snowflakes.

They played around me, swirling around my flame-wrapped limbs like sprites with minds of their own.

I felt them kiss my flesh, instantly dying when they met my heat. I wondered if Stefan had sent them, right before I plunged into a black arctic darkness.

Chapter Twenty Five

I lay sprawled on my back, unable to see. I was no longer plummeting to the ground but suspended motionless in a bitterly cold embrace. I opened my mouth and tried to snatch a breath of air, but water spilled over my lips and gurgled down my throat. I couldn't breathe in to cough the water back up. Clamping my mouth shut, I tried to fight against the weight of darkness. Something shifted. Water pooled around my sizzling flesh. I could lift an arm through the suffocating soup, but without knowing which way was up—or out—I had no idea how to escape.

A cold hand closed around mine and yanked me free, almost dislocating my shoulder. I slumped to my knees in the thick blanket of snow. My demon had all but vanished, the sudden cold chasing her away. I was myself again as I blinked up at Stefan. Snowflakes swirled around him. The cold wind tugged at his coat. I shivered at the sight of his boreal eyes. He shimmered beneath the streetlights, his skin liquid ice. The element seeped from his mortal flesh, enveloping him in pure energy. He'd called from the veil.

He held out a hand. It was only when I took it and let him pull me to my feet that I realized the entire stretch of Atlantic Avenue had been buried in at least three feet of snow. Winter had descended abruptly on Boston. Inexplicably, a snowdrift had gathered at the front of The Atlantic Hotel, exactly where I'd plummeted from the penthouse apartment above. I heard shouts of alarm around us. People wandered from their businesses and stranded cars.

"Holy hell," I wheezed.

Nica emerged from the side of the hotel, arms wrapped around herself, shivering uncontrollably, teeth chattering. She slogged through the thick snow to get to us, her court shoes disappearing in her tracks.

"C'mon, we need to get off the main street," Stefan urged, glancing up through the swirling snow at the hotel. "He'll be on us in seconds."

I took Nica's hand, pooling warmth into my hand in an effort to keep her warm. We trudged through the snow, but it's cloying weight slowed us down. I summoned what warmth I could find from the nearby buildings and focused it ahead of us so that the snow began to melt, shrinking back to create a path.

"We need to get to the Institute." Stefan said from behind us.

I glanced back. He'd shaken off his demon and had returned to his normal self. Gun in hand, he covered our retreat, waiting for Mammon to emerge and give chase.

"No." I replied, pulling Nica barefooted behind me. "It ends now." Even I was a little frightened at the growl in my voice. I was not in a good place, mentally, but I refused to stop and think about why. Now was not the time to go over the deceit Stefan had wrought upon me. "Whatever happens, it ends now. I'm not running anymore."

We emerged along Harbor Walk, a footway that follows the waterfront around the many wharfs and marinas along Boston harbor. The ink-black water of the harbor ahead of us reflected the sparkling lights from the buildings on the opposite side of the bay. Snow continued to dust the ground, but the further away from the hotel we were, the less snow hindered our escape until all that remained were lazy flakes fluttering like ghostly butterflies in the night air.

A pier stretched out across the water with smaller boats bobbing gently at its edges. I rounded on Stefan, forcing him to pull up short. "How could you?"

"Muse." He didn't even look sorry.

This wasn't the time to fight, I knew that, but I wasn't having him walk beside me any longer. I needed to know why he would lie to me before Mammon incinerated us all.

A scowl darkened his eyes. "Not now." He glanced behind him. "We need another plan."

If it weren't for the threat of Mammon, I'd have blasted Stefan with every molecule of fire I had at my disposal. "There is no other plan. He knew about the injector—"

I saw him flinch, guilt slicing through his attempt at indifference.

"You told him?" He didn't deny it; he could barely hold my gaze. "You told him!"

Nica stepped in front of me as I tensed to lunge at him. I'd have torn into him had she not stopped me. "Muse," she stuttered. "You can't blame Stefan."

"The hell I can't. I trusted him." I laughed and staggered back onto the pier. "It took me a while. I should have listened to my instincts at the beginning; they never lie. I should have known better... You son-of-a-bitch."

Nica stood in front of her brother, then stepped back, relaxing against him as he slipped his left arm around her, pulling her close. I watched, the anger simmering beneath my skin, as he kissed her lightly on the head and whispered something into her hair. I read the apology on her lips even as the breeze stole the softly spoken words. They were close. That much was clear. He'd been protecting her, but in doing so, he'd put me repeatedly in the line of fire and then screwed me for good measure.

"Hey," I snapped. "Hate to break up the family reunion, but we have a Prince of Hell bearing down on us and not a clue how we're going to get away from him."

Nica swept a rogue tear off her cheek and nodded. "Just don't be so quick to blame, Stefan. Please..."

I avoided Stefan's glance and focused on Nica instead. I'd forgotten how vulnerable she was in all of this. A half-demon for a brother, the two of us throwing elemental energy around, revealing our demon selves as though it was perfectly normal. She must have been terrified; she was the bravest of us all.

"Stefan, can you and I..." I shoved my rage aside, bottling it and screwing the lid on tightly to be opened once this was over "Together, can we out-power him?"

"It's possible. At least, I can draw from the veil, but I saw what he did when you summoned your element from the netherworld. Your attack slid right off him. You can't fight him, Muse. You wield the same power. All you were doing was feeding him energy."

Crap. I bit into my lip. There had to be a way. I racked my mind for anything resembling a solution, but didn't know enough about battling demons. I'd spent my life cowering at their cloven hooves, not standing up to them.

"Why did you tell him about the injector?" I know—not the right time, but I needed to hear it from him. "It could have worked."

Stefan moved around Nica, but as he approached me I stepped back, holding a hand out. "Don't," I warned. I couldn't stand to be near him. It only made the gaping mental wound he'd inflicted hurt all the more. That, and the fact I wanted him to hold me, I needed to feel his arms around me. It had only been a few hours since we'd lain together. I'd been stupid enough to think that meant something. It had to me.

"I didn't have a choice." Stefan stopped his advance, albeit with reluctance. "He had Nica. I had to tell him everything. If he suspected I was lying, he'd have killed her."

"But you're so good at lying." Anger spat the words through my clenched teeth.

He grimaced, glancing away before glaring back at me, jaw clenched, fist clenched at his side. "I did everything I could to protect you."

"Sure, while buttering me up for Akil. All that bullshit about teaching me to summon from beyond the veil. It was all for Akil. You were leading me right into the lion's den."

"I didn't have a choice." The wind tugged his raised voice away, carrying it across the dark water. "Nica should never have been sent in to work Akil. He knew who she was the second he saw her, so he used his advantage to call me in. I was supposed to watch over you, nudge you in the right directions, see how powerful you were—how much you knew. I did all that, you're right, but I also kept you safe. Akil's trials would have killed you."

They might as well have, I thought. "Why didn't you tell me?" I couldn't keep the bitter sadness from my voice.

"I told you as much as I could without putting Nica in danger. I did what I had to. I'm sorry. Please, Muse. I couldn't let him hurt Nica. She had no-one. The Institute—our father—wouldn't even acknowledge he'd sent her in there. I was all the hope she had."

He chanced a step closer, but I backed up. "Don't come near me."

He glowered back at me, eyes narrowing, but I could see how my words wounded him. The pain was apparent in his eyes. He had no idea what he'd done to me. I'd trusted him. More than that, I loved him. God-help-me, I loved him. He'd let me believe in him, and it had all been lies. Lie after lie after lie. Pile that on top of Aki's twisted betrayal and Damien's before him, and frankly, I was surprised I hadn't just thrown in the towel and merrily stepped through the veil myself. Stefan had been my last hope that everything would be alright. In his arms, I'd been safe. Now that too had gone.

I masked my sorrow with anger, sneering at him as he tried to make me understand. "Don't come near me. If we get out of this, I don't ever want to see you again."

"Muse," he breathed, face crumbling in pain.

"Never."

The clap of hands behind me pierced the night. The wind played with the sound, tossing it in the air.

"Bravo," Akil's deep voice purred, the single word spoken with a syrupy slowness. I turned, pooling heat into my hands as I fixed him in my sights. Back in human form, his appearance shimmered with a heat-haze. An abundance of power rolled off him. We had little to no hope of beating him.

"He does love you, Muse." Akil frowned playfully. "I knew that much when I saw you together at the lake house. Two half-bloods of opposing elements; you realize it'll never work? Aside from the fact I'm taking you home. So, no need to fret, you won't be seeing him again." His lips twitched. "Ever."

I wasn't going back there without a fight. I summoned my demon, plunging her strength into my limbs. Energy strummed through me, weaving up and down my spine and rising to the tip of my wing. I planted both feet firmly, casting my arms out and stretching my wing back. Let him see me, all of me. Let him witness the furious broiling energy thrashing inside of me. If he wanted me, he could have all of me.

I called every fragment of heat from the city behind me, finding less there than I had earlier. My attempt stuttered. The cold of the snow still piled high on the street subdued the available heat available. I hesitated only briefly before reaching further, but the cold water of the bay offered little, and the reaching tendrils of power recoiled, snapping angrily in the air, their lust for power unsatisfied. Driven by rage, I sought the heat beyond the bay, but the further I stretched, the weaker my efforts became.

Akil frowned. "I expected so much more. Stefan was very thorough in his reports of your newfound prowess."

The madness of rage spilled over me. A white-hot torrent of heat ripped across my skin, enveloping me in light. As Stefan had so eloquently said, I was about to go nuclear, and I had the source of energy I needed standing right in front of me. Akil seemed curious as my ethereal tendrils reached toward him. I wrapped the touch of them around his ankle and slid it sensually up his leg. He watched my element snap in the air around him with a look of admiration on his face. He lifted his hands as I teased more writhing ropes of power around his waist. I sensed the energy coiled inside of him: a vast abundance of fire ripe for the picking. He had torn my element from me at the marina right before he'd mistakenly or deliberately tried to kill me. Now it was my turn.

I twisted the vines of power around his wrists and then caught his hesitant glance. I had him. I didn't need to hide the fact from my face. I let him see my features twist with rage and grinned, revealing my own glistening, sharp teeth. He tugged at his right arm, but I pulled the restraining tendrils tighter. He snarled at me and arched his back, summoning his true form. Fire raced up my reaching whip-like tendrils and dove into my chest where it spun around itself, searching for an exit. My demon laughed, greedily swallowing up the power, letting it swell inside us.

Mammon staggered, his ragged wings shuddering. Embers fluttered in the air with the snowflakes. He stamped back, tossed his arms out, shook his horned head, but couldn't break free. He summoned his element, and I called it from him, drawing it out of him and sucking it into me. Our elements combined, flooding over me like a tidal wave. My eyelids fluttered closed, and undulating flames licked over my body. I didn't need to see him to know where he was. I was inside him, pulling at his mental barriers, clawing at his source, eager for more.

Bathed in a heat so intense it ignited the very air around me, I rose up inside the firestorm. The power gathered up my physical body, set off a blistering fusion reaction, and sucked every last drop of power from Mammon's ethereal body. We collapsed in unison. Through the flames, I saw Akil's demon fade away, leaving his unconscious human vessel on the pier. He wasn't dead, just exhausted in the truest sense of the word.

I, on the other hand, was about to experience exactly what it meant to summon a god-like amount of energy and not unleash it upon the world. The pain began immediately, but at first, it was barely noticeable. Just a few twitches like splinters of glass dashing my skin. Nothing I couldn't handle.

"Muse..." I made out Stefan's distinctive coat. He dropped to his knees in front of me, but he couldn't breach the wall of flame.

A snap of pain lashed up my back, wrenching a cry from my lips. "Just kill him..." I hissed.

He didn't move. It didn't matter what we did to Akil's human vessel, it wouldn't destroy the essence of him. Immortal, remember? Not the kind of immortal that isn't really immortal either. Princes of Hell don't die.

Tears sizzled in my eyes. "Stefan..." Terror clamped my chest.

He couldn't reach me. Pain tore my back. Energy lashed furiously at my insolence. A scream squeezed through my clenched teeth. I flung my desperate stare at Stefan. "Please, make this worth it. Do something. Make sure he can't come back." Energy cracked across my spine, slamming me against the ground. Fire spilled across the pier like a creeping river of lava. It was going to consume me. I couldn't contain this much power. Not even a full-demon could contain this much energy. My only other option was to release it. But if I did that, half of Boston would be destroyed. I lifted my head and saw Stefan beside

Akil with something in his hand. Ice. I saw the water running down his arm... No, not water. Blood.

My element slashed through my flesh, lancing up my entire right side. I was beyond screaming. I'd retreated from my physical self, my human mind unable to cope with the pain. Power still tore into me, slashing great talons of energy through my body.

I felt rather than saw the veil open. My demon instinctively reached for home, seeking an escape, but she could no more escape than I could. Stefan had Akil's limp body draped over his shoulders. Blood flowed down his coat, dripping over his boots and onto the pier. I couldn't think clearly enough to understand what was happening. Nica was there, beside him, her face wet with tears.

Fire scorched every inch of my flesh. I could end this. The water. If I could get to the water... I could escape. It had nearly killed me before, but death seemed like the easy way out compared to the body-sundering assault my element was dealing me. I searched for Stefan, needing to see those cool winter eyes one last time. Amid the heat and flame, I caught sight of him. He saw me too, and a weighted sadness crossed his face. I reached out, extending flames toward him and then he turned away and carried Akil through the veil. The tear in reality stitched itself back up behind him, and he was gone.

Gone.

I couldn't do this. I needed him. Someone. Anyone. I couldn't do this alone. My demon snarled at me, snapping inside my skull. She wanted to release the power. *Let it all go,* she hissed. *...the delicious release of chaos. Taste it. Let it go. Burn the city, burn the people, burn, burn, burn.*

I clawed at the pier, nails fracturing, and dragged my blazing body to the pier's edge. Better to smother the flames, to drown in the darkness, than release the desires of the demon. I was half-human, and she was mine to command. She would not win, could not beat me. I would always be human first. My life here—my love—it was mine, and she would not take that from me.

I slipped off the edge of the pier and into the water.

Chapter Twenty Six

I don't remember Nica pulling me out, nor do I recall Adam scooping my cold, limp body off the pier before bundling me into the back of a car. They later told me I was unconscious and non-responsive for a week. Had it not been for the sweltering heat I radiated, they'd have given me up as a lost cause.

At least I have no memory of the pain. My human mind had locked it all away in a box marked Do Not Touch—Ever. My demon would remember it, but I didn't have to deal with that because the Institute had their claws in me, and my demon half had been sent packing.

I had a new prison cell, furnished with steel bars.

Adam visited me daily. A man of few words, he'd sit outside my cell and scribble a few notes. It was just as well they'd taken my demon from me because I'd have spontaneously combusted him on sight had I the power to do it.

I refused to speak to them. It was all the power I had left, so I stubbornly used it, hoping they'd forget about me—maybe even let me go if I played dumb long enough. No such luck. Adam hadn't spoken Stefan's name in weeks. He'd asked me a few rudimentary questions, which I'd refused to answer, but for some reason, that day, he decided to broach the subject.

"Do you know what happened to Stefan?" he asked in a monotone way, like a doctor might ask how you are on this fine sunny day.

I kept my head bowed, letting my tangled hair hide my expression. I knew what I'd seen, but I didn't know what it meant. When I finally did speak, my voice rasped across my cracked lips. "He took Akil back to hell..."

Adam let the quiet return before speaking. "He offered himself to the veil as a human sacrifice. He took Akil to the netherworld, making sure the Prince of Greed could never return."

I remembered the blood I'd seen dripping down Stefan's coat, but I hadn't known what it meant. I did now. He wasn't coming back. *A one way trip.* He had said as much when discussing the idea of a sacrifice in the library with Ryder. I cared, I did, but numbness had descended over me. I knew it was a coping mechanism. The only way I could function was to not feel anything, but it was a tenuous solution, liable to fracture at any moment. I looked at Adam and wondered if he'd gained a few more worry lines since I'd walked out of here in a little black dress all those weeks ago. "He'll come back," I said.

Adam tilted his head to the side. "No. He's a half-blood in the netherworld without an owner to protect him. How long do you think he'll last?"

I clenched my teeth. Did this man not feel anything at all for his son? "He'll come back."

Adam stood with a weary, drawn-out sigh. "He's likely already dead."

I lunged at the bars, hissing. "He was right to despise you."

"Perhaps." Adam folded his notebook and tucked the pen into his shirt pocket before peering back at me, his soft brown eyes deceptively beguiling. "Of course, we could train you. If you worked for us, we could provide the knowledge you need to retrieve him."

"Sure, let me out of here, give me my demon back, and I'll help you." I don't think he appreciated my sarcasm.

He dragged a hand across his bristly chin then scratched at his cheek. "You'll come around."

I watched him walk away. The heavy steel door opened. A guard acknowledged him before pulling the door closed and twisting the lock.

Alone, I clenched the bars in my warm hands and tilted my head back, closing my eyes. Stefan was locked beyond the veil in a world that despised him where every rippling shadow might kill him. I'd been there. I'd lived much of my life in the netherworld, most of it on my knees in chains. Stefan was alone, and he'd trapped a Prince of Hell with him. I couldn't begin to imagine how he'd survive, but he would. I had to believe he would. He'd survive until I could get to him.

I paced my tiny cell, hands laced in my hair.

Stefan had lied to me. He'd dashed my hopes. I hated him and what he'd done to me. He'd tossed my misplaced love back in my face, but I couldn't leave him there. He didn't deserve that. Nobody deserved that. If the Institute wanted to waste their time and money training me, that was their mistake. As soon as I got my demon back, I would cross the veil. Val was there, waiting for me. So was Akil. It was madness to even consider it, but what else did I have? Anything that had ever mattered to me, gone.

I stopped pacing and stood in the center of my cell, hands clenched at my sides. I'd work for the Institute. I'd play their game. I'd lie to them, let them believe me an ally, and when they trusted me, when they thought me one of them, I'd be back with Stefan to tear this place down around them.

***

Epilogue

The light had long ago given up the ghost, but I didn't mind the dark. It suited my mood. The bleached-white light from the workshop spilled into the small office through the dusty window, pooling enough of a wan glow across the desk the I could see the scuffs on my boots.

I heard the workshop door rumble open and glanced through the cobwebs covering the workshop's little window. The white sheet covering the half-finished Dodge Charger bellowed like a skirt as the uninvited breeze slipped beneath it, then settled gently as the door closed.

I counted a few beats before Ryder poked his head around the office door. He wouldn't have wasted any time searching elsewhere for me. There was only one place I went when I needed to think.

"You're up. Demon, Class C, downtown."

I rocked my chair back, feet still resting on the desk. A Class C was a minor demon sighting, little more than a box ticking exercise. It was all I was permitted to do as a trainee Enforcer.

Ryder didn't hide his frown. He sucked in a breath and entered the gloomy office, tucking his thumbs into the pockets of his grease stained jeans. I could smell gun oil and knew he'd been working on his collection of Institute guns. He was the go-to guy for the Enforcer weaponry, and despite his disheveled appearance, he was a damn good weapons expert.

He scratched at an eyebrow and glanced back out the door, clearly uncomfortable with my silence. "Muse, you gotta talk to someone." He smiled, but it looked sheepish on his face, as though he were embarrassed to even mention his next words. "It's been months. You've not said a word about him; not mentioned him at all. It ain't healthy."

It was sweet that he cared enough to raise the subject. Talking about *feelings* wasn't one of Ryder's strong points. "What do you know about healthy?" I smiled. "I've never known a guy who could survive on coffee and Doritos before."

He lifted his hands, guilty as charged. "All right. I'm not the guy to talk to, but you gotta talk to someone. This silence, it ain't doin' you any favors."

He was talking about the Institute and their incessant reporting. Ryder was my handler. My tutor. My babysitter. Everything I did, every move I made, every screw up, he reported to the Institute. It wasn't his fault. He had a job to do. At least he didn't lie about it. Who could I talk to? Nica hadn't said three words to me since that night on the pier, blaming me for her brother's sacrifice. I might not have felt so alone if they'd given my demon back, but she was off limits. All I had was Ryder.

"I want my demon back." I plucked at a loose thread on my jacket. "I don't care about anything else."

"Not even Stefan?"

I flicked my gaze up without lifting my head, peering at him through my lashes. "Stefan's dead."

Neither of us believed it, but it was the right thing to say. The Institute needed to believe I'd given up hope, so that's what I told them. Ryder knew it was a lie, but he played the same game I did. Only when Adam and the Institute thought I was entirely theirs, would I get my demon back. Only then could I go beyond the veil and go after Stefan.

It had been months since Stefan had offered himself to the veil, locking both himself and Akil on the other side, and it would be longer still before the Institute trusted me. But if any half-blood could survive on his own in the demon realm, I had to believe it would be Stefan.

A quirky smile chased away the concern on Ryder's face. "C'mon, lil' firecracker. I'll race you there. First one on scene buys the beers."

I made a show of examining my nails, then flashed him a grin. Ryder bolted from the doorway with me in hot pursuit.

He always wins.

Author Interview

This is the first novel in The Veil Series. Did you find the story came to you easily?

BTV (Beyond The Veil) was one of those rare books that writes itself, by that I mean the plot carried me along at a blistering pace. I've slogged through many a book, practically dragging the story out by the scruff of the neck. Compared to those, BTV was a pleasure. I wrote the first draft within six weeks. Even during the editing process (editing is something I usually dread) BTV was gentle with me. I think it comes down to a concise plot and clearly motivated characters. If you can get that right, the rest flows naturally.

Did the idea of Muse's world come to you already developed, or did you have one particular starting point from which it grew?

The opening chapter of BTV came first. I had the scene in my head and was meant to be working on another novel at the time, but this damn image wouldn't let me go. It was so ripe with conflict on so many levels that I wrote a quick outline, thinking that would be enough to placate my imagination, but the idea had its claws in me now. I had no choice but to sit down and write the scene, or risk going insane trying to hold it back. Many authors will tell you that the first chapter in a book often gets rewritten by the time the ending comes around. BTV's opening chapter is much the same as it was in the first draft. Once I had a few thousand words down I attempted a rough outline for the story and the rest, as they say, is history. The world that Muse inhabits, the framework, relationships, and characters, all grew from that one scene.

What was the most challenging aspect of Beyond The Veil? Were there any surprises?

Stefan was a difficult character to pin down. In fact, his motivations were always a little sketchy and still are. To fit the genre I tried to push him in the direction of would-be hero, but he wasn't having it. After much internal wrangling, I let him have his way - hence the reveal at the end when Muse learns of Stefan's outright betrayal from the first chapter. He's consistently lied to her throughout the book; some might say he's worse than Akil in that respect. What do you think?

What is it about urban fantasy that keeps you writing more?

I was writing urban fantasy before the genre existed. Back in my teens, some twenty years ago, I buried myself in fantasy within a contemporary setting. I've been influenced by the likes of the Highlander TV series, The Last Unicorn, Dark Angel and Buffy. At one point, I devoured every urban fantasy novel I could get my hands on, including the early Laurell K Hamilton books, Patricia Briggs, and Charlaine Harris. There's something about paranormal occurrences happening in the same place and time we all live in, that really appeals, especially when you put all the ingredients in an urban setting.

Where do you write and do you have a routine?

Anywhere, and no. Well, let me explain. I have two children, aged 4 and under, so I snatch time pretty much whenever they allow it. Mostly, I write when the little devils are in bed, and I'm guaranteed a few hours in the 'zone'. I use a laptop for the first draft. I pop earphones in, and I'm gone. Editing is a little easier to work around the kids as it requires a more analytical approach, which I can dip in and out of throughout the day.

Do you plot every aspect of your novels?

I start with an idea. It could be anything; an image, a character, a conversation, and then I drum out a few thousand words to see where the story takes me.

Once that process is complete, I attempt to create an outline, but whether I stick to it or not depends on how the story plays out. Occasionally the plot can take an unexpected turn, in which case I stop and rework my outline to see if everything still conforms to the initial idea. For me, writing is an organic process; the first draft, a creative roller coaster. Each book is different. For example, for the second book on The Veil Series, draft-titled Devil May Care, I had a clear outline. It's obvious from the end of the first book, where the characters will be going (physically and mentally) so an outline was required to pin these vital plot points down.

Some readers have liked your style to Jim Butcher's Dresden Files; would you agree?

I was late to the Dresden Files and am still playing catch-up with the series. In fact, it was only when a number of readers mentioned the Dresden series that I took an interest in the books. I do write in a similarly conversational first person perspective, but beyond that the worlds and stories have very different arcs. Although, I would like to witness a conversation between Muse and Harry.

What are you planning next for The Veil Series?

Devil May Care, the second book in The Veil Series, is currently going through many rounds of editing. We get to further explore Muse's complicated relationship with Akil, resulting in a much darker book than BTV. We also visit the netherworld, where

Muse was raised. It's not somewhere you'll be holidaying any time soon. And of course, we can't have a Veil book without 'Mr Cool' making an appearance.

I'm also busy writing the third book in the series.

I'd like to explore both Stefan and Akil's lives before events in BTV, plus there may be some Institute short-stories in the works. I'm limited only by my imagination, which shows no sign of letting me rest any time soon!

Which character is your favourite? Stefan or Akil?

That's a cruel question. How can I choose between them? That's like asking a parent to pick their favourite child. But… those who know me, know I have a soft spot for Stefan, but Akil is temptation personified. He's the bad kid at school, the guy the girls lust after, and the one the parents don't want their daughters to bring home.

***

Wanting more?

Visit the **Beyond The Veil website** for exclusive access to character bio's and **Muse's personal blog:**

www.pippadacosta.wix.com/beyond-the-veil

Beyond The Veil has a Facebook page where you can comment on the book and chat with likeminded readers:

www.facebook.com/theveilseries

If you liked Beyond The Veil, why not **review the book on Amazon and Goodreads.** Let other readers know what you thought and who's side you're on; Stefan's or Akil's?

ABOUT THE AUTHOR

Visit www.pippadacosta.com

Born in Tonbridge, Kent in 1979, Pippa's family moved to the South West of England where she grew up amongst the dramatic moorland and sweeping coastlands of Devon & Cornwall. With a family history brimming with intrigue, complete with Gypsy angst on one side and Jewish survivors on another, she has the ability to draw from a patchwork of ancestry and use it as the inspiration for her writing. Happily married and the Mother of two little girls, she resides on the Devon & Cornwall border.

ACKNOWLEDGMENTS

For my Dad. For all the adventures we had together. I know he would be proud, but there was always room for improvement.
Miss you.

FEEDBACK

As an independent author, your comments are extremely important to me. Please do get in touch, either on the website or via Facebook & Twitter. Just search for Pippa DaCosta.

Made in the USA
Middletown, DE
30 October 2015